EEL RIVER

 **Book View Café**

www.bookviewcafe.com
Book View Café Publishing Cooperative

To Mark

MY BELOVED

I'm still so happy I get to keep you

AUTHOR'S NOTE
For The Revised Edition

I am so pleased to bring you this revised, clarified version of my beloved *Eel River*. It's an early novel, and an odd one for me; I am not usually a horror writer. I wrote the initial draft in less than thirty days, during my first National Novel Writing Month, in November 2006. The novel was then tinkered with, critiqued, tinkered with some more, shopped around, rejected, and then set aside for a long time before picked up by a small publisher—my first novel sale!

A number of readers bought and enjoyed that original 2013 publication, but the book didn't seem to find the audience it could have. And I was never entirely satisfied with the resolution, how it all played out. I wanted another chance to get it right.

Circumstances have now given me that chance. The book is out of "print" at its original publisher (or whatever the e-book equivalent might be). My husband, Mark Ferrari, and my dear friend Chaz Brenchley have given me extensive, insightful feedback which has helped me see the story underneath the story. And so I have rewritten accordingly. Many parts are changed very little or not at all from the earlier version, but other parts are heavily revised, especially toward the end. I'm much happier, and more creeped out, by the book now.

Thank you to Mark and to Chaz; thank you to Vonda McIntyre, who capably formatted the ebook on very short notice; thank you to Pati Nagle, who was kind and patient with me as I learned Book View Café's procedures

(I am still learning them). Thank you to everyone in Book View for welcoming me in to your august company.

And, in further thanks, the acknowledgments from the first edition still hold true:

Thank you to everyone who helped me with this weird little tale. First of all, the Critters: Todd Edwards, Kenne Morrison, and Mayuri Mandel. The Critters led me to NaNoWriMo and, thus, to the rest of my writing community. A huge hug to Mark Deniz, who bought one of my earliest short stories, then some more, and then this novel. Thank you to the Zombie Club, my longest-duration crit group: Heather Liston, Lise Quintana, Ian Dudley, Keith White, Amory Sharpe, S.G. Browne, with special thanks (and sorry) to Cliff Brooks. To the awesome Katey Taylor, whose edits made every sentence just that much better. To my beloved Mark Ferrari, who has not only cheered, critiqued, and supported so much of my writing, but also drew me a gorgeous cover.

And most of all, to my parents, who let me read everything, never dreaming where it would lead.

Last but not least, I thank you, dear reader, for stepping into my world. I hope you enjoy my hippie horror tale.

Shannon Page
Portland, Oregon
May 7, 2015

*"Once upon a time
there was a princess..."*
— TRAD.

*"What a long,
strange trip it's been."*
— JERRY GARCIA

CHAPTER 1
Summer 1973

Once upon a time there was a Princess who lived in a little house in the deep dark woods. Her parents had moved to the little house in the deep dark woods after her father quit his job as an insurance salesman in the big city, started smoking pot, and became a hippie. The Princess's mother became a hippie too. She took off her bra, and started sewing patchwork clothes and baking whole wheat bread from scratch. The parents moved to the country with all their cats, the Princess, and the Apricot Boy.

The deep dark woods, which all the grown-ups called the Land, might have seemed like a strange place for a Princess to live, but the Princess knew it was all right. Princesses had been living in deep dark woods since the beginning of time. Princesses had been kidnapped, hidden away, locked in closets, given as prizes in competitions, threatened by evil stepmothers, fed poisoned apples, trapped in tall towers with nothing to do but grow their hair, and otherwise challenged on their paths to achieving true glorious Princesshood. It was all part of the plan.

The Princess sat in the front meadow, cross-legged in the tall grass. Ants and earwigs and small grasshoppers and the occasional fuzzy caterpillar meandered across the ground, crawling up onto her toes, tickling them.

She tried to see how long she could stand to let an ant walk across the top of her foot. Not very long.

Soon she stretched out her legs and lay back in the grass, staring up at the sky but careful not to look directly into the sun. She had been playing her little-village game earlier, but now she was tired of it. She had finished reading all her library books, and her mom had said they might go into town later, or maybe tomorrow, and then she could get some more. The Princess had long since read, reread, and re-reread the few books she owned, which she kept tucked away in the small niche upstairs that she called her room, at the corner of the loft. It was not a room at all, for there's no such thing as separate rooms in a one-room house with a loft. The Princess's nest, where she slept in a pile of blankets, was a funny little space carved out over what would be the bathroom if the A-frame had such a thing. But it didn't. Instead, under the Princess's nest was the sauna, with a specially built wood-burning stove upon which her parents had placed river rocks. The adults lit the fire, then sat in the sauna on one of the built-in redwood benches. When it got too hot, they ladled water over the river rocks, which made steam. The steam was good for the lungs, and the skin. It opened their pores or cleansed their chakras or whatever it was that saunas were supposed to do.

The Princess didn't like to go in the sauna. The Princess didn't like to play in snow. The Princess only swam in the fine swimming hole down at the Eel River in the dead of summer, when the water was blood-warm and barely moving, and the sand was almost too hot for bare feet. The Princess didn't like to be particularly hot or particularly cold. Or dirty, or wet, or otherwise out of sorts.

At the sound of a car engine, far down the highway, the Princess sat back up and turned around so that she could watch the curve of the driveway, where it emerged from the trees that lined the road. Maybe Dad was coming back from his trip into town. That would be good. If he brought the car back this early, and if he had forgotten something that Mom wanted, then maybe she would drive into town, and take the Princess, and they could go to the library.

The small county library didn't have many books either. The Princess would often think she had read everything that the library had to offer in the children's section. And the adult section, of course, was way too boring. But then she would be poking about anyway and would find something new. She had found *Harriet the Spy* that way, snatched the book up from the wire display rack, taken it home, and devoured it in a day. Only the greatest book ever written since the beginning of time!

Now the sound of the approaching car grew louder. Probably it was heading to the Morgan ranch next door—"next door", three country miles down the road. Old Don Morgan drove past a few times a day, going into the big town or the little town, bumping his beat-up pickup truck over the cattle guard that separated the Land from his ranch. Morgan always gave a sort of dead-man's wave whenever he passed anyone, opening his left hand slowly, then closing it again, his elbow never budging from where it was propped on the open truck window. He'd even wave at the hippies, who nobody else would acknowledge. "Nobody else" being the couple who owned the property a mile and a half on the other side of the Land, who were only up on weekends; and the family on the far side of them, with the foster kids who swam in the river all summer at their lousy, rocky swimming hole. It might have been nice for the Princess to get to know some other nearby kids, but the foster kids came and went, they didn't go to the Princess's school in the little town, and anyway, since everyone ignored the hippies, it was a moot point.

The Princess leaned forward, holding her bony ankles in her hands, listening to the car. Pickup truck, or Dodge Dart? Whatever it was, it was laboring slowly along the road. Was it turning? Was it?

Yes! It was coming up the driveway! Dad was home!

The Dad was cruising back from town, where he had picked up his unemployment check, gone to the co-op for his wife's shopping list (organic peanut butter, fresh-ground in the noisy machine; safflower oil; baking powder; sunflower seeds, raw and unsalted), and hung out for a while at the Electric Brothers Foreign and Domestic Auto Repair Shop and Country Market, where the county's freaks tended to gather. There hadn't been anybody there, so the Dad had eventually split. As he drove, he turned up the local AM radio station, which was crap, but it was all there was. He took the highway out of Yokayo and headed north for fifteen miles. He took the turnoff, crossed the Russian River, and went through the little town of Vaughn's Corner. He was about to take the next turnoff to go over the last hill before the Eel River ford and the Land when he spotted a bearded dude standing by the side of the road. Bearded dudes always merited a second look, and this one was no exception. When the bearded dude noticed the bearded Dad in the battered blue Dart checking him out, he raised an arm laxly, thumb pointed upward. The Dad pulled over at once, leaned across the wide front seat, and opened the door.

"Come on in."

The bearded dude—an older guy, kind of scrawny—slid into the seat after the Dad shoved aside the groceries to make room. He dropped a ratty backpack onto the floor and said, "Thanks, man." He took a long drag on a hand-rolled cigarette, and didn't offer it.

The Dad pulled the Dart back onto the country road as the strong odor of tobacco filled the car. Which was a surprise, but it also answered the question as to why the dude hadn't passed the joint over: it wasn't a joint. Fair enough.

"Where you headed?"

The grey-haired bearded dude glanced over at the Dad, then shrugged. "Wherever. I got my woman and kid back in town. I'm supposed to be looking for a place to crash for a few days. Quiet place."

"Cool," the Dad said. "You can crash with us. We got a place a few miles off, on the river."

"Far out."

The Dart ambled through the valley towards the hill. It passed tidy little farms, blackberry bushes by the side of the road, picturesque tumbledown barns. The valley was very green, which made a nice contrast to the hills, which had turned a golden yellow in the August heat. The two men traveled silently for a while, then the Dad asked, "What's your name?"

The bearded dude took another long drag on his lumpy cigarette, then stubbed it out on the filthy knee of his blue jeans. He opened a small blue bag with "Bugler" emblazoned across the front and carefully unrolled the butt, emptying the filaments of tobacco into the bag. "Bill," he said, after he had rolled the Bugler bag back up and tucked it into one of the pockets in his tattered shirt.

"Bill," the Dad echoed.

"Billy Goat, the woman calls me," he added, and gave a low snicker.

Now that the cigarette was extinguished, the Dad smelled something new floating about the person of Bill. An earthy, animal smell. He nodded. "Billy Goat. I see."

Bill laughed again, this time more of a guffaw. The Dad laughed with him. After that, they continued the drive in a companionable silence.

The Mom came to the doorway of the little A-frame house when she heard the car on the driveway. She saw the Princess in the meadow, sitting perfectly still, knees folded, perched on her ankles, with her yellow Salvation Army skirt smoothed down all around her. Her hands were on her knees, her chin was slightly raised. The Princess just sat and watched, which the Mom wondered at, idly.

As the car rolled into view around the bend of the driveway past the big double oak-and-madrone tree, kicking up dust, the Mom saw that her husband had picked up a passenger. Another hitchhiker. She sighed and glanced back at the stove: yes, there would be enough soup. It was easy to stretch it. She hoped he had remembered the peanut butter, at least.

She watched the Dad bring the car all the way up to the house, circle around the side, and come to a stop. The dogs had been barking from the moment they had heard the car. Now they frolicked by the driver's door, waiting for the Dad to emerge and scratch them about the ears. Maybe he would have bags of something interesting. Everything was interesting! They quickly left off greeting the Dad in order to rush over and inspect his fascinating passenger. They bumped into him, almost knocking him over with their thick heads, and paid particular attention to the odor of his pants.

"Sauron, Galadriel, down!" The Dad rushed over and pushed the large animals off the man, pulling on their macramé collars, grinning in apology at his guest. It looked as though the dogs were grinning too: huge tails wagging, mouths open, noses aflutter. The Mom watched all this from the back door, waiting to be noticed, to be introduced properly. She still had a bit of suburbia to her.

Finally, the men and the groceries and the ragtag backpack approached the house, with the dogs following close behind. "This is Bill—Billy Goat. He and his woman need a place to crash for a few days," the Dad explained.

"And our kid—little girl, about the age of yours down there." Billy Goat nodded to the Princess, who still sat in the meadow two hundred yards away, watching.

"Well, sure, that's great," the Mom said. "Come on in. The soup's almost ready."

The Princess slowly got to her feet and walked through the meadow, up to the house, moments before the Mom came out onto the front porch to call her in for lunch. The Dad and the new arrival had gone in fifteen minutes earlier. The Apricot Boy was also already in the house. He had tried to get the Princess to let him play with her earlier, but she had sent him away. He had sniffled a little, but he was used to this by now. After his sister had banished him from her meadow empire, he had gone inside, probably up to the loft to dig around in the faded blue toy box. The Princess imagined him driving Mom to distraction with his little cars. Now she felt a little bad about not playing with him, but she knew he'd get over it. Just like she knew it was time to go into the house for lunch now without being called. And like she knew that there wouldn't be any trip to the big town today with

Mom, despite the fact that Dad had brought the car back early enough.

So she was surprised when her dad offered to let her ride into town with him. "What about it, honey?" he asked, wiping lentil soup from his beard with the back of his hand.

"Okay," the Princess said politely, secretly overjoyed. And then she ventured, "Can we go to the library?"

"Sure, if there's time." He glanced at the guest: a hairy, smelly, spindly fellow they had introduced as Billy Goat. He looked like a goat too, though not nearly as cute as the real billy goat who was tied up behind the house, far away from the nanny goats so he wouldn't sour their milk.

The guest nodded. "They're at the Auto Shop or the Laundromat."

"That's by the library. Sure, we can go to the library."

The Princess smiled.

"They might even be at the library, I dunno." Billy Goat was suddenly talkative. Over lunch he had drank two Lucky Lager beers, the ones with the puzzles in their caps. The Princess loved the puzzles. He had also rolled and smoked an icky joint from weird brown pot he kept in a blue bag and didn't share with the Princess's parents, but they didn't seem to mind. The Princess didn't really understand this new fellow. He seemed as old as her grandfather, but her grandfather didn't have long hair or a grey beard, so she didn't know quite what to make of Billy Goat.

Not that she minded very much. Strange people were always coming to the Land. And they always left again before anyone could get to know them.

The Apricot Boy pushed his soup around in his bowl, whining a little. He didn't like lentils. He liked apricots. Probably there was other food he liked, but so far, it was basically apricots. And apricot juice. And dried apricots. And apricot jam, homemade by the Mom, cooked for hours on her wood cook stove. He was a simple boy. It's good to know what you like in life, the Princess thought. She, on the other hand, did not like apricots at all. She liked strawberries very much.

Billy Goat stayed on the Land with the Mom and the Apricot Boy while the Dad drove into town with the Princess to pick up the rest of his family. The Dad wasn't exactly sure how this had come to pass, especially since he had never met the family in question. But there was only so much room in the Dart, and the woman and kid apparently had some stuff with them: sleeping bags, extra clothes, and a couple of random boxes.

"You'll know them—she's curvy and cute, and our little Morning Star is just your girl's age."

"I'm ten," the Princess said.

"Well, she's eight, but she's about as big as you. And Evening Star will be so happy to see you—she'll know you too. I've already sent her some vibes. You'll see."

Vibes, thought the Dad. *Of course.* But he smiled and nodded, packed the Princess into the car, and started the laborious journey back through the ford, over all the hills, through the valleys, down the highway, and into town.

The Princess sat quietly by her window, her face sober. The Dad watched her out of the corner of his eye when he wasn't negotiating the winding mountain road. He was happy she was getting something she wanted. The girl's appetite for books was insatiable. He and his wife almost never read. Life on the Land was too hard, too tiring. By the time evening rolled around, they were both exhausted from the work of the day—cooking, gardening, milking the goats, doing laundry by hand in the creek, canning fruits and vegetables, and the endless building and repairing of the sheds and goat fences and outbuildings and even of the house itself. Sturdy as it was, something always seemed to need fixing: a window resealed, the screen door reattached, a leaky pipe repaired. And the endless chopping and stacking of wood! He hated to begrudge his family anything, especially heat in the winter, but he had to shudder every time he saw the Mom load another log into the heat stove and open the damper. All that work, literally up in smoke!

After forty-five minutes, they pulled up to the Yokayo Library. There was a parking space right out front. This was the thing the Dad thought he loved the most about the country, about small towns. Just like in the movies. There was parking everywhere. No meters that would jam up on your dime, no tickets slapped on your windshield by uptight bitch meter maids. Just big wide streets and loads of parking. Even if the town was full of rednecks.

The Princess smiled and got out of the car. She walked to the door of the library and pulled on the big handle. The Dad saw her into the children's section. "You wait here, honey, I'm going to go find Evening Star and Morning Star, okay?"

"Okay." She made a beeline for the shelves in back.

The Princess had to sit in the back seat on the ride home, next to the other little girl, Morning Star. She was blonde and chubby, with a dirty face.

"It's not my real name," the little girl whispered to her as soon as they hit the highway.

"Oh," said the Princess.

"I'm not supposed to use my real name—it's got bad trip on it, Mom says."

"Okay."

"Do you want to know what it is?"

"Sure."

"Well, I can't tell you." Morning Star smirked and looked at the Princess triumphantly.

"Okay." The Princess looked out the window, watching the scenery go by.

Morning Star leaned over and pinched her.

"Ouch!"

"Hey—cut that out," Evening Star said from the front seat, and then returned to an animated conversation with the Dad.

Adults are so boring, the Princess thought. *All they ever do is talk.* At least the brat next to her didn't pinch her any more. She squirmed and fidgeted on her seat and kept trying to get the Princess's attention, but after some judicious ignoring on the Princess's part, the other girl was finally quiet.

The Princess was quite disappointed in the fat girl. Until she met her, she had actually considered showing her the secret, dark places on the Land. The places that only the Princess knew, and that knew her. But now—no way!

CHAPTER 2

For centuries the Land had barely been touched. Native people hadn't settled along this particular bend of the Eel River. The Land didn't even have much animal life. Deer wandered across, grazed a while, then moved to the greater meadows north across the creek. Sometimes a bear would pass through with her cubs, but she wouldn't stay long. Mostly the Land was left to the voles and mice and bugs and the tiny fish in the creek.

When new people came to the river, carving roads with their earth-moving equipment, parceling out this piece for one fellow and that piece for another, the Land remained barely touched. A hundred years ago, a man bought it sight unseen in San Francisco, never visited it, and later lost the title in a poker game. The fellow who won it also never visited it: he was killed soon thereafter, shot in the back on a dark street. The ranch and the properties that flanked it were developed, after a fashion; houses were built, fences reinforced, cattle brought in. The Land stayed fallow, quiet.

The Mom and the Dad bought the Land from a real estate agent in San Francisco. The agent was cagey about the previous owner, but the Mom and the Dad didn't care. The photos looked gorgeous. Before signing the final papers, they drove up to check it out on a fine June morning, three hours from the city. They stood in the tall grass in the front meadow, grinning in the sunlight. "This is far out!" the Dad exclaimed. The Mom turned her face to the sun, stretched her arms out beside her, and slowly twirled.

They hiked around the big wide front meadow, discovered the smaller back meadow, and checked out the great swimming hole and the fine mellow water of the river, then got into their VW and drove back to the city to complete the deal. After they had gone, the Land slowly reclaimed its solitude. The grasses they had tramped down with sandaled feet and well-worn tires stood back up, and the winds blew the beach sand around, covering up their footprints.

The Princess climbed out of the car, clutching her treasures. She slipped into the house while the others were still unpacking, snaked up the stairs to her bed-nest, then tumbled the treasures out before her. Three new books! More precious than gold! The Princess rarely experienced such bounty. She laid them out side by side on the army surplus blanket that was her bed-spread. Which one should she read first?

A sharp squeal drew her attention. It was that little fat girl, she was out behind the house somewhere, what was the matter now? The Princess got up and stretched on her tippy toes to look out the narrow back window, but couldn't see anything. She shrugged and went back into her little bedroom, where her fabulous books were waiting for her, but then her curiosity got the better of her again. She pulled the little gate to, fastening it with its hook and eye mechanism. It wouldn't keep anyone out, but it was her way of marking her space. Then she hurried down the steep stairs.

She opened the back door—the bottom half only; the top of the Dutch door was latched open against the outside wall—and padded out into the back yard on tough bare feet. She hurried across the tightly packed ground in the direction of the noise, and soon came across Morning Star. The squeal had apparently been because the little fat girl had just discovered the goat shed. Now she was in the pen trying to get one of the baby goats, Becca, to come to her. Becca was wary, but reasonably interested. Most of the goats were friendly enough; they liked people.

Morning Star had left the gate open behind her when she went in. The grown-up goats, no fools they, had already started to leave in search of fresh grass, dog food, open car doors, bags of groceries, young strawberry plants, or whatever other mischief they might be able to find. "No!" the Princess yelled at one of the goats, a big brown Nubian named Lady. "Go back!" She reached up and tried to grab Lady by the horns, but Lady was too tall, not to mention far too strong. She ignored the Princess fearlessly. The Princess and Lady both knew that the Princess would never again try to grab Lady by the tassels that dangled down from her neck. That was a mistake people made only once.

"Mo-o-o-m!" the Princess yelled. "Dad! The goats are out!"

Morning Star was still trying to get the baby goat to come to her. She would approach her tentatively, cornering her in the process; Becca would spook and skitter over to the other side of the pen, but then look back expectantly at the child, cocking her head.

The Princess's cries attracted the attention of the dogs, who came galloping up the path and into the goat pen, tongues hanging out, looking for delicious goat chow. Sauron stuck his nose into Becca's rear, startling her. She charged from the pen, following her mother down the path. She was the last goat out.

"Mom!" the Princess shrieked. She ran after the baby goat, who was more her size, anyway. Becca had no horns yet, so she couldn't do much damage. She was, however, quite fast. All the goats were soon in the front meadow, Lady's bell clanking vigorously.

The billy goat, tied to his tree by the side of the house, strained and bleated at the smell of the delicious, sexy nanny goats hurrying by. But they were more interested in food and freedom and mischief than in him.

"You're going to get in trouble!" the Princess hissed at Morning Star. But the fat girl just stared back at her blankly. Was she stupid? Probably.

Now the Princess finally heard the Dutch door slam, and then both her parents came up the path. "What happened?" the Dad asked. The Mom gasped, and then frowned, looking at the empty goat pen, the two girls standing by.

"*She* left the gate open," the Princess said, pointing at Morning Star.

"I did not." With a sullen pout on her dirty face.

The Princess's voice shrilled up into a high whine. "Yes you did!"

Billy Goat—the man, not the animal—and Evening Star appeared on the path. "What is it, sweetness?" Evening Star asked.

"I just wanted to say hi to the goats!" the little girl whimpered, running to her mother and burying her face in her full skirt.

"Far out. Goats," Evening Star said. "Where are they? Goats are special creatures."

"Front meadow, I think," the Dad said, and set off to find them.

An hour later, the Dad had finally corralled all the goats and locked them back in their pen, and the Mom had begun the evening's milking. Fortunately, as stubborn and crafty as the goats were, they were also gluttons and easily tricked. A few empty coffee cans filled with the special, expensive goat feed from the Farm Bureau and shaken around enticingly had managed to lure all but the youngest kids, and the kids soon followed their mothers.

Bill had laughed as he watched the Dad stalk around the meadow with the coffee can, and didn't lift a finger to help. Evening Star had sat on the front porch watching as well, with Morning Star in her lap, braiding her daughter's hair. *Well, probably they don't know how to handle goats and didn't want to freak them out*, the Dad thought, passing a fat joint to his wife as the whole gang sat cross-legged on the floor around the low dinner table. The Mom took a deep drag, then passed the joint to Evening Star.

"Thanks, man," she said. Took, toked, passed. The joint went around the table three more times until it was burnt down to its roach. The Dad carefully opened the roach and unloaded the unsmoked weed back into the frisbee where he kept his stash. Watching him, Bill was apparently reminded of his Bugler bag; he got it out and rolled a cigarette, then smoked it.

Why anyone would smoke tobacco when there's pot is beyond me, the Dad thought, but it was all cool, all mellow, so he kept it to himself.

Hitchhikers usually crashed somewhere in the front meadow if the weather was nice, or on the braided rug in the downstairs of the house if it wasn't. This evening, the weather was perfectly warm and mild, but the sleeping arrangements somehow seemed difficult. First, Evening Star asked if her daughter could sleep up in the loft with the Princess. The Dad had shrugged, and so had the Mom, but the Princess balked. The Apricot Boy still slept in his crib against the back window, although he was nearly four. They liked to keep him penned up, just until they were sure he wouldn't tumble over the edge of the loft in the night; he didn't mind. Just beyond the crib was the bedroll for the Mom and Dad, on the other wall was the pee-pan, and that was pretty much it for the loft.

Are they thinking about some kind of...? The Dad couldn't finish the thought. He felt excited and slightly queasy at the same time, just considering it. He looked across the table at Evening Star: indeed, very curvy and cute, full of laughter and irreverent joy and bawdy jokes. Probably in her late twenties, early thirties at the most. No, he wouldn't mind... But then there was Bill. Billy Goat indeed: ugh. The smell of tobacco, of unwashed blue jeans, of, well, old man. *He must be almost fifty.* Ancient. The Dad couldn't figure them as a couple at all. Was he even the father of the little girl? He couldn't quite remember the man's exact words. Well, it could be.

The Mom solved the quandary. "Okay!" she said, getting to her feet and starting to clear the dishes. "Want to give me a hand here, Star?"

Evening Star got up, and after a few minutes' whispering at the sink, the new guests were bedded down in the meadow with some spare army blankets and a roll of foam padding.

The next day, the Princess ventured alone into the deep dark woods. She liked to oversee her dominion and to search for the hidden worlds beyond the known realms. Her royal bare feet carried her painlessly along the path past the goat shed and the back vegetable garden, skirting the back meadow. She knew just when to leave the trail and find the low points between the trees where the hidden trail began. She padded along the fallen leaves past the little creek, past her dad's supposedly top-secret pot garden hidden in the high hills, to the abandoned logging road cut along the crest of the mountain behind the house. The Princess climbed her mountain regularly—maybe once a month, more often in the summertime. From the top, she could see down the river, past the weekenders' land and the foster-kids place to the ford, and beyond, to the guy with all the kennels right next door to the bible camp, and then on to the big hill that led into Vaughn's Corner.

She sat on the mountaintop, telling herself another story. She had already devoured the new library books. She had tried to ration them, but then she couldn't stop. The first one was less than satisfactory, so she had read the second. Then, when that one didn't do it either, she had read the last one. So many disappointing books out there. So few *Harriet the Spy*s.

A plump black spider let down a line of web from a branch above the Princess's head. It hung, dangling in mid-air, legs waving about. The Princess startled badly when she first saw it, then moved more deliberately away so that it couldn't come near her, no matter how hard it tried. The Princess *hated* spiders. Of course she wasn't afraid of them; she just didn't like them. Once she was at a safe distance, she sat and watched it and thought about the very silly book *Charlotte's Web*, with its utterly unrealistic friendly spider, the talking pig, all that nonsense. Everyone knew spiders were evil.

Evil…

She liked the word; it gave her a delicious shiver. She said it out loud: "Evil." First very quietly, then louder: "Evil!"

The spider seemed to be watching her as she watched it; it had paused on the level of her eyes. Then, after she had yelled "Evil" a few times, the spider slowly climbed back up its thread to its main web. *The Princess banished the evil spider from her realm*, she thought with satisfaction.

Then she got very cold suddenly, and decided to walk back down the mountain. Usually she stayed up here for hours, coming down only when she got hungry, which she could delay by bringing along a hunk of government-surplus cheese and an apple or something. Which she had done today, and hadn't even touched it yet.

Why was it cold?

She had already started back towards the logging road when she stopped. It was August, and probably ninety-five degrees outside, maybe a little cooler in the shade. And there was no breeze. Yet there were goose bumps all up and down her arms, and on her mosquito-bitten legs, and she shivered. She had a strong urge to go down, down, home. Safe, warm.

"Evil!" she yelled one last time, and then shrieked. She ran full tilt down the hill, not stopping until she got to the house. She was giggling by the time she got there, and no longer cold.

The little fat girl was playing with the Apricot Boy behind the house, near the dry creek bed which delineated the end of the back yard and the beginning of the meadow in the map of the world the Princess carried around in her head. In fact, they were playing in a spot that the Princess considered her own. She had set up an imaginary village there a few months ago, and had considered building more permanent roads and perhaps even bringing some water to make a pond, but then she had discovered a more interesting site in the front meadow. But she hadn't fully abandoned this site, and felt a surge of proprietary alarm at the sight of her brother playing with that awful new girl. She stopped giggling and came to a screeching halt, then turned her head away from them and loudly called the dogs. Galadriel and Sauron came running, always happy for attention. "Nice doggies!" she said, patting them both on their heads. "My nice pretty perfect doggies!"

The Apricot Boy looked up. She could see he was torn. He loved the dogs too, and he loved his sister. He was undoubtedly only playing with the new girl because he had no choice, because the Princess had slipped away to climb her mountain. After a moment of rumination, he got up and toddled over to his sister and the dogs.

The Princess gave a small, fleeting smile.

I'm spending too much time cooped up in this tiny little house, the Mom thought. Cooking, canning, cleaning, baking, then turning around and doing it all over again. Right now she was canning tomatoes. Despite the heat of the day, she had the wood cook stove cranked up full blast. Since only cold water came out of the tap, she needed to boil big vats of it to sterilize the Mason jars and their lids. She was grateful, of course. The Dad had spent weeks running the line all the way down from the spring at the top of the mountain so that she could have clean, pure running water in her kitchen. After sterilizing the jars, the tomatoes themselves needed to be cooked, peeled, and squished into them, along with their liquid, leaving no gaps of air. Then the lids would be sealed shut, and the jars set to cool on the counter.

She wiped a bead of sweat from her forehead, then went to look out the front window. No one else was around. The hitchhikers had gone down to the river for a little dip, which sure sounded good right now. The Dad was probably with them. Well, he worked hard enough. The kids were out back. It was nice that Bill and Star had a daughter that the kids could play with. Maybe the Princess would let the little girl sleep in her bed tonight. She was awfully shy, but now they seemed to be warming up to each other all right. Kids always found a way.

The jars were all sterilized, and their lids too. She fished them out of the boiling water with tongs and set them aside to dry and cool on a clean dishrag. Now the tomatoes. Maybe when she was done with those, she'd join the others at the river.

Once the tomatoes were coming along, she took off her shirt and tied it around her waist. It didn't matter, no one was around anyway. Furthermore, they'd all be naked at the river, so what was the difference?

An hour later, bright red jars of tomatoes lined up along the counter under an open window, she went out back and checked on the kids. All three of them were playing quietly by the dry creekbed.

"Hey kids? I'm going down to the river for a little while, want to come?"

The Princess looked up at her; the other two looked at the Princess to see what she would decide. "No thank you, we're busy here now."

The Mom smiled. "Okay, sweetie, I'll be back in a bit. Just going to cool off. We'll have lunch when I get back, all right?"

"All right."

The Mom walked down the path to the road, still topless. She paused just before emerging from the trees and listened for a moment. No cars coming. It would be just like that old redneck rancher to drive by right then and catch the hippie chick with her shirt off. Or this would be the moment for some of the other neighbors to be strolling by with all those kids. Whatever their names were. Unfriendly bunch of people, they were, all the neighbors. Not that she was surprised. It had been the same way in San Francisco, and in southern California before that. Nobody liked hippies. Summer of Love indeed.

She walked across the road in the bright sunshine, and was re-entering the woods on the path leading down to the river when she was suddenly startled by movement ahead of her. Her eyes were still dazzled from the sun, so she couldn't make out who it was right away.

"Far out," said Bill, as her eyes adjusted and she saw him. He leered at her small breasts. "Is it lunchtime yet?"

"Just about," she said, more crossly than she intended. "I thought I'd get a dip in the river myself. Do you mind?"

Billy Goat put his arms out, palms open, a gesture of submission, surrender. "Hey, lady, it's all cool. Fabulous swimming hole."

"I know." She moved to go past him on the path. At the last moment, he stepped aside for her.

The Dad and Evening Star were still swimming, down past the perfect rope swing site, near the bend in the river. The Dad was talking, as usual. Star was laughing, floating on her back, her big pillowy boobs poking ostentatiously out of the water so that the Mom could see them even from this distance. The Dad liked big boobs, but he had married the Mom. Still, there was nothing to stop him from looking.

The Mom eased out of her colorful skirt and panties, hanging them and her shirt on the tree with the other clothes, and then picked her way carefully down the bank. It only got steep right at the end, but that was also where the sand abruptly turned to clay, and you could slip and fall on your ass, make a fool of yourself, if you weren't careful.

Not that anyone was looking. But she got into the water without incident.

The cool water felt great on her overheated skin as it moved up her body. She waded slowly into the river until the water came up to her waist; then she paused a moment, shivering as it lapped at her belly. She took a few more short steps, letting the water rise higher, higher, and then quickly did a shallow half-dive, ducking her head under and swimming a few strokes there before resurfacing. She was across the river in a minute, then turned and swam slowly back. Instead of getting out right away, she sat in the shallow water, burrowing her feet into the soft sand. God, it felt good to sit down. Why she had ever thought that moving to the country would be like always being on vacation was beyond her.

After she had been sitting still for a while, the disturbed mud settled out of the water and little fishes came to nibble on her toes. Then an eel swam by. They were so bizarre, the eels; prehistoric. The Dad and the other men who visited laughed and made nervous jokes about them. Especially the dead ones, which turned white, bloated to twice their size and floated in the slow-moving river, giving off a powerfully bad smell. Someone, generally the Dad, would have to go pick them up with a stick and bury them a long way off, where the dogs wouldn't find them.

She heard a great hoot of laughter from Star down the river, who then started furiously splashing the Dad. He laughed as well, swimming back to the beach.

"Hey there, fair maiden," he said to his wife as he swam up to her.

"Just cooling off," she said. And then, "Ready for lunch?"

"Sure!"

Evening Star offered to help make dinner, which was nice. After getting her started on chopping a big pile of potatoes, the Mom left the adults in the house, with the weed and the Lucky Lager and the Gallo Mountain Rhine, and headed out to the goat shed for the evening milking.

"Oh, shit." She stopped on the trail and dropped the bucket in disgust. The gate was open again, and the goats were nowhere to be seen.

She stormed back down the trail to the house. Now the children were nowhere in sight either. "Damn it!"

Her husband appeared at the back door. "What is it?"

"Those stupid kids have let the goats out again. Are they in the front meadow?"

"The kids, or the goats?"

"Anyone." She went around the house, but the front meadow was empty too. "Damn it."

"Shh," he said, coming out of the house and following her. "Listen for the bell."

"I know!" But then she was quiet.

They heard nothing. "Well, they can't have gotten far," the Dad said eventually.

"I'm gonna go check the back meadow."

Evening Star and Billy Goat appeared on the front porch. "I feel a vibe," Billy Goat called down. "Check the back meadow."

"Thanks," the Mom muttered, already halfway down the trail.

Sunset was still a ways off, but shadows were growing long in the back meadow. The children were still nowhere to be seen, nor were the goats. The Mom stood there a long time, listening for Lady's bell.

Then something caught her attention, in the middle of the meadow. A dark shape. She walked up to it, then suddenly turned and ran. She made it to the edge of the woods before throwing up.

The Princess watched from the woods as the Mom was sick. The Mom had seen the evil thing. More evil even than a big black spider, although somehow reminiscent of it. The dogs had seen the evil thing too, and had made it even more evil before the Princess could make them stop. Actually, truth be told, the Princess had not been able to make them stop at all. They had eaten their fill before wandering off to nap, bellies engorged. At least she had managed to keep the Apricot Boy and the stupid fat girl away from it. It was not something that children should see.

The Mom walked slowly down the path back to the house, carrying a bloody bell.

CHAPTER 3

"I don't know *what* it was," the Mom said for what felt like the eighteenth time. "I didn't see anything—you guys saw as much as I did."

Billy Goat frowned, brushing tobacco flakes out of his beard. They fell to the floor and disappeared into the braided rug. "Are you sure there weren't any footprints or tracks or whatever?"

The Mom got up and went to the sink, where the half-chopped potatoes waited. She poured herself a glass of water and stared out the window. "You saw exactly what I saw," she finally said, in a flat voice. "You want to go look again?"

"No, we don't, hon," Evening Star said quickly. She got up and went to the Mom, giving her shoulders a squeeze. The Mom smiled at her briefly as Star went on, "Don't be uptight. We're all freaked out. He's just trying to help, that's all."

"I know." The Mom turned back to the group. She caught her husband's eye and gave him a look.

He took the cue. "The important thing is to decide what to do next," he said, looking at Billy Goat and Evening Star particularly. "For us *all* to decide."

"Far out," Evening Star smiled. "You really mean you want us to stay, then?"

"Yes," said the Dad, at the same moment as the Mom said, "Of course." *The more the merrier*, she thought.

"We never meant to live out here all alone," the Dad added.

Billy Goat grinned. "Here's to our new community!" He raised the bottle of Mountain Rhine to his lips, took a generous swig, and then passed it to the Dad, sitting next to him.

The Dad took the wine and sipped. "Right. So, about what to do…"

"Right," Evening Star agreed. "Well, the rest of the goats are safe now, right?"

"Those were our two best milkers," the Mom said quietly. She sat back down next to the Dad, cross-legged on the floor, and accepted the wine bottle from him. "And they weren't cheap." She felt awful, thinking of them as commodities. They'd been creatures, living beings who had names and personalities. Sure, Lady had been a bitch, and Fatima had been sort of difficult too, but she had never wished them dead.

"I imagine they're safe in their pen," the Dad said. The Mom noticed he didn't meet Evening Star's eyes when he said this, though he did glance briefly in the direction of the loft, where all three children were playing quietly.

"She didn't mean to let them out," Evening Star said.

The Dad patted her knee. "I know. But now she knows to be even more careful when she visits them."

"Speaking of being careful," the Mom said, then hesitated. They were all skirting around the real issue here. "I mean, um, whatever it was…"

"You think it might come back?" Billy Goat seemed almost amused at the concept.

The Mom couldn't figure him, not at all. Why wouldn't the thing come back? "Well, who knows? We don't even know what's out there. And you guys were talking about getting a tent or something…I mean, a tent isn't much protection."

"It was probably a bear," the Dad said. "The goats must have surprised it. Bears aren't very vicious unless they're surprised."

"But Lady wore a bell," the Mom said. "It's not like a bear wouldn't hear her coming."

Everyone nodded. The Mountain Rhine bottle worked its way around the circle.

"We'd still like to get a tent, maybe a big army surplus one," Evening Star finally said. "Those are sturdy."

Billy Goat nodded and grinned again. This time he seemed to leer at Evening Star.

Yeah, I know, I know, the Mom thought. *It's hard to ball in full view in the front meadow.* Though she doubted he was very modest about such things, when it came to it. "Do you really think that's safe?" she asked.

"Let's give it a few days, and see if anything else happens," Evening Star said. "The dogs are outside, they'll bark if they hear anything."

The Mom frowned. There hadn't been any barking this afternoon. "Well…" She paused. "Maybe you guys should sleep in here for now, anyway."

"Mom?" came a plaintive voice from the loft. "When's dinner? We're hungry."

"Soon, honey," she called. And then, to the adults, she added, "Anyway, we can't afford new goats. We'll have to make do with the flock we've got." She got up and went back to the sink.

"I'll finish those," Evening Star said, also getting to her feet.

The Mom stepped aside to let her chop potatoes. "Thanks." She started building a fire in the cook stove. "Jeez, how late is it?"

"I don't know," the Dad said. The sun had gone down a while ago. "There's three kids in the flock," he added. "I mean, baby goats. Two of those are female, right?"

"Right," the Mom said.

"So we can sell the male, and the females will be grown soon. We can mate them with the billy goat—sorry," he grinned, looking at Billy Goat. "I mean—"

"Yeah, I know," Bill said. "But isn't he their father?"

"Well, yeah," the Dad frowned. "Is that a problem?"

Everyone shrugged. Billy Goat said, "Hey, it should be cool. They won't do it if the energy is wrong."

Of course they will—they're goats, the Mom thought, but she wasn't sure. Actually, she had no idea about animal husbandry, what the goats would and wouldn't do. It had just seemed like a cool idea, to buy goats and raise them, milk them, make cheese, all that. Who knew they would be such a pain in the ass? They were strong, stubborn, willful. And smart enough to act stupid, when it suited them. At least the milk was good. And even if they were damned frustrating sometimes, she did enjoy milking them, spending the time with them.

"Can we go outside and play?" the Princess asked, leading the other kids down the steep stairs from the loft.

"No," the Mom said. "It's dark, and I told you, it's dangerous. You guys play inside. Dinner will be ready soon."

The Princess gave a theatrical sigh and flopped down on a pillow. The Apricot Boy and Morning Star sat down next to her.

"What we need is more folks here," Bill said. "A bigger community would be safer, not to mention better energy and all."

"Well, like I said, we've always wanted more folks, but so far, nobody's come along who wanted to stay," the Dad pointed out.

"Nobody knows we're here," Bill said. "We need to put fliers up at the Laundromat or the auto body place, or the health food store, they have that billboard there. No one can find us out here."

"You found us," the Mom pointed out.

"That was just luck."

"Yeah, we were thinking of heading up to Eugene, actually," Star said.

"But this is much better—incredible energy, great vibes," Bill added.

"It sure is," Star agreed.

The Mom nodded and smiled as she filled a pot with water. Fliers might be a good idea. Behind her, she heard the sound of another joint about to be rolled, Dad shaking his Frisbee full of stash, separating the seeds and stems from the good weed. "Sure, make some fliers," she said. "But sleep in the house for a few days, all right?"

"Sure, Mama," Evening Star agreed.

The Princess sat with the other kids at the front of the house. They'd been lurking upstairs, listening to the Land meeting. It had taken all of the Princess's powers of persuasion to keep them quiet so she could hear what was being decided. She absorbed the news that the Stars and Bill would be staying on. She had guessed as much already, so she didn't react, but still, she didn't like it. They were the wrong kind of people for the Land. She couldn't have said why, exactly; they were just wrong.

Now the Princess wanted, more than anything else in the whole wide world, to go back outside and investigate. It had all been too crazy earlier. As soon as she had found the goats, the dogs had started in on them, and then her mom had come along. And then the other adults had all trooped out there. How was she supposed to find clues with everybody tramping all over the place?

Now she was locked in the house, and there was no way to slip out unnoticed. *Stupid small house*, the Princess thought. One room; both doors in full view of everyone. Well, she'd soon find a way to get outside and figure it out.

"Here's a snack," her mom said, bringing the kids some sliced carrots.

"Thanks," the Princess said. Morning Star whimpered a little, but didn't refuse them. The kids all chewed on carrots until dinner was ready.

A week later, the Mom cleaned up after breakfast. The children were squabbling at her feet, Morning Star shrieking about something, the Apricot Boy whining. Outside, the Dad was chopping up some more wood outside. She didn't know what Bill and Star were up to. They hadn't come in yet this morning from their new tent.

The Mom still felt anxious about them in the tent, especially since they'd insisted on setting it up near the vegetable garden, along the path that led to the back meadow. That seemed to be asking for trouble. In any event, the Mom still wasn't willing to let the children play outside, at least not where she couldn't see them.

They usually played upstairs, driving their little trucks and matchbox cars on the patchwork carpet in the loft, but today for some reason they had decided to make their game downstairs. "Vrooooom, vrooooom," the Apricot Boy said studiously, moving his truck along the outer edge of the braided rug.

The Mom scraped the dishes into the compost jar, tuning out the kids, trying to calm her annoyance at the Dad. "It must have been a bear," he had said, yet again, this morning. "There's nothing else that dangerous out here."

"What about mountain lions?" the Mom had asked.

"But those are way smaller than the goats. You know Lady could have held her own against a mountain lion."

"No, those are huge. You mean bobcats. Mountain lions eat deer, I heard."

"Whatever." Then he'd immediately gone out to chop wood.

Actually, the Mom had no idea what anything ate. She had thought bears just ate honey and berries, for that matter. Which was why they'd been having this exact same argument for a week now. An argument that just made her feel more helpless and frustrated.

At least she had Evening Star, who had been a godsend. It was so nice to have a like-minded person around, even if she did insist on moving into the tent. She had artistic talent, too; she'd drawn up gorgeous fliers advertising the community, inviting like-minded, peace-loving individuals to come and hang out, swim, consider joining. The whole Land community had loved the fliers, so they put them up at strategic places in Yokayo. They didn't bother putting any up in tiny Vaughn's Corner—it was all rednecks anyway.

The Mom turned to wipe down the counter by the stove and almost tripped over Morning Star. Overbalancing, she leaned back, her foot coming down hard on the Apricot Boy's stupid little jaggedy metal truck, which she could hardly see against the rug. "Son of a bitch!" she yelled, flailing, catching her elbow on the counter with a hard slam. The Princess looked at her, eyes wide.

Ever since the evil, the Princess had been locked in the house with the Apricot Boy and the fat girl. Boring! Unfair! Nobody seemed to understand that the evil would not hurt the Princess, and that furthermore, she had already protected the younger children from it. In fact, she was now convinced that somehow she had only let the Mom see what had happened after the threat was long gone. Even the dogs had been safe. The evil had come and gone quickly. It had done its work, then slipped back into the woods.

The Princess knew about evil. She had read plenty of books about it. She had seen the spider on the mountaintop and had commanded it to leave. But she had been prevented from finding out any more details about this particular evil, and that would not do.

She had not actually seen what had happened to the goats. But she felt she understood it all the same. It was part of what made life interesting, more like the books she read, particularly the scary ones. Scary things were thrilling, exciting.

She had tolerated being cooped up for an entire week now, waiting for her mom to relent, but now she had had enough. "Okay, listen to me," she had told the Apricot Boy and the fat girl, whispering in the loft. "This is what we're going to do."

Within an hour, they had moved their game downstairs, tripped the Mom, and gotten shooed out of the house. Freedom! The Princess smiled. "Come on," she said to the others, heading up the path to the back meadow.

"My mom says we're not supposed to go there," the fat girl whined as soon as she realized what the Princess was doing.

"Well, all right, if you're scared, you don't have to come." She took the Apricot Boy's hand. "We'll go by ourselves."

The fat girl started crying again, fresh tears running down the tracks left on her face from five minutes ago. "I want to come! I'm coming!"

"So come *on* then," the Princess said.

They walked up the path, silently except for the last lingering sniffles out of Morning Star. The dogs came with them, trotting happily along, making the Princess feel even more safe. They passed the tent where the fat girl's parents were, walking even more quietly on their bare feet so as not to disturb them. The Princess especially did not want to look. She had already seen Billy Goat and Evening Star earlier, in the front meadow. She knew what balling looked like—when her parents did it, when the goats did it, even when dogs did it, when they weren't supposed to—and she didn't like to see it. Besides, Billy Goat and Evening Star did it wrong. From everything the Princess understood, the man was supposed to be on top.

The children reached the back meadow. The Princess immediately walked out to the spot where the goat carcasses had been found. Her dad had cleared the area well. The dogs were no longer interested; after a perfunctory sniff, they flopped down in the shade at the edge of the meadow. But still, the Princess thought there might be something to see, some clue.

The ground was still stained dark from the blood. The Princess sat down right next to the dark spot, tracing the edges of it with her finger.

"Ew," the fat girl said. The Apricot Boy stood quiet, watching his sister warily, but adoringly all the same.

The Princess just looked back at the others for a moment, then returned her attention to the spot of evil.

For some reason, it made her feel really, really good to be here. Beyond just the excitement and relief of being freed from the house, during a week of such nice weather. She got a little thrill in the base of her tummy, which grew stronger as she poked her finger at the spot. She closed her eyes and enjoyed the feeling. It was better than when her dad drove the car really fast over the whee-bump on the road, down past the ford.

The Princess removed her finger and thought about it. If the evil had left some bit of itself in this spot, then it was a magical place, like the wardrobe with the winter coats in it, like the road to Mordor...

"What are you doing?" the fat girl asked, interrupting her train of thought.

The Princess turned slowly to face the annoying child. "I am looking for clues. I am solving the mystery."

"It's not a mystery," Morning Star answered. "My dad said it was a bear, and then the dogs maybe even finished up the job. Maybe the bear just hurt the goats a little, and then the dogs came and ate them."

"Not Galadriel and Sauron!" the Princess protested. The dogs looked up at their names, then returned to their nap. "They wouldn't hurt a fly!"

"My dad said you never know with dogs. He gets a vibe."

The Princess stood up to face her. "Well, *my* dad says your dad's vibes are a bunch of bullshit."

Whereupon the stupid fat girl burst into tears yet again, and ran from the meadow back to her family's tent. Good riddance.

The Princess returned her attention to the spot, again tracing the dried blood with her finger, avoiding a small spider web holding two blades of grass together. But now the magic was gone, and she felt nothing. Magic was like that. You had to believe really hard in it, and nothing could distract you or it would scatter. Stupid Morning Star anyway.

That night in the main house, Evening Star got out her I Ching coins, offering to throw them for everyone. The Mom and her husband sat forward, watching her with polite interest. The Mom did some astrology from time to time, casting horoscopes for everyone in the family, including her parents, who weren't the slightest bit interested, but astrology was different: that was scientific. There were books and charts and everything for astrology, and it all depended on the actual movements of actual stars and planets and the like. The I Ching seemed, well, kind of made-up. Ancient Chinese divination coins indeed. But the Mom didn't say so. She was always reluctant to make fun of someone else's religion. However ridiculous it might seem to her.

"Yours first," Evening Star said, sitting across from the Mom. She closed her eyes as she tossed the three coins, then stared down at them, reading meaning where there seemed to the Mom to be none. Eventually, she got out a big book and started looking something up.

"It says we are at a crossroads," she told the Mom. "You especially, but all of us, our family, our community. We have a big choice ahead of us, and one of the paths is dangerous."

The Mom struggled to keep a straight face. *Life is always a crossroads, isn't it?* "Which path is the dangerous one?" she asked.

"It doesn't say." Evening Star picked up the coins. She looked at the Dad and said, "Now I'll do yours, and maybe it will answer her question. Because your destinies should be intertwined."

She shook the coins in her hands again and tossed them onto the braided rug, then repeated the process of staring, then going to the book. "The left road," she finally said.

Now the Mom couldn't help a small snicker. "Which one is that?"

"The one opposite the right one," Billy Goat put in, from where he reclined in the rocking chair across the room, with his beer and his hand-rolled cigarette.

Hippies are such bullshit-purveyors, the Mom thought, as Evening Star picked up the coins for another throw. *Except us, of course.*

The Dad was driving back from town a day or two later. The car was full of groceries and dog food and goat food and a day-old free newspaper and clean laundry and other stuff. Someday they would be totally self-sufficient on the Land…but not yet. That was cool. It took time to do something right, after all.

He took the turnoff past the Russian River and into the little valley that led into Vaughn's Corner, driving almost without noticing, just cruising along. The radio was playing, and it was a good song, for once. He was close to the spot on the drive, but not quite there, where it was far enough from town so that the reception wavered, and then faded altogether. He sang along to the Grateful Dead, narrowing his eyes to croon with Jerry, one finger on the steering wheel.

When he got to the place where the valley opened up, separating into East Side Road, which was long, straight, and flat, and West Side Road, which was shorter, but winding and slow, he suddenly skidded to a stop, almost ramming into a barrier laid across the road. "What the…" He peered out through the dirty, buggy windshield at a sign: *Detour. Road Closed.* An arrow pointed to West Side Road. Just beyond the barrier, a few road crew workmen milled about on a little bridge. "Shit, man," he said to himself. If they were replacing that bridge or something, that would be a colossal pain in the ass. That would take weeks, at least. Maybe the rest of the summer!

He checked his rear-view mirror, then backed up, making the left turn onto West Side Road. "Think they could put up a sign or something," he muttered, wondering if he had simply missed one in his last few minutes with the music.

Three bends into the poky, frustratingly slow detour, he saw an old faded yellow GMC pickup with a hand-built wooden camper shell on the back of it: a classic hippie-mobile. It was parked on a wide dirt shoulder by the side of the road, and a couple was standing beside it, puzzling over a map. The Dad pulled over behind them and got out of the Dart.

"Hey, you folks lost?" he asked, in his friendly, hail-fellow-well-met voice.

The couple looked up at him. The man was tall, a little stout, and bearded. The woman was small and dark, with long thin hair pulled to either side in leather pony-tail holders with fringes dangling down, matching her long earrings. The man broke into a smile at the obvious sight of another hippie. "Hey, man, cool. We're trying to find this place." He held out one of the fliers Evening Star had made. "But we're completely lost, and that construction…"

"That's great! That's our place—our flier!" the Dad exclaimed. "Far out. Just follow me."

The woman smiled too, but got back into her truck without saying anything. Even so, the Dad thought, *Nice folks. Probably should have gotten their names.*

Twenty minutes later the two vehicles pulled off the dirt road and made their way up the long driveway. Galadriel and Sauron went into their usual frenzy of excitement, paying particular attention to the camper shell. The new couple got out and looked around, stretching; the woman yawned. The Dad parked next to them, then came over and stuck his hand out, introducing himself properly.

The stout man said, "You can just call me Weed—everyone does. It's better than Walter!"

The Dad laughed. "Weed, cool, any particular reason for that?"

The woman smiled and said in a low, melodic voice, "Pretty much what you'd think. I'm Astrid."

"It's *great* to have you guys here," the Dad said, because it was. You advertise, and not a week later, kindred souls show up. Why hadn't they thought of this sooner?

Weed went to the back of the camper shell and opened the door. Two big dogs scrabbled out. The black one immediately ran to Galadriel and started sniffing her butt. The brown one approached Sauron a little warily, with its fur up, but wagging its tail.

"Elf—easy now," Weed said to the brown dog. Meanwhile, the black dog was already trying to jump on Galadriel's hindquarters, but he wasn't lined up properly.

"Granola! Cut it out!" Astrid yelled.

The Dad laughed. "It's all right—we had her spayed, after the litter. They can have all the fun they want."

Astrid gave him a bit of a dirty look, but said nothing. She grabbed Granola by the collar and yanked him down off Galadriel.

The Dad shrugged. Not everyone approved of spaying or neutering dogs. But even on land as big as this, who wanted thousands of puppies running around? Puppies that would grow into dogs and need to be fed, taken care of, watched out for.

"So come on in." He ushered the new folks to the house.

"The left road!" Evening Star shrieked, thrilled. "You took the left road and there they were! It's just like the coins said!" She gave the Mom a huge grin.

Yeah, so what, I didn't believe you, the Mom thought, but smiled kindly back, then even more genuinely at Weed and Astrid, who had expressed an entirely satisfactory level of delight at her lovely home.

"I didn't have any choice—everyone had to take the left road," the Dad pointed out. "The right road is closed."

"It doesn't matter! The coins said the left road, and you took it, and now our community is growing! Your destiny—ours, all aligned together—perfect!" She sat on the floor, rocking back and forth with delight.

"I thought they said the left road was dangerous," the Mom said, frowning as she tried to think.

"No, the left road was the good one." Evening Star shook her head incredulously. "Because remember? The *right* road was the *wrong* road."

"Whatever." The Mom shrugged.

Weed and Astrid grinned at everyone. Beers were opened, and freshly grown weed was passed around in generous joints. The Mom could almost see the newcomers deciding to move right in, no further discussion necessary. At least they had a camper to sleep in. All they needed to do was find a level place to park it.

The Princess watched her dominion grow. More subjects came to her realm, but they were just more boring grown-ups. Astrid especially was very unfriendly to the children: cold, silent. She only smiled when she was talking to one of the grown-ups.

The Princess did not mind this all that much. The last subjects who had come had brought the stupid Morning Star, who was as worthless a playmate as the Apricot Boy. The Princess was destined to live out her days in solitude, even when surrounded by other people. That was all right. It was the way of princesses. Some day she would be rescued. Somebody would understand.

The Princess watched from the low branch of the doubled-up madrone and oak tree in the front meadow as the new folks settled their truck in. After much debate amongst all the grown-ups, they had chosen a spot near the road, at the edge of the front meadow. It looked reasonably level, but every time Weed positioned the truck and parked it, Astrid would get into the camper shell, come back out after a minute, and make him move it again. A few inches forward, a few inches back.

The Princess watched all this with detached amusement. She could have told them a perfectly level place to park, but nobody had asked her. Besides, they probably wouldn't want to park in the back meadow anyway. Although it was by far the nicest meadow on the property, nobody seemed to want to spend much time there. They never had, even before the goat thing.

The Princess now went to the back meadow every day. Usually alone, though sometimes the Apricot Boy managed to tag along, or the dogs—now a pack of four. Morning Star never joined her. Which was fine.

At last, Astrid seemed satisfied. Weed turned the truck off one last time, then got out and started doing something at the back corner, tying something down or untying something. Astrid went into the camper and didn't come out. The Princess grew quickly bored, leaned back on the thick branch, and began daydreaming.

The Princess was sitting in her tree watching her realm grow when the evil monster came to talk to her. He had a huge fat hairy body and way too many legs, like an ugly demented spider. "You do not own this realm! I do!" the evil monster challenged in a deep and booming voice. "You all must leave! You have been warned!"

"No, evil monster, it is I who own this realm, and you who must leave!" the Princess answered in a strong enough voice of her own. "Go and do your evil in some other realm!"

"Ha ha ha ha ha," the evil monster laughed.

"I will kill you!" the Princess cried, raising her magic wand.

"No, not the magic wand!" the evil monster cried.

"Yes!"

"Aiiiiyeeee!"

A sharp pain bit into her ankle. The Princess blinked her eyes, coming back to the here-and-now and reaching down for her leg so fast she almost fell out of the tree. She pulled up the leg of her jeans to inspect. A red ant had stung her, and was still crawling around, obviously looking for its next bite. She crushed it and flicked it to the ground, then looked around. Weed was still fiddling with his truck, and Astrid had not come out again. Boring! The Princess slipped down out of the tree and went into the house to find her little-village toys: the matchbox cars, tiny ceramic animals, and scraps of rugs and shells and other little decorative bits with which to build their homes.

"We're going down to the river in a few minutes, honey, if you want to come along," the Mom said, as the Princess came back downstairs with her basket of supplies. The Mom was wiping the Apricot Boy's face with a rough washcloth. He made faces but didn't protest.

"No, thank you. I'm going to play outside," the Princess answered.

The Mom smiled. "Okay. We'll be back in an hour or so."

"Okay."

At dinner, the six adults and three children crowded around the octagonal folding table. The Dad would have to build another one if the community wanted to keep eating together. Which was kind of the point of a community, wasn't it? He dug into his soy vegetable loaf with enthusiasm as he pondered the problem. Should he build a second table, or just replace this one with a larger one? The eight-sided table had worked very well for smaller groups. He had designed it himself, and was rather proud of it. It was cut from thick plywood, hinged in the middle, and painted a cheerful red. Four little stubby legs, a little under a foot and a half long, were hinged onto the bottom and snapped into place for use. The whole thing folded up to only a few inches thick and could be tucked away when not needed, when you wanted to do anything else but eat in the little one-room cabin. And there was no need for chairs. You sat cross-legged on the floor, as nature intended.

"This is great," Astrid said, meaning the soy vegetable loaf.

"I know!" Evening Star said, meaning the whole scene. Everyone smiled, everyone agreed.

The Dad was proud not only of his table. He had pretty much built the whole house as well, with help from his sister's boyfriend, and the Mom of course, a little, and this one builder guy who had drifted through at just the right moment last year and had been happy to work for weed and food and a place to crash. But it was the Dad's vision, his design. His wife had been reluctant to move out of the city in the first place, though she hadn't said it in so many words. She had relented somewhat on their first visit to the Land, when they stood in the gorgeous front meadow and turned their faces to the welcoming sun. But she hadn't really warmed up to the place until the cabin was built. He'd felt a little bad about pushing her, but happy that she'd come around.

"My brother would love it here," Weed was saying.

The Dad perked up, returning his attention to the conversation. "Really? Bring him—why not? You can call him from town."

"Yeah, he's having a tough time with our folks. He came and crashed with us in the city for a while, but then that scene fell apart, so we headed out…"

Astrid grimaced. "Ugh, the city. Bad scene. Wrong drugs, bad energy. Bad people."

"Bummer," the Mom said.

"Bummer," Astrid agreed. "Anyway—you'll like Junior, he's a good kid."

The Princess looked up from her soy vegetable loaf. The Dad noticed and smiled. "He's probably not a kid-kid, is he, Weed? How old is your brother?"

Weed laughed. "Junior? Nah, he's not a kid—he's seventeen. A little too old to play with your kids here!"

The Princess' gaze darted back downward, and she took another reluctant bite.

"Don't push it off your plate, honey," the Mom said.

"I'm not." The Princess refused to look up.

"Yes, you are—look, it's all over the place!" She sighed and got up to get a washcloth—the same one that had scrubbed the Apricot Boy's face earlier.

"I'm full," the Princess announced, pushing her plate away from her, and into the mess she had made.

"Stop it!" the Mom said, her voice raised as she returned with the washcloth. She pushed the plate back towards the Princess and out of the mess. "Now look what you did! You mushed it all up."

The Princess burst into tears. "I'm full!"

"Well, that's fine, but don't smear food all over the table!" The Mom picked up the plate and started wiping up the mess. The Princess sobbed loudly. The Dad patted her shoulder for a second and then shrugged as he looked around the table. The rest of the adults all looked back at him, uncomfortable. The cozy mood of a minute ago had evaporated.

Kids, the Dad thought. *Well, what are you gonna do?*

He went to see the Princess up in her little cubby an hour after she had left the table for bed, still sobbing. "Hey," he whispered, in case she was asleep. He carried a kerosene lantern, but the cubby was tiny and it was hard to see in there. Especially when a little girl had wrapped herself in her blankets to work through her misery and didn't especially want to be bothered. Or, rather, wanted somebody to take a lot of trouble to bother her. Which would mean they really meant it.

The Dad smiled to himself at the thought of his strange, bookish daughter sniffling upstairs, waiting for someone to come to her. He had done the same thing himself as a child. The important thing was not to come too soon, before the mood had worn itself out; but not so late that the child felt abandoned and forgotten, or fell asleep.

"Hey," he whispered again, leaning in with the lamp.

"Dad?" came a small voice from under the covers and the jumbled fur of two or three cats.

"Hey Princess, I thought we were going to read more of *The Two Towers* tonight. Don't tell me you forgot?"

The covers shifted slightly, then a little face appeared. Solemn, but happy underneath. "I didn't forget."

He crawled into the cubby next to her, though there was barely enough room for his head and shoulders. The rest of his body stretched out into the main part of the loft, next to the Apricot Boy's crib. He propped himself up on his elbows. The book was still in its niche, just under her tiny window. He settled the lamp so that enough light came in, found their place in the book, and started to read aloud, in a calm, practiced voice. Within three pages, the girl was asleep.

A day or two or three later, the Mom was coming back from milking the remaining goats, trying not to think about how much easier the task was now that there weren't so many of them, or about how the two most belligerent goats had been the ones killed, when she heard something coming up the driveway. It didn't sound like a car, exactly, or a truck. It was a thin sound, but loud. She hurried down the trail, trying not to spill any milk, and found a guy on a motorcycle. He pulled into the cleared-off, tramped-down place by the house where all the cars parked, wheeled around showily, and came to a stop under an oak tree, facing away from her.

He had no shirt on, and wore very faded, holey, and patched blue jeans. His slender butt on the motorcycle seat stretched the denim almost to a breaking point. Below were thick black leather boots, equally worn, ragged at the heels. His long brown hair flowed down his back all the way to his waist, gorgeous and clean and wavy; she only knew he was a man because she'd seen him briefly from the front before he spun around. He wore no helmet. Helmets were uncool. Helmets were for cops. Hippies never wore helmets. He did, however, wear dark sunglasses, like a beatnik.

Behind him on the bike, where a second passenger might ride, was tied a bedroll, a canvas knapsack, and a guitar case. The Mom didn't know anything about motorcycles, but she knew this was a pretty big one.

The Mom stood there, milk pail in hand, watching. The guy turned off the engine, then swung a long leg over, getting to his feet. He turned around and seemed to just notice the Mom, although she had the feeling he knew he had been watched the whole time. Call it an intuition, but it was just how he moved. Languorous. Easy. Self-assured.

Now he smiled at her and took a step forward. She suddenly felt self-conscious in her Indian-print skirt, crummy faded red t-shirt with a fresh squirt of milk across the front, and the utterly bucolic milk pail dangling at her side. Because the guy was simply gorgeous. His huge dark brown eyes matched his hair and long eyelashes. He was deeply tanned, his skin was flawless and smooth. His cheekbones were prominent, his chin was perfect. His nut-brown chest was firm and well muscled, though there was no excess on him. The blue jeans fit him perfectly, where they weren't about to fall apart.

"Hi," the guy said. "I'm Junior."

CHAPTER 4

The Princess's realm just kept growing! Though she had been warned, it was nonetheless disappointing that the new kid had turned out to be another grown-up. Not that she was terribly interested in new kids, but you never knew. She liked his guitar playing, though, and he was nice to the Princess. Since his brother's camper on the back of his truck was too small for more than two people, Junior had been sleeping on the floor of the main house while he built a tiny cabin of his own, close to the creek which separated the Land from the cow ranch next door.

The Princess liked to watch him while he picked at his guitar. He had the longest eyelashes she had ever seen on anyone, man or woman or boy or girl. Her mom liked to sing along with the guitar playing too. It all seemed very nice; so nice, in fact, that sometimes it would come to the point where the Princess would have to get away from it all, go outside and up to the top of her mountain with the evil spiders and the other monsters.

Today was one of those days. She felt suddenly that there wasn't enough air in the house, though that was silly, because it was a sunny, pretty day, and all the windows were open, narrow as they were, and the double-Dutch back door too. But she knew when it was time to go to the woods. Nobody questioned her as she slipped out the back door and up the path, past the goats, past the burned-out trees, past the hidden pot garden…to her mountaintop.

The Princess had spent a few hours alone and was on her feet, ready to go back down the hill, when she thought she heard a voice. She stopped and listened. There was an ancient logging road up here, and theoretically someone could walk along it, but it didn't really lead anywhere. It didn't come from anywhere either. This wasn't even technically the Land anymore; it was government land, Forest Service or Bureau of Land Management or something, nobody was really sure. It didn't matter. There were no fences or signs, and nobody used the government land. It stretched hundreds or maybe even a thousand acres off towards the north and east, and was very inaccessible.

As she stood there near the top of the trail, all she heard were the normal sounds of the woods. But as soon as she started walking again, her bare feet rustling leaves on the path, she heard it again: *I'm here*, it might have been. Or, *Come here*.

She froze, ears alert. "Who is it?" she finally asked.

Fun here.

She wheeled around—the sound had come from right behind her—but there was nobody there.

For the first time, she felt a tiny bit frightened, an edgy feeling in her tummy. But it went away quickly as she could easily see that she was alone.

She took a few steps back the way she had come, looking for the source of the sound. "Who is it?" she asked again, trying to make her voice brave like Peter in the Narnia books. Peter was always taking charge, despite being so young. That's what oldest children did. And it all worked out, one way or another.

One fear. Or was it that? It might have been another *Come here*. It was so faint, and now it seemed to come from behind her again, on the way down the hill.

She turned slowly around and looked down the trail. Though there were shadows, it was still a bright sunny day, and nobody was there. Not even a talking deer.

The Princess steeled herself, straightened her shoulders, and said out loud, in a firm, calm voice, "I am going back down the trail now, and if anybody wants to talk to me, they are going to have to let me see them." She promptly started walking. *I won't stop, even if I hear it again,* she thought. *They're just playing tricks on me.*

Don't fear, she thought she heard, but she kept walking.

She had gotten past the crest of the mountain where the logging road crossed the trail when the sound changed. *Can't see,* it maybe whispered. Or *Cat thing.* The voice was very unclear. *Camping?*

She couldn't stand it: she stopped again. The voice still seemed to come from whatever direction she wasn't looking. "Is it the mountain talking to me?" she asked.

Eeeeeeeehhhhh, the voice sighed, whispered, exhaled. If a shout could be whispered, that was. An anxious breathing, but a relief as well.

Was it just the wind making a tree branch creak? If so, why hadn't she heard it before? It wasn't particularly windy. The Princess frowned and sat down on a fallen log by the trail. "What do you want to say to me?"

Go away, she thought she heard. Or maybe, *Come and play.*

"I don't understand you," she said. "You have to be more clear."

On the day...

"This is my mountain," she said, much more boldly than she felt. "My mom and dad bought all this property, and they said I could walk up this trail if I wanted to. So you can't scare me. Okay?" Of course, this wasn't exactly true. They had never discussed where the Princess could and could not go. And this probably wasn't their property right here at all. Or maybe it was. Hard to tell without fences.

But now the voice was silent.

The Princess sat on the log another minute, then got up and started slowly back down the trail. She heard no more voices all the way down the hill. But she wasn't going to stop again, even if she did.

The Mom sang all morning as Junior played his guitar. For such a young guy, he knew so many songs, and she hadn't sung in such a long time, she had forgotten how much she loved to. The others hung around for a while, singing along, but eventually everyone but the Mom drifted away. She was happy to have him to herself, though Junior didn't talk much. He expressed himself through his music. Weed had told them that he had trouble with his parents—their parents. But Junior didn't say anything about it, to the Mom or to anyone else. He seemed very relaxed and happy on the Land. He was quiet, but that was just fine. Everyone had come to the Land to make a fresh start, in one way or another.

At lunchtime, the Mom made cheese sandwiches and poured glasses of fresh co-op apple juice for the two of them. "This is delicious," Junior said politely. He ate the sandwich as though he was starving, so she made him another one. He had been here more than a week now and he always ate this way, not putting on an ounce (and she could easily tell, because he still didn't wear a shirt). Teenagers. He drank three glasses of juice as the Mom tried not to think about how much it had cost. It was an extravagance she allowed herself, at least until they found a source of apples and she could make her own.

"Do you want another?" she asked, as he wolfed down the second sandwich as fast as the first.

"Um…" Now he looked a little sheepish. "No, I'm fine, thanks. I don't want to eat you out of house and home."

"Nonsense," the Mom said, getting up and going back over to the cold-box for the cheese. "It's practically free—the cheese is government surplus, and I made the bread myself."

"It's delicious," he said again. She smiled as she made him a third sandwich.

After lunch, he leaned back from the table and said, "Well, I guess I should work on my cabin some."

The Mom tried not to feel disappointed. Of course he had work to do. Hell, she had plenty of chores of her own and she had wasted the whole morning singing. It just felt so good to let her hair down once in a while, so to speak, to have some fun. "Do you need any help?" she found herself asking.

Junior gave her a long, lazy look from underneath those incredible eye-lashes, sending a flutter of confusion through her chest. "Nah, you got stuff you want to do here, remember?"

"Of course." She gave a small laugh, gathering herself. "It's past time to milk the goats, anyway. And I was going to do some laundry…"

"Well, I guess we better all get to work then!" He got to his feet, putting his guitar back in its case. "Mind if I leave this here?"

"Not at all." She was pleased to keep his guitar in the house, though there was really no room for it, alongside his knapsack and bedroll and the extra pillow they had rummaged up, and the folding table coming out three times a day, and all the people hanging out here all the time. No matter. She'd make room. "Good luck building. Let me know if you need anything."

"Will do." He tipped an imaginary cap to her and went out the back door.

The Mom was just trying to find her brain again, and decide whether to do the milking first or go straight to the laundry, when the Princess came in the back door. "Hi, hon," the Mom said.

"Hi." The Princess went to the cold-box, got out the hunk of cheese, and put it on the counter, which was almost too high for her. Then she got out the bread and a knife, and started sawing away at the loaf.

"Hold up there, you're going all crooked." The Mom rescued the project and her food supplies. "I can make you a cheese sandwich, okay? Go wait over there, it'll be ready in a second." She pointed to the floor-pillow by the front window.

"Okay." The Princess went to the pillow and sat down.

After the Mom brought the sandwich to her daughter, she began gath-ering the laundry together and performing triage on it: what absolutely needed to be done today, what could wait a few days. The mending pile needed a similar triage, but that could wait another day… By the time she looked up again, her daughter had gone upstairs, leaving three-quarters of a cheese sandwich on the plate by the floor pillow.

The Princess was glad that when she got home, the scene with the guitar and the singing and the not enough air in the house was over and done with. In fact, by the time she got home, there was nobody else around except for her Mom. Which suited the Princess just fine. She always liked to be alone. After she ate as much as she could of her sandwich, she climbed the stairs to the loft and her little room-niche, got out *The Lion, the Witch and the Wardrobe*, and settled in to read the Narnia books just one more time. She had liked thinking about Peter, and the duties and responsibilities of oldest children. She knew she was supposed to identify with Susan because she was a girl, but Susan was boring. She only got to be a Queen. Peter got to be the main King, and the leader of all the rest. Now that was a role worth aspiring to.

A few days later, the Dad was driving into town when he saw a woman by the side of the road, her thumb poking at the air. He dutifully pulled over and opened the door for her.

She got in, tossed her huge green bag in the back seat, smiled at him, and said, "Far out, thanks!"

"Where you going? I'm only heading into Yokayo, but I can take you that far if you like."

She pushed her long dirty blonde hair out of her eyes and settled more comfortably into the seat, exuding essence of patchouli oil, and something darker underneath. The smell of the road. "Oh, nowhere in particular. Do you live in Yokayo?"

"No, we have a community out in the valley, by the river. I'm just going to the store and stuff. I'm the designated town-goer."

"A community! Far out!"

Aha, another convert, the Dad thought with satisfaction. She was pretty cute, too, although there was something weird about her eyes. Too pale, and they didn't seem to track together. It didn't matter. The more, the merrier.

So Bliss came home with him after he had finished his chores in town. She was friendly and talkative, and nineteen years old. She had left Memphis six months ago and was traveling the world, or whatever part of the world she could hitchhike to, anyway. She was just now heading down from Alaska, where she had spent a "wild" couple of months enjoying being one of the few females around with a bunch of horny guys. "But they're all rednecks, you know," she said as the Dart wound its way up the last hill, on the way to the ford. "And I knew it would be a bummer to be there in the winter. So when the energy started getting a little hostile, I said, 'Eat me,' and got out." She gave a private smile. "I'm always welcome back, though!"

"I'll bet," the Dad agreed.

Bliss would fit in nicely with the rest of the community, he thought. Maybe she and Junior would even get together. They were almost the same age. He was mature for seventeen; he certainly looked older than his years. The Dad saw the two of them making eyes at each other over dinner, or at least he could imagine they were making eyes. It was hard to tell with Junior. He was pretty shy and soft-spoken.

Bliss also made an attempt to talk to the children, the Princess especially. Most adults tried for a while, if they did at all, and then gave up in the face of her bland resistance, her polite one-word answers, her slinking away and finding a book the moment the adult glanced away. But Bliss kept on trying, even offering to read tonight's bit of *The Two Towers* to the girl.

"Okay," the Princess said, surprising everyone, no one more than the Dad himself.

Bliss stayed a long time upstairs with the girl. The Apricot Boy was long asleep in his crib, and the Stars and Billy Goat back in their tent, Astrid and Weed settled out in their camper-truck, by the time she came back down. Junior plucked away at his guitar by the stove. The Mom and the Dad shared a last glass of Mountain Rhine. Well, a last handmade pottery mug of the wine, anyway.

"How did it go up there?" the Dad asked Bliss.

She smiled and nodded, putting a finger to her lips and glancing up at the loft. Then she whispered, "She's just fallen asleep now. You know, she's an incredible girl. She's so wise. She told me the forest knows we're here, that the trees can talk. They say things to her."

The Dad smiled back. "That's far out, I didn't know she thought that." He was silent for a moment. "You know, nobody's ever loved this land before, and now here we are, making a home of it."

The Mom said, "You don't know that exactly."

The Dad, mellow with wine, just kept smiling. "Sure I do. We built the first house."

Bliss asked, "Who else lives around here? Are there other communities nearby, up or down the road? I saw other driveways when we drove by."

Junior looked up at her briefly, then returned to his strumming.

The Dad noticed the look and tried not to smile at it. He loved the idea of playing matchmaker, but hated to seem obvious about it. "A few people— mostly farmers and ranchers this side of the hill, though. I know there's other mellow folks who have some property down in Vaughn's Corner, but we don't see much of them. They're cool, though. It's just that everyone's always doing their own thing, you know."

"Far out," Bliss said, cozying herself onto a pillow and scooting closer to the stove. "I'd love to go check out more of the Land tomorrow."

"I'll show you all around, unless someone else wants to." That was about as direct as the Dad felt like he could be, but Junior didn't take the bait. Oh well. There was plenty of time for that. At the moment, it seemed that what was called for was another joint.

Bliss saw the Dad reaching for his frisbee, and what was in there. "Oh, man, I just remembered something." She dug into her pocket and pulled out a plastic baggie filled with some mysterious brown stuff. "Shrooms! Psychedelic mushrooms." She handed the bag to the Dad, who took it and peered inside.

"Far out," he said.

"There's enough for the four of us," Bliss offered.

"I don't know," said the Mom. "How long does it last?"

"You never did shrooms before?" Bliss asked, disbelief lacing her voice.

"No." The Mom looked uncomfortable. "We haven't really... I can't just..."

"It's not a long trip—a few hours, maybe. We'll be cool by morning."

The Mom glanced uncertainly at the loft, then at her husband.

Junior spoke up, startling everyone. "I love shrooms. I'll do some with you."

"Me too!" said the Dad. He too was feeling a little self-conscious. Everyone knew you couldn't be a true hippie until you had done hallucinogens, and so far, he and the Mom had only smoked and grown pot. Hash at the most. Often, in fact, just wine. Being so isolated out in the country, they didn't come across other drugs very often. But here were free shrooms!

The Mom looked around at the other three, then finally shrugged. "Okay, I'll do a little, like a half a dose. I need to stay together in case the kids wake up."

"They'll be all right," the Dad said. "Besides, Evening Star and Bill are just up the path."

"I don't think there's enough here to share with them," Bliss said.

"We don't need to tell them—only if there's a problem." The Dad was turning the bag over in his hands, looking at the mushrooms from every angle. Yep, they looked like mushrooms, all right. Little dried-up brown ones. How did you tell which ones were hallucinogenic or not? How did you know they were not poisonous, even? There were plenty of wild mushrooms growing all over the place on the Land, but so far, nobody had been adventurous enough to try and eat any of them.

Bliss reached out for the bag, so the Dad handed it back to her. She dumped the contents out onto the counter and started dividing them into little piles.

"Remember, half a dose for me," the Mom said. She sounded worried.

The Dad went and put an arm around her, scratching her back a little. "Hey, hon, it's all right. You don't have to do any if you don't want to."

She frowned. "No way, I don't want to sit around and watch all you guys trip." She glanced at Junior, then quickly looked away.

"It's cool, I've done them before," he assured her.

"No, I wasn't worried about that," she said. "I know you're old enough.

I just wonder if it's too late in the evening, you know. Maybe we should wait till tomorrow."

Bliss chuckled. "Hey, man, whatever you like. But I don't have a schedule. I feel like tripping now—and anyone who wants to join me..." She had separated the shrooms into three equal piles, plus a fourth, slightly smaller one. "Climb aboard." She picked up one of the piles—a pinch between thumb and forefinger—and ate it. Then she made a face. "Ew. I'll never get used to that taste."

Junior got up, ate a pile, grimaced and then laughed.

The Dad looked at his wife. "Go ahead," she said. So he pinched up his pile and put it in his mouth. 'Ew' was right! It tasted awful—like dirt, a dried-up old pile of dirt, or even old cow shit or something. Had they even been washed? He chewed and swallowed as fast as he could.

"Pass the wine, that helps," Bliss said, reaching for the mug.

"There's more in the bottle," the Dad said.

There was one pile left: the small pile. Everyone sort of casually looked at the Mom. The Dad didn't want to pressure her, though he understood not wanting to feel left out. Staying sober in a group that was getting high was no fun at all.

She gave an uneasy smile, got up, and picked up the pile of mushrooms. Then she ate them, grimacing like everyone else. "They taste like mildew," she said. "Wine, oh god, right now!"

Bliss laughed and handed her the mug.

They passed the wine around a few more times until Bliss said, "That's probably enough of that, if you don't want to see it again in an hour."

Oh, right, the Dad remembered. *I forgot they're supposed to make you sick.*

"An hour?" the Mom asked. "How long does it take to get off, anyway?"

"About an hour and a half," Junior said. "More if your stomach's full."

"Oh, god."

The Mom knew it was a bad idea from the moment Bliss had pulled the baggie out of her pocket, but for some reason, she took the mushrooms anyway. No, not for some reason, she knew the reason. She didn't want to look foolish in front of Junior, to look square, like an old stick in the mud. She wanted to be cool and fun and seventeen, just like he was.

Probably she wanted even more than that, but she wasn't willing to admit it, even to herself.

Anyway, what was done was done. She had taken the drug, and now all they had to do was wait till they got off. And how late it was! With no clocks, nobody really knew for sure, but the sun had gone down hours ago. They had finished dinner some time back, and then Bliss had read to the Princess for another long while, and then…well, it didn't matter. It was late; they'd have a mushroom trip; then they'd come down. It would be fine. It would have to be. Besides, what choice did she have, at this point? Besides sticking her finger down her throat.

The Mom noticed the jug out on the counter. There was only a little wine left in it. She got up and screwed the cap back on, and put it in the cupboard. Too bad there wasn't room for it in the cold-box, but she was getting used to room-temperature wine.

Then she came back and sat down next to the others. Bliss laughed: "Waiting to get off. The most boring time of day."

The Mom laughed weakly in response, then saw another little thing that needed tidying up.

"Come on, give it a rest," the Dad said. "Let's play cards or something."

After much discussion and searching for a deck of cards, and then finally finding one upstairs in the loft, which had to be done quietly and with just a little flashlight, so as not to wake the kids, the four of them settled in for a game of Hearts. Halfway in the middle of the first hand, the Mom's stomach started feeling queasy. She took a few deep breaths to calm it, which helped for a minute, but then it came back again.

Sharp-eyed Bliss noticed, and smiled gently. "It'll be all right—go barf if you need to. It's already in your blood. You'll feel better in a few minutes either way."

The Mom got up and hurried out to the dry creek bed next to the house. She leaned over and gagged a little, but there was nothing in her stomach. After a few minutes, she sat back on her heels. The night was cool, but not too cold, and the air was incredibly fresh. It felt great, sinking into her lungs. It was like water, only breathable: if you could breathe crystal-clear, sparkling, pure water and it was good for you, if it was what your lungs needed, this is what it would feel like. It must be what being a fish felt like! Oh god, why couldn't she be a fish!

She sat back a little further and looked up at the night sky. *Wow*, there were so many stars up there. Since they had moved to the Land, she had enjoyed the clear nights, the views of the stars, but she had never really *appreciated* them until just now. Why hadn't she noticed before how incredible they were? She stretched out on the grass so she could see them more easily. And ah, the cold air felt so good on her body. And in her lungs!

"Hon?" came the Dad's voice, from the back door. "You all right?"

"I'm incredible," she said. That was fun to say, rolling the R off her tongue, so she said it again. "I'm *incredible*. Have you seen the stars?"

He chuckled, and then she heard, "Wow." She couldn't really see him, other than in profile; the light from the house was behind him. But he had looked up at the sky. She understood in that moment—even though she was thirty yards away—that they were seeing *exactly* the same thing, and understanding it in exactly the same way. They were so connected! Her man—her lover, her mate, her husband, father of her children.

Her children! Her gorgeous perfect sweet children! A sudden rush of anxiety clutched at her heart. Where were her children?

She sat up, and got a head rush. "Whoa."

The Dad came over and sat next to her on the grass, taking her hand. "Hey, you're right, those stars are incredible."

"The children!" She was about to panic.

"They're fine…they're in bed upstairs, they're still asleep. I know they are fine."

Relief flooded her. "Oh, good." Then she truly felt his hand in hers, the warmth of his skin, his strong flesh, the muscles, the hardness of the bones underneath. When had she really appreciated his hands before? And they did so much! They chopped wood, they drove the car, they caressed her breasts, they carried the children…

The children!

No, they were fine.

"You are so beautiful in the moonlight," the Dad said to her, in her ear, too close.

Moonlight? She hadn't even noticed the moon! It was just rising, poking up through the trees at the horizon, three or four nights past full, waning but still bright. "Oh my god," she said. She could see every detail on the surface of the moon. It wasn't a man in the moon…it was a devil! "Look!" She pointed.

"I see," he said, and she knew that he saw. She didn't have to say anything. She leaned into his arms. He would protect her from the devil in the moon. Funny how different it was from the drawings of it in children's books.

Children!

The Dad held his wife outside for a while, keeping her calm. He was getting off pretty hard himself, but he channeled all his energies into holding her steady, steering her away from her panic, again and again. Finally he convinced her to come back inside the house, promising that they would check on the children.

Once they got in, however, the narrow stairway leading to the loft defeated them. "I'll just rest here a minute," the Mom said, sinking down onto one of the floor pillows.

"That's fine," the Dad said, settling in next to her, marveling at the soft pillow, trying to stay focused.

Bliss and Junior were still sitting over the abandoned card game, but they weren't playing. They were facing each other, holding hands—both hands—but not exactly looking at each other. In fact, Bliss's eyes were rolled up into her head; Junior just looked incredibly stoned, his eyes bloodshot under those ridiculous lashes.

"Hey," the Dad said to them. Junior didn't budge.

"Shh…we're channeling," Bliss murmured.

The Mom started to giggle.

"What are you channeling?" the Dad asked, in what he hoped was a calm and reasonable voice. Because he suddenly had a very bad feeling about the two of them. He no longer wanted to be a matchmaker, or anything. He kind of just wanted Bliss to leave. Were these really just mushrooms? How much had they taken? What did she mean, channeling?

Bliss gave a gentle laugh. "The spirit of the forest. What else?"

Junior blinked.

"In fact, it's calling to me." Bliss paused. "I think I need to go out there."

Junior let go of her hands.

Bliss got up, quite steadily. "I'm going outside."

Everyone nodded. She walked to the back door and out into the dark.

The Princess woke up in the middle of the night. She got up and felt her way out of her cubby to the pee-pan. She lifted the lid, set it carefully on the floor next to the pan, and squatted. After doing her business, she replaced the lid and started to find her way back to her bed, then paused. A scrap of light filtered up over the edge of the loft from downstairs, which was what had made it hard to find her way to the pee-pan in the dark; it didn't illuminate anything, it just distracted her eyes. Were there people still awake downstairs? It was very late, she thought. And quiet.

She crept to the edge of the loft and got down on her belly. From here, she could peer over without anyone seeing her. Probably.

She inched out, looked down, and saw her parents downstairs with Junior. Her mom was tracing her fingers along the coils of the braided rug, with a fascinated smile on her face. Her dad was sitting up at the desk with every drawer pulled out, most of them on the floor around him, one of them in his lap. He was drawing something and peering at it very closely, almost putting his face right on it. She couldn't tell what it was. Maybe a map? She didn't know.

Junior was sitting in the corner, staring straight ahead, grinning. The weird lady who had read and talked to her for such a long time before bed was nowhere to be seen.

Hmm. This was strange. Why didn't they go to bed? What was going on?

The Princess waited at the edge of the loft for a while, but nothing else happened. She could hear the slightly adenoidal breathing of the Apricot Boy in his crib behind her as he slept on.

She was getting a little cold and was about to go back to bed when she must have fallen asleep right there or something, because she suddenly had the strangest dream. The creature who had whispered to the Princess in the woods the other day was back, and now she could understand him perfectly, even if she couldn't see him exactly. He appeared as a dark shape in front of her, floating under the high-peaked ceiling. Her parents and Junior still sat downstairs. They did not look up and notice the creature.

Hello, little Princess, the creature said.

The Princess cocked her head, trying to see him more clearly. She rubbed her eyes, but it did not help. What a strange dream!

Hello, she said to him. Still nobody downstairs noticed, though he was right over their heads.

Thank you for sending me that fine morsel, the creature said.

The Princess understood exactly what he meant, although she hadn't sent him anything. The weird lady had decided to go outside on her own, in the middle of the night. She had told the Princess that she wanted to go explore the whole property, but the Princess had merely shrugged it off after a mild warning about the trees. Hitchhikers were frequently impressed by the property, and full of all kinds of great ideas about what to do with it. Then they would leave again, and that would be that.

Did you eat her? the Princess asked.

I made a good start, the creature said. *But something about her didn't agree with me.*

Oh. The Princess still kept trying to see the creature, but he was blurry, and the night was very dark. He seemed to have too many legs; she couldn't bring him into focus.

I'm sure it will pass. I had no trouble with the goats.

Oh, the Princess said again. *Everyone thought a mountain lion or a bear got the goats.*

But you knew better, didn't you?

The Princess shrugged.

Well, it's back out into the night with me, the dark shape said. *This is about all I can take of confined places.*

Okay, goodbye, said the Princess.

Goodbye.

The darkness dissipated; the Princess shook her head. Then she was awake again, and even colder than earlier, in her thin nightgown. She inched back from the edge of the loft as quietly as she could, although clearly the adults downstairs were paying no attention to her. And they could easily have heard her using the pee-pan earlier, for that matter.

She got back into bed, snuggled under her covers, and tried to get warm. The fire must have gone out downstairs. The night was very cold. She shivered a long time, thinking about her strange dream. Eventually, she fell asleep again, and dreamed no more that night.

CHAPTER 5

The Mom spent the rest of the Shroom Night on the floor in the cabin, exploring every little nook and cranny of the braided rug. So many different fabrics had gone into it! She had never realized this! And they were all so incredibly gorgeous. And they spun and twisted—she could almost see the hands that had woven it as the fibers themselves moved, undulating. She was vaguely aware of the others in the room with her—her husband going through his desk and writing something, the silent Junior sitting in the corner doing nothing—but she paid them absolutely no attention. She forgot all about Bliss. The energy in the room was better without her anyway.

In the middle of the night, it got very cold in the cabin. The Mom was sort of vaguely aware of this as well; the fire must have gone out. She thought maybe she should do something about that, and two or three times she actually started to prepare to do something but got distracted again by the rug, then finally gave up. It actually wasn't that cold after all, now that she thought about it.

When the eastern sky just barely began to brighten with dawn, she finally realized how tired she was. She looked up at the Dad, who was staring now, just like Junior had been. Although Junior had actually fallen asleep, she now saw.

"Wow," she said. "That was half a dose?"

"I don't know how you measure," the Dad said, after being momentarily startled by her voice. He put the drawer that was on his lap back into the desk and got stiffly to his feet. "Are the caps stronger than the stems, or what?"

"Like pot? I don't know." The Mom got up too, and went to put a blanket over Junior. He still sat, though he was sound asleep. She eased him down so that he was reclining on one of the floor pillows. She made sure his neck was not twisted uncomfortably, and that his legs weren't on top of each other so that one of them would go to sleep. She admired his long dark lashes atop his cheekbones, and then left him.

"Bed?" the Dad asked.

"Absolutely."

They climbed the stairs to the loft. Her legs felt like they weighed a million pounds each.

The Apricot Boy slept in his crib and the Princess was tucked in her nook at the back of the loft, two of the cats curled up at her feet. The Mom and the Dad crawled into their foam-pad bed on the floor, snuggled under the blankets, and both were asleep almost instantly.

The Dad awoke to bright daylight streaming through the narrow back windows. He sat up, confused and horribly thirsty. The Mom slept on beside him, heavily. Her mouth was open, and a bit of drool eased onto her pillow. He left her sleeping and rolled out of bed, pulling on the jeans that lay on the floor where he had dropped them last night, or this morning, or whenever.

He rather creakily made his way downstairs, gripping the rail as he went. *Good lord, I feel like I was pushed over a cliff!* Damned if he was ever going to do hallucinogens again. Although it was pretty cool... He smiled as he remembered the visuals, all the incredible little tiny things he had found in his desk. And the stars! Yeah, those were pretty cool. Maybe he was just stiff from staying up so late. Like when he was in college and had taken a bunch of reds to study for a final. This actually felt better than that. He still had a little of the drug-euphoria in his system.

When he got downstairs, he found Junior standing over the wood cook stove, heating a pan of cowboy coffee. Astrid sat in the desk chair, watching him. She gave the Dad a knowing smirk as he slowly descended, gripping the rail, then returned her attention to Junior.

"Wow," the Dad said. "That was some night."

Astrid laughed. "I'm glad we turned in early—I hope you don't feel as bad as you look."

"Well, thanks." Then, walking over to the stove, he asked Junior, "What's cooking?"

"Coffee," he said. A man of few words.

"Good." Two could play this game. The Dad could be unspeakably cool if he set his mind to it.

He went to the sink and poured himself a glass of cool, clear spring water, and drank it all down. Ahhh, that was good water. He took particular pleasure in it, because he could envision it traveling all the way down from the top of the mountain where the spring emerged, a little trickle that eventually became the roaring creek separating the Land from the Morgan ranch next door. He could easily envision it because he had laid all that pipe himself—3/4 inch white PVC, all the way down the mountain. And he tended it himself; whenever a piece got broken or clogged, or frozen in the wintertime, he hunted it out and fixed it. Really made you appreciate your water.

He filled the glass a second time and started to drink it, but then his stomach balked a little. Oh, yeah. Maybe he should be gentle there. It had had kind of a rough night, his stomach. He took a sip, savoring it, then set the glass down. Then he got a head rush, and had to sit down.

Astrid watched him the whole time, still smirking in a kind of ugly way.

Finally the Dad said, "What? You've never done shrooms before?"

"Oho, shrooms, were they? I didn't know we had shrooms in the *community*."

Ah, that's the problem. "Sorry!" he said. "I didn't know either—that chick brought them, the hitchhiker—Bliss. You had all gone to bed when she brought them out. I had no idea."

"Where is she, anyway?" Junior asked.

"I don't know." The Dad looked around the room, as though he could have missed seeing another person somehow in a fifteen-by-twenty-five-foot cabin. "She didn't crash down here?"

"No, she split, she went outside, remember?" Junior kept stirring the coffee on the stove but looked sidelong at the Dad.

"She never came back in?"

"I never saw her."

"Hmm. Well, maybe I should go out and look for her."

"Maybe."

The Dad left the cabin soon thereafter. The mood in there was enough to chase him away, even if he didn't have somebody he felt he should go looking for.

Though certainly Bliss could take care of herself, he thought as he walked around in the front meadow. Hadn't she just hitchhiked all over the country and lived in Alaska with a bunch of rednecks? She was young, sure, but it wasn't like she was some kind of teenage runaway, fresh from the suburbs. She knew what was what, even in the woods. Alaska was pretty much all woods, wasn't it? And snow.

Still, he felt responsible. He had brought her here, anyway. He felt a little foolish, walking around the woods half-heartedly calling out, "Bliss, Bliss!" She wasn't anywhere in front of the house, or across the road, or down by the river. No clothes hung in the clothes-tree. After the cold night, the day was warming up quickly...mmm, a swim actually sounded pretty good. He took his clothes off, hung them in the tree, and dove in.

The Mom slowly awakened, with incredible cottonmouth. The bright sunlight from the window had reached her face, making her sweaty and uncomfortable. She rolled over, groaned, and tried to sit up slowly, pushing herself up with an elbow.

The Apricot Boy stood up in his crib, smiling at her. "Ma!"

She smiled back at him and got up, lifting him out. "Oh, there's a good boy...and you let Mommy sleep so long!" Goodness, what time was it? It felt like half the morning was gone.

She helped him get dressed and carried him downstairs, after glancing into the Princess's empty sleeping nook. The Princess had obviously gotten her own breakfast by now, and was probably out playing in her little village in the meadow.

Downstairs, she found the house empty, but a fresh pot of camp coffee on the stove and the fire still warm, though burning down. The Mom didn't like the boiled-grounds coffee that much, but it almost sounded good this morning. Water first, though.

After she had fed the Apricot Boy and tried to eat a little something herself, she started to wonder where everyone was. Probably at the river: the day was heating up, as usual. As the summer drew to a close, everyone was trying to get in as much river time as possible. Autumns here were brisk, and winters were downright freezing. She and her husband knew that well enough after last year.

"Want to go to the river?" she asked the Apricot Boy.

"Ya!" he agreed. He was such a sweet kid.

The Princess sat on a rock in the creek dividing the Land from the ranch, back behind the back meadow, looking down at what remained of Bliss. Apparently, the dogs had not found her yet. This was nothing like the goats. The strange woman had been fairly neatly disemboweled. Her middle was almost completely gone, eaten away by something with an incredibly large mouth, because it looked like it had happened in one bite. Her arms and legs and head remained intact, though moving gently as the water lapped around her.

The Princess had been horrified when she had first seen the body, but now she studied it with almost clinical detachment. It hardly seemed real. She knew she should feel scared, but somehow she just couldn't.

She looked up, across the creek. Three cows stood in the small field, two grazing, one chewing its cud and looking at her blankly.

She looked back down at the body. There was almost no blood; it had been washed downstream. Which was part of what made the body not look real, perhaps. The dead goats had been much more believable. With them, there had been quite a mess. Plus, she had known the goats better.

So you found my little secret. The creature's voice was around her again, but still no body, just a formless dark space, a fog.

What secret? You told me yourself.

But I didn't tell you where. You are a clever little girl.

She nodded. After a few minutes, she ventured to say, *You probably shouldn't have done that. People are going to get mad.*

Some things are already mad. And I still haven't recovered from the poison in her system.

Maybe you should have started with the arms and legs, instead of the tummy. The Princess kind of couldn't believe she was having this conversation, but on the other hand, it had a bizarre sort of reasonableness to it. It was like something out of a book, a fairy tale. The monsters are real; they do their evil things, but then you talk to them and make them be good; and then everyone lives happily ever after.

Oh, I don't mean the drug, that's perfectly natural, the monster said. *I mean the poison in her mind. She was a bad woman.*

Well, she was a little strange, the Princess allowed.

And I thank you again for sending her to me.

I didn't send her to you.

All right.

I still think you shouldn't have done that. I'm going to go tell my mommy.

You don't need to tell her. They will know soon enough.

Why shouldn't I tell her? But the Princess already let the doubts cloud her mind. There were all kinds of reasons not to tell Mommy things.

I don't want you to tell her. You're good at keeping secrets, aren't you?

Yes, I am.

The Princess startled back to reality, which still consisted of a disturbingly dead body moving gently in a creek, draped over some rocks. She was, in fact, good at keeping secrets. She had learned it was better that way. Sometimes, when you told the parents something they didn't want to hear, like about the time the visitor took her out to his truck at night, and touched her down there, and she had liked it, but then she hadn't liked it, and she hadn't known what to do about that; but then the visitor left the next day, and so she was trying to tell her mom about what he had done, because she felt like she should, but she really couldn't find the right words for it, and then her mom wasn't really listening, and was doing something at the stove, and didn't seem to understand her anyway...well, sometimes it was just better to keep the secret.

Then she heard the dogs on the trail behind her, and she got up to head them off. Something about the dogs eating dead bodies seemed just, well, wrong. Even though there was meat in dog food. Somehow, this seemed different. Dog food wasn't made out of *people* meat.

As she hurried back down the slight trail, she again had the thought that she really should go get someone—tell someone, go for help, get her mother, her father. But what kind of help would be any good at this point? Nothing. Bliss was dead, utterly, thoroughly dead. In fact, she had looked rather peaceful there in the creek, with the whole middle of her body eaten away. Maybe the monster would want to come back and finish his meal when his tummy stopped hurting. It might be dangerous to interfere with that.

And he had told her not to tell. If she hadn't imagined the whole conversation.

Because she wasn't entirely sure that she would be believed. About the monster, that was. The dead body was quite real. But monsters. That was another story.

The monster was certainly gone now, that much was clear. If he was ever there in the first place. The Princess looked all around her. Rocks, creek, cows, trees. And here came the dogs. Galadriel and Sauron and Elf and Granola all came bounding down the path, delighted to have found her.

"Hi, doggies!" the Princess said, distracting them by letting them all jump into her arms, rubbing their bristly fur and pulling gently on their soft ears as they licked her face. The dogs loved the Princess. Galadriel and Sauron were still wary of the Apricot Boy even though he hadn't pulled any tails in at least a year, and they didn't seem to like Morning Star all that well either, but the Princess had always gotten along with all the animals. Even the cats, who really hated children. Except for the Princess.

So she went back to the house, bringing all the happy dogs with her, leaving them outside with freshly filled bowls of water from the hose. When she went inside, she found that nobody else was around, not even her mom. Maybe they were all at the river? Everyone loved the river, and the Princess even liked it all right, if the day was really hot. She was not a strong swimmer. She generally had to rely on inner tubes if she wanted to go any distance at all. Fortunately, the Land had an ample selection of fabulous inner tubes from old truck tires.

But she didn't feel like going to the river. She felt kind of icky and blank. So she went upstairs instead, found a pile of Fabulous Furry Freak Brothers comics, and settled in.

Late in the afternoon, the gang all came back up to the house. The day had turned blisteringly hot. The Dad had spent most of the day at the river, and everyone else had eventually joined him there. Every time he was ready to leave, someone else had shown up, so he stayed. In the back of his mind, he sort of figured Bliss would show up too, but he didn't really worry about it when she didn't. Some folks were swimming, some lying on the beach, the guys yet again discussing the possibility of hanging a rope swing from the big oak tree, which had a perfect branch stretching out over the water. Evening Star and Astrid sat talking on the beach for a long while. It was good that everyone was getting to know each other.

The day wore on and the Princess didn't show up either, but nobody worried about that. The Princess had always liked to spend a lot of time alone. Or maybe she and Bliss were off somewhere together. They had seemed to get along well enough last night, with the story-reading and all. That was what was so great about the Land. Nobody was laying any heavy trips on anyone else, everyone just did what suited them.

Of course, it was harder for the kids when they had to go back to school and put up with the crazy shit there—at least the Princess, since the Apricot Boy hadn't started school yet—and the Dad had to put up with a certain amount of it when he went to collect his unemployment check, but on the whole their new life was a pretty mellow scene. Just what he had always dreamed it would be.

The Dad had especially enjoyed observing the variety of naked women in the river as the community grew. The Mom—his wife, his love, mother of his children—had a nice, healthy body: slender, small of breast but wide of hip, very feminine in her own way. And he also held the memory of her during her two pregnancies, when her belly and breasts had swelled in a most beguiling way. He could still see her that way with very little imaginative effort on his part.

But beyond the Mom, now there was Evening Star—short, very busty, very curvy in the hips—probably she would be fat in a few years, but now she was very nice to look at. She would probably be even nicer to touch—the Dad tried not to think too hard about that. But she looked like she would be soft, yielding, pliable… Okay, he *really* tried not to think too hard about that. Although, if he were to slip, it wouldn't be an insurmountable problem. Free love and all that. The Mom would probably forgive him. Eventually.

After finally drying off in the hot sun and putting their clothes back on, the group got to the gravel-covered road, pausing to put on sandals or flip-flops, and crossed over, then walked up to the driveway. The Dad continued his ruminations. Because now there was a third woman, Astrid. Astrid was very small, petite, almost boyish: not the kind of woman who generally attracted the Dad at all. But the funny thing was, he also found her terribly exciting. There was something almost forbidden-seeming about such a small woman—like a child? Like a young man? But that couldn't be it. Certainly Junior was even prettier than Astrid, and the Dad felt no attraction for Junior.

Then there had been Bliss. Where had Bliss gone? She had wandered out into the night last night, stoned on mushrooms. She was cute, too. Blonde, a little tall and lanky. Her nose was kind of big, and she had those weird eyes. She wore her clothes baggy, so it was hard to determine exactly what her figure might be underneath. Too bad she hadn't turned up in time to go to the river with everyone. Oh well. There would be another chance.

The Mom was similarly lost in ruminations on their way up the hill. Everyone was tired and sun-baked from the day at the river; she and the Dad, and no doubt Junior, were also blasted from the night of shrooms and very little sleep. Her thoughts did not wander to the delights of Junior's fine physique, though on another occasion they might well have. She was just too tired.

Instead, she started fretting about what to prepare for dinner. Suddenly the community seemed so large, but she had remained chiefly responsible for feeding everyone. Sure, others helped, but she was the planner, the list-maker, the main cook, and the chief cleaner-upper. It didn't seem fair, exactly. But then again, whenever she had tried to delegate it to someone else, they just screwed it up.

"Okay, here's the deal," Evening Star suddenly said. She had been uncommonly antisocial all day, the Mom realized, just sitting and talking to Astrid on the beach. "We are a community, correct?"

They were at the first turn in the driveway, near the creek. Weed caught up, stepping closer so he could hear what was being said.

"Yeah?" the Dad asked.

"So, I think it's time for another community meeting," Evening Star said.

"Okay," the Mom said. "Can we get to the house first?"

"You mean *your* house?"

The Mom was taken aback. She and the Dad had bought the property, built the house, bought everything in it, furniture and food alike. They paid the property taxes. She cooked for everyone, with not a whole lot of help. But she'd been nothing but friendly and welcoming to the newcomers. She'd thought of Evening Star as a friend already. She'd sheltered her and her family from the wild animal that got the goats. "Yeah, our house," she said, finally, eyeing the other woman.

"Sure." Evening Star tried to make it casual.

"Okay."

They continued on in silence. When they got to the house, everyone filed in and found seats on the floor, pulling up floor pillows, Billy Goat grabbing the desk chair. Little Morning Star clambered onto his lap. The Mom thought she heard the Princess upstairs, moving around in her little room. Good. She gave the Apricot Boy a slice of cheese, then had to cut one for Morning Star as well.

"So?" the Dad asked Evening Star. "You've got something you want to talk about?"

"Yeah, I do," she said, sitting forward, clearing her throat lightly and pushing her curls out of her eyes. "It has always been our understanding, in joining this community, that all is to be shared and shared alike. From each according to their needs, or whatever. But just today, it has come to our attention that there was something of value here last night, that was secretly consumed, by you guys, after most of the rest of us had gone to bed. A valuable and rare commodity, one that would be desired by all. All of us, I mean. And I just think that's not fair, and I wanted to just say, I think you should have shared the shrooms."

The Mom just watched her make this self-important little speech. *Typical,* she thought. *Everyone wants to share and share alike when they didn't do anything to make it happen in the first place.* She shifted on the floor, crossing her legs the other way. Lotus or even half-lotus was always hard for her, and she felt vaguely resentful of people who sat easily in it. And she still felt hurt at Evening Star's unfriendly new attitude.

"Hey, man, I'm sorry about what happened," the Dad said, sincerely. "I had no idea Bliss was going to bring that stuff out."

"You already keep the pot garden secret," Evening Star groused.

"Where is Bliss, anyway?" Billy Goat asked. "Maybe she has more."

"I don't know—I haven't seen her all day," the Dad said, looking quizzically at the Mom. "Was she here when you got up?"

"Nope." The Mom felt bad, but she'd kind of forgotten about her. Well, she wasn't supposed to be responsible for everyone, was she? Anyone else could have looked for Bliss, if they wanted to find her so badly.

Everyone looked at each other. Junior offered again, "She went out in the night while we were tripping."

"And that's the last anyone's seen of her?" Billy Goat asked.

"I went to look for her this morning..." the Dad started, but then stopped. Obviously, he hadn't gotten very far before he had tumbled into the river.

"Well, then, never mind about her—maybe she hitched a ride into town or something," Billy Goat said. "Our point is, you all had a great little trip, and we didn't. And we were talking about it, and we think that would be a nice thing for the whole community to do together. It would help break down the artificial barriers between us—make us more of a family, you know."

Astrid nodded, and Weed did too, a moment later.

"All right, fine," the Dad said, rubbing his eyes. He looked as tired as the Mom felt. "But we took all the shrooms last night. What do you suggest?"

"I'd like to get some acid," Evening Star said. "Shrooms make me sick, actually. And they're too introspective, too small. You just end up staring at tiny things the whole time."

The Mom shrugged, looking self-consciously down at her toes, and the actually quite dull braided rug beneath them.

"Acid is totally cool—totally mind-blowing, mind-opening. You see *huge* stuff on acid—and you think huge thoughts. And the love! Your heart gets filled with love." Evening Star smiled, leaning back, looking around the room until her glance fell on the Mom. "It's incredible, really, thoroughly trippy."

"Sounds great," the Dad said. "So, does anybody have a connection to get some?"

Billy Goat paused in the middle of rolling another cigarette. "Well, there was this dude in Yokayo who sold me some peyote a while back, I could try to find him."

"Cool. We don't know anybody locally—we've just been traveling around since we left the city." Astrid shrugged, pulling her skinny arms to her chest. "And we're not going back to that scene."

"Or we could put up more fliers!" Evening Star offered.

"Wait a minute." The Mom frowned at Evening Star and shot a quick glance at the Dad. "I'm not so sure about this, you guys. Especially not fliers—come on, be serious. Last time I looked, acid was still illegal."

"Oh, we wouldn't say 'acid' straight out." Evening Star rolled her eyes. "There's ways to say shit so that people know."

"No fliers, no way," the Mom said. "And I'm not even so sure I'm ready to do another strong drug. Those shrooms knocked me for a loop."

"Well, it wouldn't be any good if we don't *all* do it," Evening Star said, significantly.

The Dad watched the debate, seemingly content to stay out of it now that it was rolling along, ignoring the Mom's subtle glances. Anyway, knowing him, she figured he liked the idea of the community coming together in that way, bonding, having a shared experience that was intense and transcendent. It was the sort of thing he'd talked about even before they bought the Land. And he had seemed to enjoy the shroom trip very much. In any event, he wasn't talking to her about it.

Finally, it was put to a vote and decided: tomorrow, the Dad and Billy Goat would drive into town and try to score some acid from the guy Billy Goat knew. Failing that, they'd hang around the health food store and the auto body place and try to hook up with other hippies, see what they knew. If they remained unsuccessful, well, they'd still keep their ears to the ground, and maybe ask the other community down in Vaughn's Corner. They seemed like pretty un-druggy hippies, but you never knew.

The Princess sat upstairs, listening to the adults talk down below. Actually it was mostly pretty boring. She got excited when she heard them wondering where Bliss was, but then it sounded like they started talking about something else and forgot about her.

She felt a little sick in her tummy, still. She kind of wanted to tell some-one where Bliss was, but she also didn't want to. She wasn't afraid of the monster, exactly. She didn't think so, anyway. It was more just not wanting it to be real, not wanting to talk about it. And not wanting to be the one to show them. Assuming she could get someone to come out to the creek with her, even if she did say something. In her short years, she already had long experience in taking care of things for herself. If you had problems, you could read books to figure out how to make them go away. Or you could just wait. Usually, if she just waited, the Princess found that problems went away.

She didn't know about a dead body in a creek, though. Well, maybe it would wash downstream and go into the river. If it did that, then would it be like one of the dead eels, and the Dad would carry it off on a stick and go bury it far away from where the dogs would find it?

The Princess felt a little queasier. No, of course the Dad couldn't carry a whole dead human body off on a stick like a dead eel. Even if all its middle had been eaten away.

And what if the monster had come back? Maybe it had. She should go look.

The adults stopped talking. She heard her mom start to make dinner, and some of the others started to leave the house. Her dad lit a joint. It was not dark out, and her mom had just started chopping vegetables. The Princess could leave now and be back in time for dinner without anyone noticing.

She padded downstairs and was about to slip out the front door, but her mom did see her. "Hi, sweetheart."

"Hi, Mom."

"Where are you off to? Dinner's soon."

"I left something in the meadow—I'll be back in a few minutes."

"All right." The Mom returned to her vegetables.

Outside, she found Morning Star and the Apricot Boy playing on the front porch. "Hey," Morning Star said. "Where were you?"

"Upstairs."

"Where are you going now?"

The Princess glanced out into the front meadow, then at the little deer path that led back into the woods, and the creek. "Nowhere—I just have to get something."

"We're coming with you." Morning Star got up, and the Apricot Boy's face lit up with joy at the unexpected bounty of getting to be with his sister.

"No, you're not. I have to do something, I'll be right back, it's too far, you can't come."

"Where are you going?" Morning Star started to follow her down the front steps.

"Nowhere! You can't come!" The Princess sped up, trying to outpace the other kids. She got to the bottom of the stairs, careful not to trip on the last step, which was a little steeper than the others.

The Apricot Boy, unfortunately, wasn't so careful, or perhaps his shorter legs just weren't up to the challenge. He tumbled into the dirt and immediately let out a huge wail, then began that long process of catching his breath in preparation for the even louder sobbing fit that would follow.

The Princess paused long enough to make sure that he wasn't bleeding or broken; as soon as her mother opened the front door, coming to see what was the matter, the Princess was off through the front meadow. She turned back once, seeing that Morning Star was still at the house, not following.

When she got to the path leading into the woods, she slowed down, listening for signs of the monster. Maybe it didn't want her to come back and see it? Maybe it would eat her next? But she kind of didn't think so. If it was going to eat her, why hadn't it done so already? It wouldn't be talking to her if it wanted to eat her. Right? But still, she hesitated.

Eventually, she realized she had to go into the woods. She had come this far. She had to get back to the house by dinner. Now she just needed to see if the body was still there.

She slipped into the woods silently on the tiny path. Once hidden, she doubled back to get to the spot in the creek where the body was. It was darker in here because of the tree-shadows, but still light enough out to see. The sun hadn't gone all the way behind the hill yet, but it would soon. She quickened her pace.

When she got to the creek, she stood on the bank. Now Bliss's body had turned a really weird shade of purple-blue, and what was left of it looked a little bloated. The Princess stared for a moment, then turned quickly away.

And bumped into Morning Star, directly behind her on the path. The Princess shrieked and pushed at the fat girl. "Run!" She didn't wait to see if the other girl followed her; she just turned and ran back through the woods, towards the meadow.

Morning Star said, "Hey," and then a moment later, she screamed. "Mooooooommmmmm!" Now the Princess could hear her thumping footsteps on the path behind her.

CHAPTER 6

Yet another Land meeting was hastily convened. In groups of two or three, all the adults trooped down the path, saw the awful situation in the creek, and came back to the house. There they sat staring, horrified, at each other, the floor, the house plants, the windows. Beer and wine were passed around.

The children weren't allowed back there, although two of the three of them had already seen it, and the third one was arguably young enough, and the body sufficiently inhuman-looking by now, to not understand what he was seeing. But still, it was thought that the children should be kept away.

When everyone had seen it, and the sun had finished going down, the whole community sat in the cabin. "All right," Weed said. "I'll ask it. What do we do?"

"Obviously we have to go get the cops," the Mom said.

"No way!" Evening Star said. "Not the pigs! Fuck the pigs!"

"Yeah, we're out here to get away from all that," Astrid agreed.

"We can't just leave her there," the Dad said.

"But that doesn't mean we have to bring the fuzz down on us," Billy Goat said. "There must be other ways of dealing with it."

"What are you talking about? Are you all crazy?" The Mom couldn't believe what she was hearing. "When you have a *dead body*, you are supposed to inform the police! Even you guys know that."

"Well, only if it's foul play, right?" Evening Star asked. "This is obviously some kind of wild animal—the same thing that got the goats."

"Yeah, and you don't want the cops or Fish and Game out here tramping all over the property, hunting down some poor mountain lion or whatever, stumbling across your pot garden in the process," Bill said.

"Hmm," the Dad said.

"No way!" The Mom turned to her husband. "What do you mean, 'Hmm'? What's a pot garden compared to human life?" She got up and began pacing around, but could only take a few steps in each direction in the small and crowded room. "And Bill—you talk about 'some poor mountain lion'—didn't you see the body? Didn't you see what it did? You guys sleep out in those woods every night in just a little tent. Do you seriously feel safe out there now?"

"She's got a point, man," Evening Star said. "Maybe we should crash in here for a few nights."

"That's a good idea," the Dad said. "At least till everything settles down a little."

"It's funny the dogs don't bark when this wild animal comes through," Astrid said. "Usually Elf is all over something like that."

"Yeah, Sauron too," the Dad said. "Well, both of them—Galadriel's a good watchdog."

"Both incidents were a ways from the house, and we were at the river all day," Weed said. "Maybe they did bark, and we just didn't hear them. Or were they with us?"

"Do you think it happened today? She left last night." The Dad thought about the dogs, but couldn't exactly remember if they'd been at the river today or not.

"She left in the middle of the night," Junior added.

"Who knows how far she wandered, if she was really tripping?" Evening Star said, with a slightly harsh look at the shroom-doers. "You guys shouldn't have let her go out by herself like that."

"I didn't even know she left," the Dad said.

"Yes you did, you were right there," the Mom said, and Junior nodded.

"Oh, right." He frowned.

"Does it matter when it happened?" the Mom asked. "No, it does not. It matters that she's dead in the creek, right now, and even if it's just some wild animal—which does not, by the way, put my mind at ease about it at all—we still have to go to the authorities. I mean, doesn't she have family, wouldn't they want to know?"

"She was a runaway," the Dad said. "She told me she hated her family—they kicked her out. They never wanted to speak to her again, after she became a hippie."

Everyone nodded.

"We could give her a nice burial, here in this loving land—a secluded place near the back meadow maybe," Evening Star said.

"I didn't really know her, but I can say some words," Billy Goat offered. "I've spoken over a few gravesites in my time."

"You people are all insane!" The Mom shook her head.

"Let's vote," the Dad said.

The Princess watched the entire discussion in silence, waiting for the monster to speak to her again. She had no control over his visits. She assumed he was listening, since he seemed to know everything that went on, just like any good monster. So he hadn't come back to finish his meal after all. He probably wouldn't want it now. It was all cold and waterlogged and that funny blue color.

The community voted, of course, to not go to the cops, but instead to retrieve the body from the creek and give it a proper burial. They would do this tomorrow; it was already too late to go back out there tonight. The men would dig the grave first, and then take the body directly there and put it into the ground. Work would start first thing in the morning.

In the meantime, anyone not sleeping somewhere bear-proof or mountain lion-proof would crash on the floor in the cabin. That included dogs.

Galadriel and Sauron would sleep here, and Elf and Granola would go into Weed and Astrid's camper. The goats would have to be safe enough where they were. Anyway, they had only gotten attacked when they were out of their pen. The billy goat would be let into the pen for now, even though it would sour the milk. That would at least facilitate the process of creating more baby goats.

The cats—well, nobody had control over them. It was hoped that they could take care of themselves, as they had thus far. Well, most of them, anyway. Who knew?

The Mom started preparing dinner, tight-lipped, furious. She could not believe, just absolutely could not *believe*, the utter stupidity of the whole situation. She didn't know for sure, but she was fairly certain that it was illegal not to report a dead body. Of course, it was illegal to grow pot, and it was illegal to take shrooms and acid, and all that, but those things were *completely different*. Anti-drug laws were just created by the Man to keep everyone down. Why was liquor legal and pot illegal? Liquor killed far more people every year than marijuana. It was just that liquor was the drug of the fat cats in their country clubs, and dope was the drug of the freaks.

But there was nothing whatsoever cool or groovy or freakish about being torn to bits by wild animals and then just buried in the woods like some late lamented family pet. It was just wrong, wrong, wrong. The Mom brushed a strand of brown hair out of her eyes, then started chopping Pippin apples for the salad with ferocity, whanging the knife on the counter, the blade a blur. She had argued her side until she was blue in the face (but not as blue as poor Bliss), and in the end everyone but her had voted the other way.

And since she had agreed that they were a community, that she would abide by the majority rule, she had to go along with it. However stupid their decisions might be. In her heart, she truly believed in pure democracy, in reasonable people getting together and hashing out their differences, and letting the will of the people decide the direction of the group. It was simply too bad that she had surrounded herself with such complete lunatics.

She sighed, dropping the apples into the salad bowl and reaching for the walnuts. She took a good deal of satisfaction in cracking them against the hard wooden countertop with her little mallet, then pulverizing the nut-meats with the knife as well. The Dad had, wisely, gone to help Billy Goat and Evening Star move whatever stuff they would need in from their tent; the kids were all playing quietly upstairs; Weed's family had gone off to their camper for a while. Everyone knew she needed a little space. She would simmer down soon enough. She already was.

It wasn't that she was so fond of the pigs—no way! She too had left the city to get away from all of that. And she absolutely didn't want big fat rednecks in uniforms crawling all over her private property, leering at the women, trampling the garden. And if it was true that the girl had no family that wanted her...

She sighed again, and started washing homegrown carrots, rinsing the mud down the sink.

Upstairs in the loft, the Princess heard the sighs and the gentler chopping. "Okay, we can go down now," she whispered to the other kids.

A lot of Gallo Mountain Rhine was drunk at dinner that night.

The Dad, Weed, and Junior dug a large hole at the far edge of the back meadow. Billy Goat hung around supervising, as usual. A big oak tree would provide shade for the gravesite. It was a peaceful spot, and the men agreed that if the situation were different, they too would like to be buried there. They were all privately grateful that the situation was not different, that they were still alive, and that the weird hitchhiker chick was the one who was dead.

They took turns as the hole got deeper and the sun rose in the sky, bringing sweat to their brows. The ground was relatively easy to work, but still, a grave for a whole person was a big thing. Plus, everyone had heard news reports of bodies being found in "shallow graves." Serial-killer victims and crazy shit like that. That was undignified. So they dug and dug and sweated and didn't talk much.

When they all agreed that the hole was deep enough, they left their shovels leaning against the oak tree and headed back down the path. "I'll tell the others," Weed said, and went to the house.

The other three men stood in the front meadow, looking at each other. Nobody really knew how to tackle the monstrous task of getting the body out of the creek and back to the gravesite.

Finally, the Dad shrugged. "I guess we better just go for it."

"How about a blanket?" Junior asked.

"Good idea." The Dad went to the shed and rummaged around, finally coming out with a tattered old army blanket. He had used it to cover the chicken coop last winter, before all the chickens had died of the cold anyway.

They stood around a little longer, but Weed didn't come out of the house. "We three can handle it," the Dad said, finally.

So they walked down the narrow path to the creek, where they were all secretly disappointed to discover that the body had not washed downstream in the night, been eaten by wild animals, or otherwise vanished. It was still there, waiting to be dealt with. Waiting to be rescued, handled, buried.

The Dad held the blanket under one arm and picked his way carefully into the creek, trying not to slip or stumble over the large mossy rocks. Junior followed, and Billy Goat stood on the bank. No matter. Two could pick her up.

The Dad felt a little sick as he got closer to the body, although it was so stiff and blue and clean, there was nothing classically disgusting about it. There was no smell, no flies, no drippy sticky blood. But it had been a human being, and now it was just some soggy meat in a creek. He shuddered and tried to make it a task to be dealt with, a problem to be solved: a heavy, awkward weight which needed to be extracted from some rocks amid rushing water and conveyed to the back meadow. Seen that way, it became a little easier. And Junior was very strong, clever, and helpful. Between the two of them, they managed to get the body pulled from the water and wrapped in the blanket in only about ten strenuous minutes. Then it was just a simple matter of each taking an end, and hefting it to the back meadow.

It. Not her.

The others joined them along the path, making a slow procession. They must have been watching from the windows. Even the children came. No one had discussed it, but how could they be left out, barred from such a special ceremony? Death was a part of life.

Junior and the Dad laid the blanket-covered body carefully in the big hole. The grave. It fit fine, with room to spare, and the Dad was glad of that. Nobody wanted to do any more digging.

"Here," Astrid said, producing Bliss's backpack. "This should go in with her."

The backpack reminded the Dad of something he'd thought about earlier, and forgotten. "Oh, we should look through that, see if there's a wallet, any ID, or… I don't even know her last name."

"I did look through it," the Mom said, frowning. "She had six different driver's licenses, and none of them said Bliss. None of the photos looked much like her, either. In fact, a few of them were guys."

"Oh." There was an awkward silence.

"Well, I guess we should bury her, then," the Dad finally said. Her. It. And then they had to say some words. Which part came first?

The Dad stood at the head of the grave. Although Billy Goat had offered to deliver a eulogy last night, now everyone was looking at the Dad. Well, he was sort of the leader here, if not the elder. He shrugged his shoulders and began speaking.

"We're gathered together today to lay to rest our friend Bliss. She was a happy soul, although we were only really beginning our journey of knowing her. She brightened all our lives during the brief time that she was with us. I feel sure that she must have brightened others' lives, too, wherever she met them." He paused, trying to think of what else to say, realizing he needed to avoid some shaky ground there, about whatever other lives, and wallets, she may have touched. Oh, right, the earth and all that. "We are returning her body to the land from which it came, and hope that she may rest peacefully here, in the land she loved so much, though she had only begun to explore it. And we ask that the spirits of the Land receive her body and welcome it wholeheartedly, and keep her safe in it." *I feel like I'm repeating myself,* he thought. *I don't know what to say.* But Astrid gave him a warm, encouraging smile; he saw a few tears at the corners of her eyes. So he went on. "We are deeply sorry to have lost Bliss, but we understand that life is a mystery, and death is the next adventure." *Okay, now I'm really out of things to say.* He looked around the group. "Does anyone have anything they want to add?"

Everyone glanced around at each other, looking at him without exactly meeting his eyes, smiling vaguely, mouths clamped shut. The Mom stood stolidly, arms folded across her chest. Even the Princess had that vague, serious "don't call on me" look on her face.

"Then we shall cover her with earth, and let the next phase of her journey begin." *Whoever she really was.* He went to get his shovel, and Junior and Weed got theirs. Burying was much easier than digging, and they had her covered up in fifteen or twenty minutes.

Before they left the meadow, Astrid produced a small sign. It was hand-lettered with the children's paints, on a pale block of wood, nailed to a sharpened stake. *BLISS*, it said. She drove the sign into the soil at the head of the grave.

"That's wonderful," the Dad said, giving her a light hug. "What a nice touch."

She hugged him back, letting go quickly and glancing at the Mom, who was already starting back down the path.

The Land received the body of Bliss, as the Dad had requested.

CHAPTER 7

The sheriff's deputy looked up from his desk at the woman standing before him. The first thing he noticed was that she was nervous. But then again, most people were nervous talking to cops. Especially hippies. His cop brain noted the usual details: she was white, late twenties to early thirties, maybe 135 pounds. She wore a bright paisley-patchwork granny-length dress, plastic thong sandals, and had straight brown hair down past her shoulders. No makeup, no bra.

The deputy gave a quick, surreptitious glance to see how this woman had gotten past the reception area, but the front desk was empty. The girl must be taking yet another coffee break. He smiled professionally and said, "How may I help you, ma'am?"

The woman frowned. "I want to report a, um, an accident, I guess."

The deputy reached for a pad of paper and wrote the date at the top. "Yes? What happened?"

"My husband picked up a hitchhiker, and she… Well, she died."

The deputy looked up, startled. He'd been thinking traffic mishap, and had been about to send her to the local police, but this was more serious. "How did she die, ma'am?"

"Well, we're not really sure." She glanced behind her, shifting from one foot to another. "It was probably a wild animal or something. And nobody wanted to report it, but I thought we should." She looked around again and added, "Nobody knows I'm here."

"Have a seat, please." The deputy indicated the chair in front of his desk.

The woman perched at the edge of the chair. "Now, tell me the whole story, starting with your name."

The woman blanched, then said quickly, "Mary Smith."

The deputy wrote "Mary Smith—real name?" and then "Hippie" on his pad, keeping it tilted up so she couldn't see. "Address?"

She hesitated again, and then gave an address in the country, at least twenty-five miles out of town, he thought. He wrote it down. It could be legit. He'd have to look it up later; she already looked ready to flee. The trick with these dropout types was to keep it calm, bland, professional. Not to frighten them. They were always out of their minds on drugs anyway.

"Tell me what happened," he said gently.

But she was already clutching at her string bag, and not meeting his eye. "Well, there's not much to tell. Like I said, my husband brought her home, and, um, she went out that night, and we didn't know where. The next day, we found her." She paled a little and said, "Something…had bitten her."

"You don't know what bit her?"

"Nobody saw anything. We just found…her body. In the creek."

"Is the body still in the creek?"

"No, we buried her." She glanced up at him, fearfully. "We shouldn't have done that, should we?"

It started to sound familiar, to fall into a known pattern. Stupid hippies, getting these ideas in their heads from their LSD trips and then thinking their hallucinations were real. Or else it could be some kind of Weathermen-like group, fucking with the cops. But she seemed to at least believe what she was saying.

Of course, these groups always used pretty women to do their dirty work. Scum. He leaned forward slightly. "And no one thought to phone the authorities?"

"We don't have a phone."

He wrote "no phone" on his pad, after "SDS-Weathermen-LSD?" and glanced back at her.

Suddenly she stood up. "I'm sorry, I have to leave. I shouldn't have come here."

The deputy stood up fast, trying to come around the desk without scaring her further. "I'm sorry, ma'am, but you can't leave just yet. I need more information. We'll need to send a car out to the scene. And if you're a witness…" His hand unconsciously moved towards the gun at his hip, and then relaxed smoothly away and fell on the notepad instead, turning it over on his desk.

Her eyes grew wider as she backed towards the opaque glass doors at the front of the building. "No! I didn't see anything. I just wanted…"

Just then the doors opened, and the front desk girl came in. In the confusion of the near-collision, the hippie woman got out and hurried into a Dodge Dart. The deputy almost pursued her, but instead noted the car's license plate number. The woman sped out of the parking lot and was gone.

It was almost two weeks after the burial of Bliss before the Dad and Billy Goat finally made that trip into town to look for freaks selling acid. The tragedy had faded somewhat, and nothing else had been attacked. Of course, everyone had been very careful. Nobody was wandering around in the woods in the middle of the night, or even sleeping in tents, though there was already some discussion that maybe it would be all right, in another day or two.

It was lucky, in a way, the Dad thought, that no one had known Bliss all that well. Or whatever her name really was. She had just arrived on the Land the day she was killed, after all. So, although everyone felt real sad about what had happened to her, they just didn't have anything specific to hold on to, to think about. He remembered talking to her in the car on the drive out. He remembered her exuberance, her cheerful crudeness, her easy ways with the kids, how he thought maybe she and Junior would get together. Her weird eyes. But she was already growing vague in his mind, and he had probably gotten to know her better than anyone else. And so they all went on with their lives.

The Dart came to a smooth stop outside a ramshackle house on the east side of Yokayo. "I'd better go in first, check out the scene," Billy Goat said. The Dad nodded.

Bill slid out of the car in one smooth, easy motion. He sure moved well for such an old guy, the Dad thought. However old he was. Bill walked up and rang the doorbell, then knocked, after a wait. The Dad saw someone come to the door, but he couldn't see what they looked like, or what was going on.

After a while, Bill came back to the car. "He's not here anymore, but I got the address where he's probably crashing."

"Far out."

Ten minutes later, they pulled up in front of a trailer at the south end of town. Again Bill went to the door. Again he came back. "Nope—but they said check out this other place."

Fifteen minutes later, they were down the highway in Green Valley, the next little town to the south, and this time they hit pay dirt. Billy Goat returned to the car, a big grin on his furry face. "Come on in! How much cash do you have?"

It was three days till the next unemployment check. "Uh…not much. Maybe twenty?" And he was supposed to get groceries too. Somehow he had thought everyone would be chipping in on this. Funny how it hadn't gotten discussed.

"That's plenty—he's got potent shit. Come on!"

The Dad followed Billy Goat past a parked Harley and into the front part of a small duplex just off the main highway. The door let them right into the kitchen. A living room or bedroom was right behind it, the floor strewn with clothes. A sullen dark-haired woman was stirring something at the stove. She barely glanced at them as they came in. A beardless man with long hair tied back in a ponytail sat at the formica kitchen table sorting little pills into groups; a huge stack of plastic-wrapped bundles of pot sat next to him. The Dad's shoulders tightened. This whole scene felt unbelievably seedy, like something out of a bad movie. He felt as though he were being watched from behind, though no one was there.

"Danger, my man!" Bill was saying to the guy at the table. "It's great to see you!"

The man pushed one last bunch of pills aside, then stood up. "Goat-man, where you been keeping yourself?"

"Got a community out in the woods." He turned to the Dad. "This is the guy I was telling you about—Danger."

"Your name is Danger?" the Dad asked, shaking the man's offered hand.

"It is now." Danger laughed loudly, then stopped abruptly.

The woman at the stove stirred and stirred. The Dad wanted to acknowl-edge her, but apparently that wasn't going to happen.

"It's Dan Gerson. Get it? Dan-ger?"

"Yeah," said the Dad. "Clever."

"So what can I do you for?" Danger glanced at the pills and the pot. "Got a nice shipment of reds just in, brought up from the city. And some excellently potent weed."

"Nah," said Billy Goat, "we're looking for more of a trip than that. Got any acid?"

"LSD? Ah, you were always a man of discriminating tastes, Goat-man. Let me see..." Danger rummaged around on the cluttered kitchen table for a minute. "Hang on, I'm sure I do. Let me get the rest of my stash."

He went into the next room, where he muttered to himself for a long few minutes. The woman at the stove stopped stirring, wiped her hands on a grimy dishtowel, and came and sat down at the table. Billy Goat and the Dad remained standing. The Dad glanced around, unsure what was called for here. "How you doin'?" he finally asked her, politely.

"Fine," she said, and then got back up and left the room to join Danger.

The Dad shifted from foot to foot. Billy Goat grinned at him and made the "she's crazy" sign, twirling his finger around his ear. The Dad nodded.

Eventually Danger came back into the kitchen with a baggie in his hand. "You're in luck, my good man. The finest tripping tabs in the country, right here. How many doses do you need?"

"Seven," the Dad said.

"Ten," Billy Goat said. The Dad looked at him, puzzled. "You want some for everyone, don't you?" Bill asked.

"Yeah, but there's you and Evening Star, Astrid and Weed and Junior, and then the two of us. That's seven."

"Don't forget the kids."

"The kids aren't going to do acid!" The Dad was horrified.

"Why not? It's perfectly safe."

The Dad looked at Danger, who merely shrugged.

"Well, my kids aren't going to do acid!"

"Suit yourself," Billy Goat said. "Okay, eight."

"Eight doses?" Danger asked, sitting down at the table, opening the baggie and pulling out a small sheet of brightly colored paper and a razor blade. He tapped the razor blade down the sheet of paper, counting out eight tiny increments, then razored off a slice. "That'll be thirty-two bucks."

Billy Goat looked at the Dad. "I've only got twenty," the Dad said.

"Well, let me see what I've got." Bill dug around in his jeans pocket, pulling out some wadded-up bills and change, and spread it on the table.

"Hang on, don't mess up the stuff," Danger said, pushing the money away from the drugs. "It's all right, Goat-man—since you're such a good customer, I'll give you a break. Three a dose. So, twenty-four. And here's four." He gathered it from the pile of Bill's money. Then he looked at the Dad, who dutifully dug into his own pocket and found three fives and a small handful of ones. After they paid Danger off, he was left with three dollars. Well, at least he could get a few things at the store.

Such a good customer? the Dad wondered as he and Billy Goat walked back out to the car. *I thought he'd just bought peyote or something from the guy once.*

Upon the hunters' triumphant return from their mission, the Great Land Community LSD Trip was scheduled for the following day. *Might as well get it over with*, the Mom thought. She was abashed at almost giving everything away by going to the cops. What had she been thinking? Thank goodness she had had the presence of mind to give a fake name and address.

She was also still a little wary of the drug, still unsure of her experience with the mushrooms, but everyone assured her acid was completely harmless, it was much easier on the system than mushrooms, she'd love it, all that.

She agreed with her husband on one thing, though: it was insane to consider giving the drug to children. "What are you thinking?" she asked Evening Star as Bill looked on, amused. "It'll stunt her growth!"

"Oh, it will not, it's not like she's smoking tobacco or something." Evening Star shrugged. "She'll be fine."

Morning Star sat close to her mother, her eyes shining. "I'll be fine."

The Mom frowned, closing her eyes and shaking her head. "It just seems like a bad idea to me. I'm sorry."

Evening Star smiled and put a hand on the Mom's shoulders, giving her a little relaxing neck rub. "Mellow out, love, it's all right. I'll give her a small dose—half a dose. You can give her the other half." She nodded at the Princess.

"I will not!" The Mom shrugged off Evening Star's hand. "I just can't believe you people."

"It does seem like kind of a waste," Astrid put in. "Kids are already trippy—they don't need their minds opened. We adults are just trying to get back to a kid state of mind. You know?"

The Mom looked at her gratefully. *Well, that's not my point at all, but at least someone has some sense.*

"Well, I'll let her decide," Evening Star said, rumpling up her daughter's hair. "She always knows what's best for herself."

The Mom rolled her eyes but didn't trust herself to answer.

The Princess watched the debate silently, as she had watched so many debates lately in this house. Inside, however, she was livid. First of all, she hated, hated, hated that annoying little fat girl so much! Always getting in the way, ruining her toys and her little villages and taking the side of the Apricot Boy, then sneaking up behind her on the trail and scaring her half to death and then screaming bloody murder at finding Bliss in the water, and now! Now she got to do *acid* and the Princess didn't! And the Princess was two whole years older!

But she knew her mother well enough to tell it would be futile to say anything. Just like with wine and pot and hash, her mom had this funny notion that kids shouldn't be able to do the things that all the adults got to do, just because the adults should be able to have more fun and to be a kid was to have no fun at all.

She slunk over to the stairs and retreated to her room, as she so frequently did. From there, she plotted what she would do. She hadn't seen the drug, but she knew that it was on little pieces of paper. If they cut the paper up, and everyone didn't take a full dose…well then, once they started tripping, it should be easy to scour the house for the leftover scrap. She'd show them: she'd do acid too!

She wouldn't give any to the Apricot Boy, of course. He was too young.

The next morning dawned bright and clear with an autumnal crispness in the air. The Princess arose early, got herself a sloppy slice of bread with a thick layer of strawberry jam for breakfast, and took her things out to play in the meadow. The Mom watched her from the narrow front window, smiling. Such a good little girl. She was lucky to have such self-sufficient children. It made the upcoming adventure much easier to contemplate.

The Mom tsk'ed to herself as she thought of Star and Bill giving their poor daughter drugs. That child was doomed, absolutely doomed. Probably she'd be selling herself in truck stops in ten years, needle tracks all down her arms. Well, the Mom had tried to talk sense into them. She really had.

She had to put it out of her head, though. They had made their decision, and it was going to happen. Morning Star was their child. It was up to them. And here came Weed and Astrid up the path, Junior right behind them.

As the three came in, letting the door bang shut after them, Evening

Star and Bill started waking up, emerging from their sleeping bags in the middle of the floor. Morning Star took a little longer. Then the waking-up sounds of the Apricot Boy awoke the Dad. He came downstairs with the boy in his arms, smiling at the gathered company.

"Does anyone want breakfast?" the Mom asked, after lighting the stove.

"Probably not a great idea," Evening Star said.

"Yeah," Junior laughed. "Remember the shrooms?"

"I thought acid wasn't supposed to do that," the Mom said. "Didn't you prefer it because shrooms made you sick?"

"Well, all hallucinogens do," Evening Star admitted. "It's just that acid's so much better—a more powerful trip, so loving, mind-opening. And I've never done it in such great nature before—the space here is incredible! You're gonna love it, you really are."

"All right."

Everyone looked at everyone else, then at Billy Goat. He had scored the acid, and he still had it, tucked away in the pocket of that nasty shirt of his. "Okay then," he said. "So we're ready?"

The Mom was suddenly really nervous. "Shouldn't we, I don't know, have a cup of tea or something first? Or just sit and talk about what we're doing here?"

"Plenty of time for that while we're waiting to get off," Evening Star said.

Waiting to get off. The Mom was suddenly transported back to the night of the shrooms. Bliss had said exactly that, with a laugh. Of course, this would be like that, and unlike pot or wine, which hit you right away. She felt chilly and stoked up the fire, willing it to warm the room faster, though she had just lit it.

Billy Goat sat down at the desk and got out the brightly colored blotter paper. "Anyone got a razor?"

The Princess's realm was getting out of her control. It used to be that she was the Princess. She had the Mom and the Dad and the Apricot Boy, and that was it. Other courtiers came and went, causing trouble or not, but nobody ever stayed long. The Princess always remained, if not *exactly* in the center of things, then at least central enough so that she knew that she mattered. Everyone knew that she mattered.

Now there were all these strange new courtiers who had come, and they weren't leaving. And they were changing the way everything was done. Her Dad hardly had time to read *The Two Towers* to her in the evenings anymore; also he didn't take her into town as often. The library books she had in her little cubby were almost overdue. She had read them weeks ago, and then read them again. School would be starting in less than two weeks. The Princess was surprised to find that she was actually looking forward to it. At least there would be different books to read.

And then there was the monster, the strange evil monster on the Land. He didn't seem to be a part of the Princess's dominion. He didn't do what she told him to do; he didn't appear when she wanted to talk to him. Maybe he was gone. Maybe eating the strange hitchhiker lady had been enough for him.

But she kind of didn't think so.

The Princess gathered up her toys and walked back up to the house. She knew everyone was in there, and that they would be doing the acid now. She wanted to see what it looked like, and where they put it when they were done with it, whether there was any left behind that she might be able to scavenge for herself.

But her timing was off. Everyone had already dosed by the time she got into the house. They were all sitting around the octagonal table, looking a little nervous. "Did you get some breakfast, honey?" her mother asked her.

"Yes."

"Are you going to watch your brother for me today?" The Apricot Boy sat in the Mom's lap, smiling, pulling on her hair, and her large hoop earrings. A training cup of apricot juice sat on the table in front of him, half-drunk, the plastic mouthpiece well chewed.

"Okay."

"He's already had his breakfast. He should be fine."

"Okay."

"There's bread in the cold box, and cheese, and apples on the counter…"

Evening Star laughed. "Relax! The kids can take care of themselves."

The Princess looked at Morning Star, who had a look of incredible smugness on her face. Little brat! The Princess looked away quickly. Stupid acid anyway, who would want to do acid? Astrid was right: kids already had plenty of imagination, and they got to live in a fun world, fun enough for anyone.

But she didn't really believe that. She was still terribly, terribly jealous.

After a long while, the adults started behaving strangely. The Princess wasn't exactly sure what to expect out of them. There had certainly always been a lot of talk about tripping on various drugs, but other than pot, she had never seen it. She watched them all carefully, especially her mother. She was watching her brother too, of course, but he didn't need any more attention than usual. He was always perfectly content, no matter what was going on. He slipped down off the Mom's lap when she started fidgeting, and came to his sister.

The other adults were laughing and talking to each other, but the Mom looked as though she wasn't feeling well. "Jeez, it's like cramps," she said to the Dad.

"Want to go outside?" he offered.

"Oh, yeah."

The Princess and the Apricot Boy followed their parents outside, but kept a discreet distance from them. "Is Mommy okay?" the Apricot Boy asked.

"Yeah, she's just taken acid, she'll be fine," the Princess said, with authority.

The Mom sat down under an oak tree, the Dad next to her. He held her hand and stroked it, gently, murmuring in her ear. For a while it looked like she was going to throw up, but then she didn't. Then she and the Dad started talking to each other really intensely, staring deep into each other's eyes. It got quite boring to watch.

The Princess took her brother's hand. "Come on," she said. "Let's go play in the back meadow."

The Princess really liked the back meadow. It was much smaller than the front meadow and beautifully self-contained. The tall mountain rose up right behind it, making it so much more picturesque a place. Like something out of *Heidi*.

"Okay," the always agreeable Apricot Boy said.

"But wait a minute." She wanted to go into the house again. She suddenly wanted to see Morning Star on acid, even though at the same time, she didn't want to see her at all. "I need something else to eat," she lied.

"Okay."

They left their parents under the tree and went back into the house. By now, Junior and Weed and Astrid had left, gone somewhere, out in nature, presumably. But Billy Goat and Evening Star and Morning Star were there. And it was not pretty.

Morning Star was having a tantrum, pulling off all her clothes. "No!" she screamed at her mother. "I don't want to!"

"Sweetheart," the exasperated Evening Star said. "It's way too cold out—you've got to wear something."

"I don't want to!" She was nearly naked; only her little pink underpants remained, and she was tugging at them violently. Her mother was tugging back, in the opposite direction. But Evening Star was clearly having a hard time of it.

"Oh, leave her be, she'll be fine," Billy Goat said, his eyes wide, pupils huge black holes.

The Princess stared at the family, impressed and a little awestruck. Imagine, wanting to take all your clothes off! Of course, they all did it at the river. But not in the house. What if you wanted to sit down somewhere? It would be scratchy.

Morning Star succeeded in getting her underpants off. She threw them; they struck her mother in the face and fell to the floor.

"Fine!" Evening Star yelled. "Be that way!" She kicked at the little pink panties, which flew up about a foot in the air before dropping back to the floor in a pathetic little heap. "I'm going outside, where it's far trippier than in here. You can spend your whole first acid trip of your entire life cooped up in this stupid little cabin if you like." She banged out the back door, leaving both halves of the Dutch door rattling against each other.

"She seemed mad," the Princess said, because it was so obvious.

Billy Goat laughed. "She's a spitfire!" Then he took his naked daughter's hand. "Come on, little one, I'll help you." They both went outside as well, but without the slamming.

That left only the Princess and the Apricot Boy in the house. "Ready to go to the back meadow?" she asked.

"Okay." He didn't remind her that she had said she wanted to get something to eat.

The Mom was having what would technically be called a bad trip, if there was any technical way to measure such things. Every time she regained her equilibrium, she suddenly felt that she was slipping again. The ground wasn't steady, it felt crooked, it would never be still. It was like living in a constant earthquake that nobody else could feel.

That was, when she was able to talk to anyone else about it. She had a really hard time finding her language, and she also had a hard time finding the other members of the Land community. For something that was supposed to bring them together, it had done a remarkably good job of scattering them to all corners of the property.

Not that she was very good company. She spent what felt like months hugging her own arms, trying to steady herself. The earth was alive, and that felt all wrong. If this was what mind-opening was all about, she wanted her mind tightly shut.

She huddled under the same oak tree she had first escaped to, when she'd fled the house. The tree seemed more or less solid. Except when it wasn't. Sometimes it wavered and undulated along with everything else. She told herself that it was just a hallucination, but she didn't really believe that. She understood now that all of her previous perception had been the illusion, the hallucination, and she was now boring down to the reality underneath. And the reality was damned scary. And she didn't like it.

She moaned softly, hugging her arms tighter, trying to make it all slow down, stop. She told herself it would eventually. But how much longer?

Stymied, the Dad wandered off, and immediately forgot his wife and her distress. He really did love her, care about her, was concerned for her and her troubles and her bad trip—but hey, check this out! The way the hills touched the sky, the tiny trees poking into the skyline—green against blue—oh my god, it was fucking incredible. He had never seen anything like it, even on the shroom night—although of course it had been dark on the shroom night—maybe that was the same way and he hadn't known it! He should do shrooms again! They all should!

Who all? Oh yeah, there were other people…but it all seemed so complicated. Who needed other people when you had all this incredible nature? Rocks and trees and grass and sky, oh such gorgeous blue sky. Blue was such a pretty color; it had all the other colors nested in it.

Or was that black? Or white? He had read something about that in school, but he couldn't remember now.

He wandered through the front meadow, skirting the edge of the driveway. He passed one of the places where the Princess had her little villages, the one that she made in the dirt by the little creek, damming up the water and building her little roads and all. She was so creative. She was so incredible, his daughter! Fruit of his loins—oh my god, that little girl had come out of sex! Sex with his wife, his beautiful, gorgeous, precious wife…

His wife: where was she? Oh yeah, she was wavering. He should go check on her. He would go there right now. She was having a little bit of a stomachache or something, she didn't feel good. Maybe he could help her.

Maybe he could bring her a drink of water or something.

Look at this rock!

At the end of the day, everyone meandered back to the house, utterly spent. The Princess and the Apricot Boy had spent a fun and undramatic day in the back meadow, playing the little village game in a new spot, far away from the goat-evil spot and the Bliss-grave spot, but close enough to see them both. She knew when it was time to go back; she picked up the game and guided the hungry, tired Apricot Boy down the path.

The Mom was exhausted and demoralized. But still, everyone had to be fed—except for Weed and Astrid, who had simply retreated to their camper. The Mom lit the fire and got some tofu out of the cold box, then tried to find the knife to chop it up. She had a kind of stir-fry in mind, with diced firm tofu and root veggies from the garden and whatever spices seemed fitting. They could put yogurt on it at the table. That would be plenty. Nobody was very hungry.

Morning Star was still naked. She was shivering, and a little blue at the extremities, but she screamed if anyone tried to bring any of her clothes even near her.

"She'll get over it," Evening Star said, and Billy Goat nodded agreement. She wouldn't sit down either.

"How much did you give her?" the Mom asked.

"Half a dose," Billy Goat said. "I guess. It's not exact."

"Because she's smaller than half your size, don't you think?"

"She'll be fine," Evening Star said, in a tone which stopped the debate.

Junior sat in his habitual corner, his guitar in his lap, his eyes wide, silent as usual. The Mom glanced over at him, then looked away. He was always so mellow, so accepting, so mature for his age. She hated feeling old and petty, small-minded. She hated that she had had such an obvious bad trip. Everyone was so solicitous around her now. Except they still didn't offer to help her cook.

She turned back to her chopping block, finished assembling her ingre-
dients, and got out the big cast-iron skillet. In a few minutes, she stood over
the stove, stirring, listening to the general conversation stumble around
the room. Everyone was still half-tripping, but they knew it was time to be
indoors, time to wind it down. In a little while, it would be time to bring the
dogs in. Time to button it up for the night.

Time for bed, and she looked forward to the oblivion of sleep. She tried
not to worry about what dreams she might have. She just kept tossing the
food in the skillet, stirring, trying to get through it all.

CHAPTER 8

The Dad went to check on his secret pot garden. As the summer had progressed, he had not exactly neglected it, but the novelty had kind of worn off. It was a really long hike up there, halfway to the top of the mountain. When he had first planted it, he had wanted it to be remote. That had seemed safer, like the wise choice. In case any cops came by, they wouldn't stumble across it accidentally next to the tomatoes and lemon cucumbers.

Now it just seemed ridiculous to have it all the way up here. What cops would come all this way? Heck, they couldn't hardly get fellow hippies to come by the Land itself. Until lately, that was. And none of them had climbed the mountain. At least as far as he knew. Still, he kept the exact location to himself.

He hiked up the path, breaking a slight sweat, shifting his bag to the other shoulder. He was really out of condition. He should come up here more often. Not that the plants needed much tending, since Northern California was the perfect climate for marijuana. He hardly even needed to water them. They just grew like weeds. *Like weed, ha ha.*

He kept hiking. It was even farther than he remembered. Had he missed the turnoff? The garden wasn't exactly on the path, but he thought you could see it from there, anyway, if you knew what to look for.

He turned another corner. Ah, there it was.

It wasn't fenced, but tucked away in a natural clearing amid a bunch of fir trees. The greens were similar—the tall, fragrant pot plants and equally aromatic trees. It was a mystical place, peaceful, serene.

The Dad stepped into his garden. The plants were about a foot taller than the last time he had been up here, almost as tall as he was. He moved among the gorgeous plants, sniffing their aroma deep into his lungs, touching each plant gently. He bent down and felt the soil beneath them, digging his index finger in an inch or so: perfect, just a little damp. They were growing fine. They needed no attention.

He pinched off a few lower leaves from each plant, then a few buds from the tops of the females, careful to leave enough behind for future harvesting, and so that the plants could propagate. He tucked his harvest into the bag, gave the plants one last, lingering caress, and headed back down the hill. Now would begin the process of drying the harvest, combing out the seeds, and getting it ready for consumption. Which should be finished just about the time the current stash ran out, assuming a whole bunch more drugless hippies didn't show up any time soon.

The Mom was out behind the house, hanging clothes on the line. A gentle breeze stirred the air, lifting a strand of hair and blowing it across her face. She brushed it back with a forearm, her hands still full of wet sheets.

"Do that again," came a voice behind her.

She turned around quickly. There was Junior, watching her, with a small smile on his face. "What?" she asked.

"What you did just then—you leaned over, reached into the basket, and brushed the hair away—it was like art, you were like a painting."

The Mom blushed furiously, even as she thought, *That's the most words I've ever heard out of him.* "You've got to be kidding."

He shrugged. "No, I'm serious. It was the most beautiful thing I've ever seen, in all my years."

"You're seventeen."

"Seventeen is plenty of years."

They stood there, looking at each other. "I'm thirty," she said finally, as if he had asked. As if it mattered. Because she understood, thoroughly, the look on his face.

He just shrugged again.

"I'm trying to get some work done here," she said, turning back to the basket, the clothes line.

"All right," he said.

She tried to ignore him, but she felt his eyes on her for another minute. Then he turned and went down the path, towards his brother's camper.

At lunchtime, she sliced more of the endless brick of government surplus cheese, along with more of the all too quickly consumed home-baked bread. Since it was colder out than usual, she had kept the cook stove stoked after breakfast, so she decided to make grilled cheese sandwiches for a change. The kids would like it, anyway.

Actually she would like it too. Though it also reminded her of her childhood, in the stark, sterile suburban landscape, in that big flat house in a new subdivision, with bedrooms for everyone and no trees or plants for years, and all the houses looking the same. She flashed back to her own mother standing over her new-fangled electric stove, making grilled cheese sandwiches twenty years ago. The Mom looked down at herself: apron tied over her blue jeans, spatula in hand. She had sure come a long way in twenty years, hadn't she?

Then she had to smile to herself. Of course, this was entirely different. She wasn't trapped in the kitchen, as her mother had been. She and her husband had decided together to move out here, to make a new life in the country. To homestead. Of course the traditional roles made sense here. He brought in the water supply, chopped the wood, did the heavy work.

As far as work being done by the other members of the community, well, that still had to be worked out. She sensed another Land meeting in the works. Well, more than sensed—she was going to call one, just as soon as she had her thoughts worked out more clearly.

As if she had conjured them up by thinking about them, Weed, Astrid and Junior came in, heralded by the barking of Galadriel and Sauron as they came up the path. "Hey," said Weed. "Lunch almost ready?"

"Sure," she said, ignoring the tension that rose in her shoulders at his casual question. "How many sandwiches does everyone want?"

As they sat around the table and started in on the first pile, the Mom watched Junior surreptitiously, glancing at him when she felt that he was looking away. What had that all been about, earlier at the clothes line? He wasn't seriously hitting on her, was he?

And so what if he was?

She smiled slightly at the thought. This was far more rewarding to think about than hassles about chores. She and the Dad had been married more than ten years, and in all that time, she had remained faithful to him. And, presumably, he had to her. She intended to remain faithful still, but she could always fantasize. It was pretty cool that such a desirable young man—okay, boy, technically—could find her attractive—an older woman, thirty, with two children. She wasn't dead yet.

The back door opened, and the Dad came in with his bag of pot, newly harvested. "Hi, hon," she said, smiling. "There's sandwiches."

"Great, I'm starved." He sat down on the floor between her and the Princess. She scooted over to make room for him.

After lunch, the Dad went onto the front porch to start dealing with the pot. Astrid and Weed ambled back in the direction of their camper, holding hands, with that look in their eyes. Junior stayed behind, plucking at his guitar. The Mom started to clear the dishes, still glancing over at Junior, but he seemed to be paying no attention.

Then Evening Star and Billy Goat showed up, rattling through the back door with Morning Star. The child was still naked, although it had been days since the acid trip. "Did we miss lunch?"

The tension in the Mom's shoulders ratcheted up a notch. "Yes, you did," she said, lightly. "And I've just washed the skillet." She punctuated this statement by setting the clean skillet on the still-warm stove, where it hissed and steamed.

"I'm hungry," whined Morning Star.

Billy Goat grinned and settled himself in the desk chair.

"Hey, Mama," Evening Star said to the Mom. "Did we miss grilled cheese sandwiches? We love your sandwiches."

"Feel free to make some, I've got stuff to do. I just put everything away." The Mom turned and started wiping the counter.

"Oh, but yours are so much better than mine," Evening Star said. Morning Star started to whimper and pull at her mom's skirt. "And I've got to take care of her." She picked up her daughter and cuddled her, then set her back down. The whimpering stopped for a minute.

The Mom glanced over at Junior again, but he was still strumming his guitar, picking out a difficult chord. She hated to be bitchy in front of him, but she didn't see, for the life of her, why she had to be the one to make the sandwiches. It was just grilled cheese, not rocket science. Although she did have a pretty good technique with them. And she did like being appreciated.

Furthermore, this was her community, and she wanted to get along with everyone. But she tried one more feeble protest. "I'll get the stuff out for you, but you make the sandwiches."

Evening Star simply looked back at the Mom, her eyes wide and sad. Then she picked up Morning Star again and sat down on a floor pillow with her, crooning in her ear.

Finally the Mom sighed and reached into the woodbox to stoke up the fire again.

By the time the latecomers had finished their lunches, it was almost time for the Mom to start working on dinner. Okay, definitely she needed to call a Land meeting to discuss the meal prep situation, especially if people weren't going to show up on time and each meal was going to last two or three hours. If only she could concentrate and get her thoughts in order. She hated how weak she was, but she had never liked arguing with people.

"We were thinking about heading into town, if we can use the Dart?" Billy Goat asked, pushing back from the table and pulling out his Bugler bag.

"Sure, I guess," she said. "It needs gas, though." That seemed like the least they could do. If he had enough money to buy that filthy tobacco, he had enough to put gas in the car.

In fact, that gave the Mom a good idea. But as she opened her mouth to speak, the Princess spoke up, startling everyone: "Can I come? Are you going to the library?"

"I don't see why not," Evening Star said.

"Take him too," the Mom decided, indicating the Apricot Boy.

"Sure."

"And let me give you a shopping list." *Excellent, excellent idea,* she thought. "Just a minute." She grabbed a scrap of paper and started to scribble on it. This would be a great thing for them to do—not just the hassle of shopping but also paying for the groceries. That would be a fair trade for cooking all day long.

Evening Star took the list, eyes downcast. Was she annoyed? Hurt? The Mom couldn't tell, exactly. "All right, we'll be back in a couple of hours."

"Great," the Mom said. Then, pressing her advantage, she said, "And let's have a Land meeting at dinner. I got stuff to talk about."

"Okay, Mama." Now Evening Star grinned at the Mom.

Eventually, they all left, even the naked Morning Star, squished into the back seat with the other kids. The Mom hoped they'd at least put a blanket over her when they got into town. She shook her head as she wiped the last of the latest set of clean dishes and put them in the tall redwood cupboard above the sink.

The Dad came back in from the porch. "I'm going back up to the garden. I want to get another bag of dope—there was plenty, and if we have that party like we're talking about before the end of summer..."

"Yeah, right," the Mom said, remembering. "We should have had those guys take fliers to put up about it."

"Well, we can do it next time." He kissed her goodbye and headed up the back path.

"Gee, everyone cleared out," Junior said, looking up from his guitar at the Mom and smiling.

She turned to face him, putting her hands on her hips. "And just what do you mean by that?"

He shrugged yet again—it was a perfectly adorable gesture; had he practiced it? "Nothing."

"Good," she said firmly. "Because nothing is what's going to happen here. I'm married. Got it?"

He just looked at her through those unspeakably long eyelashes, obviously trying to decide whether he could get away with denying that he was talking about what he was clearly talking about. Then he grinned. "Okay. Got it. Sorry."

She smiled back. "No problem."

What did happen instead was that he played his guitar for what was left of the afternoon, and she sang along, as she went through her various chores. God, she did love to sing. When all too soon it came time to start dinner, and she needed the big soup pot down from the high shelf for the chili, she asked him to get it for her. He obliged, then offered to chop vegetables. No one ever offered to help chop any more! She handed him a knife.

This is more intimate than if we'd gone upstairs to ball, she thought, smiling as he diced the garden tomatoes. She was immensely pleased with herself for resisting the temptation.

When the Dad came back down from the mountain a second time, he bustled through the house, then paused, taking in the scene of the two preparing dinner together. "I'll be out on the front porch if you need me for anything," he said, a note of wistfulness in his voice.

"Thanks, but I think we're fine here," the Mom said.

Over the next few days, the Dad watched as Junior spent more and more time at the house, offering to help the Mom—and the Dad, too, must be fair about it—with all kinds of chores. The energy he had felt when he'd walked in on the two of them making dinner had been odd, unsettling. He trusted his wife. They'd talked about this kind of thing happening, and had agreed that if either of them had felt any urges, they'd talk it over first, decide as a couple what to do about it. Because it was perfectly natural to want to sleep with someone other than your mate, especially if you'd been mated for as long as they had. Heck, he thought about other women all the time, enjoyed thinking about other women, watching them at the beach, watching them walk around braless, topless, naked. But so far, he hadn't felt moved enough by any one woman to want to open that particular can of worms. Which wasn't to say that he wouldn't, some day. It just hadn't happened yet.

Or maybe, if he were to be perfectly honest with himself, he was a little frightened of other women. His wife he understood, and she understood him. He wasn't sure he was up to the challenge of a new woman. And he trusted his wife to hold to her side of the bargain, so although he sort of wanted to ask her if anything was going on, he didn't. He did find himself, however, not exactly sneaking around and spying on her, but showing up at odd moments—popping into the house when he'd said he was going to be out cutting wood or mending the goat fence, quietly climbing the stairs to the loft after she'd said she was going to go lie down for half an hour, that kind of thing. But although he frequently found her and Junior in each other's company, they were never doing anything untoward. Most often, Junior would be picking at that guitar of his, the Mom humming or singing along, or else he'd be holding the other end of a sheet she was folding, or fetching something for her from the shed, or filling a pot with water and building a fire in the wood cook stove.

Should he broach the subject? Just ask her? He didn't want to seem uptight. No, they'd agreed to be open with one another. It was up to her to tell him, if there were something going on.

Ultimately, the Dad told himself that there was nothing there, and that he should just get over himself.

But a slight unease remained with him.

The Mom sang and sang through the next days. As the big party approached, there was even more work to do, but never had her heart felt lighter. At the Land meeting, Evening Star and Billy Goat had claimed a lack of funds, so Star had been assigned garden duty while Bill was to help repair the fencing that was always coming down. Everyone had been giving something to do. It was a real community.

Ever since they had spoken of it, albeit briefly, the sexual tension between her and Junior had muted into a genuine pleasure in one another's company. It was *wonderful* to have so much help, and he was such a strong young man. She didn't feel at all disloyal to the Dad; he was busy enough, he did plenty. It was just that, with the community as large as it was, there was far more to do than there had been the first year. It was nice that the work had been spread around more evenly, but it still wasn't enough. Weed and Astrid seemed to be working out some issue, spending lots more time in their camper, or else Weed spending time there alone, brooding, as Astrid wandered the trails through the forest—always careful to take all the dogs with her when she did, in case the wild beastie came back. And Billy Goat and Evening Star—well, they seemed to be trying, but it wasn't worth much. Maybe they would get more energetic in time. For now, it seemed that they were always just hanging around, eating, drinking up the wine, smoking up the pot.

Anyhow, she really did enjoy Junior's company, above and beyond the use of his strong back. She slowly got to know him better, as he let slip details of his unhappy growing-up years, his shitty family with too many kids and not enough love or sanity. She opened up to him a little too, though by contrast, she thought her own story was pretty dull. He listened with avid interest, asking questions, prying gently, almost lovingly, into her child-hood, her university education, and her marriage.

And then one day, as they were up in the loft folding yet another batch of laundry together, he asked, "Are you happy?"

She looked up sharply, but he still had a friendly, innocent look on his face. It was an honest question. And actually, she had to think about it for a moment.

She brushed a bead of sweat off her forehead. "Yeah, I think so."

"You think so?"

"Well, it's hard here. It's isolating—I miss my old friends, I miss the excitement of the city sometimes. Corrupt as it was," she hastened to add. "I used to like to go downtown, when we lived in San Francisco. I'd bundle the Princess up in her stroller and take the streetcar down to Union Square. We couldn't really afford anything in the shops, but it always felt so elegant to go, to look in the windows, to imagine I was the kind of person who'd just waltz into one of those stores and say, 'Put it on my account,' or something like that." She flushed, glancing down at the laundry for a moment. "I guess that's silly."

Junior looked earnestly into her eyes. "No, it's not silly. It's important to have dreams. I don't know what my dream is—I have so many, and they change all the time."

"Well, I guess that wasn't really my dream, or I wouldn't have ended up here." She looked around her at the dark unpainted walls, the foam pad bed on the carpet-scrap floor, neatly made up with its army blankets.

"Maybe you can have all kinds of dreams. Maybe we don't need to just make one choice in life and live with that for the rest of our days." He took a step closer; she could feel the heat coming off his skin. She wanted to step back but didn't.

"Right now my dream is to just get a little more rest," she said softly.

He reached up and brushed a strand of hair out of her eyes. "Right now, my dream is to give you a kiss."

Oh god, do not do this, she thought as she leaned in ever so slightly. He leaned in too, and they were kissing.

She moaned softly as she began to explore the taste of him, still thinking that she was going to pull away at any moment, but just somehow not doing it. Instead, her mind was racing: where was everybody? Was anyone likely to walk in on them? Because she really did not want to stop kissing him.

The Dad was in town and wouldn't be back for at least an hour. That was the most important person to keep this from. Everyone else—well, her mind blurred with desire, she just couldn't remember what everyone else was up to. She hadn't been paying attention. What was she, everyone's mother?

She sighed and reached up, gathering Junior's soft hair in her hands. He was keeping his hands rather politely to himself, it seemed. She inched closer, kicking the laundry aside, kissing him more boldly and brushing against him with her nipples erect under her cotton shirt.

That was enough of an invitation for him. He pulled her suddenly, tightly to him, and kissed her hard, fever on his lips, his tongue. She kissed right back and leaned into his grasp. Her movement rocked him back on his heels, then brought them both down to the bed conveniently right beneath them. She started to push the itchy army blankets aside to get to the soft sheets underneath, while at the same time trying to not let go of him and to divest him of his shirt all at once. His hands roamed all over her body, seemingly not knowing where to go first, where to linger, where to simply graze.

She nibbled and bit at his delicious mouth. His new young beard was soft, intriguingly different from the beard she was accustomed to kissing. She sighed and rolled over a bit, trying to get closer to him, still worrying at his t-shirt. In the tangle, Junior pulled away a little, taking his mouth off of hers for a moment. "Are you sure about this?" he whispered.

"You started it," she whispered back, then kissed him again.

He kissed her back, fervently, but then drew away once more. "Because if you…"

She reached down and felt the firm bulge in his jeans, giving it a gentle squeeze. His eyes rolled back in his head, his eyelashes fluttering. "Oh my god…"

"I thought so," she said. "Now, shut up and kiss me."

He stopped protesting and did as he was told. She ate him up, rolling over and under him on the bed, and finally got that damned shirt off. She was slightly astonished at her sudden need, her desire for him. How long had it been since she and her husband had made love? She couldn't remember—it had certainly been a while; they were always so exhausted when they dropped into bed every night. And it was hard to pull off with the kids sleeping a few feet away, and half the commune hanging around right below the open loft.

But now the house was empty, the afternoon was warm, and this incredible hunk of eager young man was in her arms. She ran her hands over his smooth, muscular chest, then did the same with her lips, kissing him everywhere, enjoying the salty taste of his fresh sweat. He moaned again as she reached for the button fly of his jeans, peeling them open with a single motion, then trying to slide them down his narrow hips. He responded by undulating and writhing in her arms, actually a little counterproductively, but with so much enthusiasm it only inflamed her more. She managed to worry them about halfway down his hips before they got so tangled up that she gave up for the moment. His hands still wandered all over her body; she reached up and guided one under her blouse, where it might do more good, and then gasped as his finger touched her bare nipple.

She sat up for a moment and shrugged out of her Indian-print blouse as quickly as she could, never letting Junior's hand leave her breast. "Ohh," he sighed, and leaned in to kiss her right nipple. He bit, a little too hard; she gasped and drew back.

"I'm sorry," he said, looking shocked.

"I'm fine." She growled and pulled his head down to her breast again.

He kissed more gently this time. She squirmed with pleasure, and then tried again to get his jeans off. She rocked back on the bed, bringing him with her, and with her right hand, she managed to reach back and scoot the jeans down his ass. He finally got the idea and helped her slide them down.

Now he was naked, and she still had her jeans on. His hand went to her fly, but it was zipper, not button, and he got all jumbled up, trying to do it one-handed, backwards, and not looking. "Let me," she said, reaching down and unzipping them smoothly, then rocking her own hips. He helped, and soon she was down to her panties. They vanished with one swipe from her hand; she kicked them off her toe and didn't even look to see where they landed.

He was atop her, still kissing and caressing her breasts. She turned her attention to his erect cock, taking it into her hand, and it jumped with anticipation. A few beads of moisture collected at the tip, threatening to fall onto her belly. She reached a hand down, checking, although she knew: she was soaking wet. She could hardly stand to wait a moment longer. She eased her thighs open and invited him in.

He sank in as far as he could go and gave another loud moan. She rocked her hips under him, encouraging him, though he needed no encouragement. He pulled almost all the way out, then dove back in again, and then thrust again, and again, his fever building.

"Whoa, slow down there," she whispered after a minute, putting her hands on his shoulders. She knew about teenage boys; her husband had been a teenager once.

Junior obligingly slowed down, and she began to pace her own enjoyment, moving against him, letting it all build back up again. She reached back and took his firm, small buttocks in her hands and squeezed them tightly, pulling him closer to her, closer, as far in as he could go, and then farther, and farther...

He sighed and shouted and came, gasping for breath, collapsing onto her. It was a little too soon for her, but she had seen it coming, and she gave herself that one final push, getting herself over the edge. He stayed hard as a rock, which certainly helped. She let herself go, falling into the moment, into the deliciousness of him, his body above her, her own eyes rolling back into her head, waves of orgasm coursing through her body. Then she sighed and relaxed under him, still shuddering a little.

After a long moment, he rolled over and out to lie beside her, still in the tangled army blankets. "Wow," he said. "That was incredible."

"Not bad," she murmured, smiling and caressing his soft bearded cheek.

"I love you," he said.

"That's so sweet," she said. *Oh shit*, she thought. And then, "I need a drink of water."

He sat up slowly, looking around them at the laundry and discarded clothes strewn everywhere. "I'll go get you some."

"I'm getting up too—we can't stay here. Anyone could come in."

He blinked and seemed to come back to the reality of the situation a little. "Oh, right. Okay." He dug his jeans out of the pile on the floor and put them on.

She got up and gave him one last kiss, and started looking around for her discarded clothes. "Don't say anything to anyone about this, okay?"

He looked at her seriously, eyes filled with seventeen-year-old love. "I won't. I promise."

"Good." She found her jeans and blouse, and then snagged a clean pair of panties from the laundry pile. Where was the pair she'd been wearing earlier? Oh well, they would turn up.

She followed him down the narrow staircase, and spotted her panties on the floor just as the back door opened and Evening Star came in.

The Mom froze. Junior, walking ahead, didn't notice anything amiss, but Evening Star took in the entire situation at a glance. She gave a cold, quick smile, and then said to the Mom, "Lose something?"

The Mom hurried down the rest of the stairs and snagged her panties. "We were folding laundry." But she blushed furiously as she said it, and stuffed the soiled panties in her jeans pocket.

Evening Star's smile widened. "Far out. Looks like a lot of fun. I never realized how much fun laundry could be."

Now Junior seemed to clue in. He turned and looked at the Mom for guidance. "It's all right," she said, patting him on the shoulder. "Everything's mellow."

He nodded, and his previous shyness overtook him. "Um—I gotta go." He quickly slipped out the back door, leaving the two women together.

"I had no *idea* you guys had an open marriage," Evening Star said, her voice mocking.

"We don't—I mean, we do, of course, but we haven't—you know—"

"I do know, yes," Evening Star said carefully. "When you sent us out to the meadow the first night we got here, I guess I misunderstood. It wasn't that you didn't want to party with anyone. You just didn't want to party with *us*." She glared at the Mom, then gestured towards the back door. "But with him…"

The Mom shifted her weight from one foot to another. "It was just, it was nothing. Please don't tell anyone."

Evening Star grinned. "Oh, no, Mama, I wouldn't dream of telling anyone. I can keep a secret, for my very good friend, can't I?"

Fifteen minutes earlier, the monster said to the Princess: *Don't go to the house.*

"Okay," she said, startled. Had she imagined his voice? Where had he been all this time? "Why not?" she finally asked, just to see if he'd answer.

Just don't. Trust me.

She did not trust the monster but still sat in her tree and waited, peering down the driveway, even though she wanted to go in and get a piece of cheese.

Finally, the monster said, *It's okay, it's safe now.*

"Where have you been?" the Princess dared to ask as she climbed down.

I am always here.

"But you haven't talked to me in a long time."

I am always here.

The deputy had been called out to enforce an eviction way out in the country, past Vaughn's Corner, and it reminded him of the crazy hippie woman from a few weeks ago. Now, the eviction done, he drove his cruiser slowly, just poking along the winding road beside the Eel River. Long gravel and dirt driveways forked off from the road at semi-regular intervals, five-digit addresses nailed onto mailboxes by some of them. Others were unmarked: abandoned logging roads? Privacy lovers? Hippie enclaves? He found no address that matched the one the woman in the patchwork dress had given him, which didn't surprise him. He had run her car plates as well, and had found that the Dart was registered to a man in San Francisco. Stolen? Or just not reregistered? He had looked through the property records for the man's name, but found nothing. Of course, the county's property record-keeping system was notoriously unreliable, as well as being out of date.

He turned another corner and came to a cattle guard. After bumping over that, he crossed a well-maintained little bridge onto the Morgan ranch. Don Morgan was a longtime local, a good man, quiet and reliable. The deputy was married to a sort of second cousin of his. In small towns, everybody became kin to everybody else sooner or later. Don would know if there were any hippies in the area. And he'd give him a cup of coffee, anyway, if he was around.

The deputy drove up to the tidy white ranch house and parked his big American cruiser out front. There were no cars or trucks here; the place felt empty. A dog barked from somewhere behind the house, unseen. The deputy got out of his car and walked up to the front porch, peering into the windows. It was dark inside, but he knocked anyway. After a few minutes, he shivered, got into his car, and drove back down the road.

He made another slow circuit of the winding Eel River road, double-checking, but still didn't find the address. Eventually, he drove back over the hill and into town.

CHAPTER 9

The Dad awoke, rolled over, and looked at his sleeping wife. She was so peaceful, her dark brown hair strewn across the pillow, her mouth slightly open, her forehead smoothed in slumber. She had seemed particularly uptight lately, as if she had never quite gotten over her unpleasant acid trip. He'd hoped that the chore redistribution would give her some relief. She and Evening Star had some sort of dust-up, he could tell that much, but neither of them were talking to anyone else about it. Whatever it was, Evening Star was doing basically no work at all, and the Mom wasn't complaining. Not out loud, anyway.

For a while there, the Dad had been thinking that his wife was finally getting accustomed to life in the country, to the different pace, to the lack of television and modern comforts, but now he wasn't sure. Now he felt a bit guilty for dragging her out here, but he told himself that she had been just as enthusiastic as he had. It was true that it had been his idea, originally, but she had embraced it at once, when he had broached it. Well, not at once, but soon enough, after he had explained all his thinking. And she had never complained about the idea—just the reality. She had plenty to say about the little day-to-day inconveniences, the minor things that got in the way of seeing the larger vision. It was a lot of work, and they fell into bed exhausted every night, even still, and probably always would. But she still agreed with that vision. Now that the community was growing, they faced new challenges, of course. But the Dad was hopeful that it would all get worked out in time.

He was particularly worried about Weed and Astrid. They were getting the bare minimum of their chores done, but then they were spending *lots* of time in their camper, hardly emerging even for meals, this last week or so. At first he had thought they were rushing down there to ball all the time, and that that was why Junior was hanging around the house so much more, to give them some space, some privacy. But then the tension coming off of them when he did see them caused the Dad to rethink his theory. Tension: especially Astrid. Something was going on with her. Maybe they were getting ready to move on. Maybe community life was not for them. Maybe they were having troubles in their relationship. People were complicated, that was for sure.

The Dad gave his wife one last look and considered waking her up, but then decided to let her sleep. He could get the breakfast ready. He didn't have much else on his plate today in terms of chores.

The whole community was getting geared up for the big Land party this weekend. They'd gone to town and put up fliers, talked to the other community they sort of knew down in Vaughn's Corner, and done everything else they could think of to get the word out. It would start on Saturday morning with a big swim gathering down at the river. He hoped the warm weather would hold. It was a little iffy this late in the season, but the water was still slow and warm, so even if the day wasn't real hot, the river should be inviting enough. Maybe they could finally get that rope swing hung. Then, after everyone was tired of the river, or at least hungry, they would work their way up to the front meadow for a huge potluck. He hoped enough folks would bring stuff to share, but at least the Land denizens would have a lot prepared. And they'd meet all kinds of new people! It would be so cool, connecting with the other freaks in the area. They had been isolated far too long.

He got out of bed, shaking his head to clear the last vestiges of last night's wine and pot, found some clothes that weren't entirely grungy, and made his way downstairs. He poked around in the kitchen looking for a skillet. He'd make pancakes. Yum. Everyone loved pancakes.

The Princess found her way through the woods at the south edge of the front meadow, an area she didn't generally have much interest in. But it was near where Weed and Astrid had parked their camper, even though it wasn't the very best site, because nobody had asked the Princess's opinion about it.

Generally the Princess wasn't all that interested in adults. All they did was hang around and talk, and not even about very interesting stuff. When she made her little villages and populated them with the tiny ceramic animal characters who drove around in their matchbox cars, she made their lives far more dramatic and fascinating than what she saw of her parents and their friends. But lately, she had known that something strange was going on with Weed and Astrid, and she wanted to find out what it was. Maybe they were fighting! That would be interesting. Her parents never fought.

She spied their camper parked under the trees above the road, a light glowing inside even though it was the middle of the day, the door shut tight. She was a spy, she was *Harriet* the Spy, gliding along noiselessly. She would get to the bottom of the mystery. She would find out what was making everyone tick. She was the Princess and this was her domain, and there should be nothing that went on here, if it was interesting, anyway, that she did not know about.

She padded up to the camper on her tough little bare feet. Their dogs didn't hear her; nobody heard her. She got right up to the front of the truck, but of course, since they were in the back, this wouldn't help any. She had to get to where she could see and hear inside.

The only opening other than the back door was a tiny high window, way over the Princess's head, on the left-hand side. The window was open, but even as she crept all the way up to the side of the truck, she could only hear indistinct murmurings. This was no good.

She faded back into the woods to think about it, stopping twenty or thirty yards from the camper, turning back to look at it.

From this distance, she spotted another opening: a little skylight or vent on the roof. It was propped open.

So somehow, she had to get on top of the camper. Then she could hear, and maybe even see, what was going on inside.

She stood there, pondering the impossibility of this. The truck and camper combination looked incredibly rickety. Even if she moved very, very silently and carefully, and as small and light as she was, she couldn't imagine being able to climb across the top of it without them knowing right away that she was there. It would creak, it would make noise, it would wiggle. No, that wouldn't do.

But several big trees overhung the truck. Did any have branches that would support her? If anyone could climb a tree, it was the Princess.

Unfortunately, most of the trees were pines: not climbing trees. There was one live oak, but its branches were kind of spindly, and she didn't like live oaks anyway because their leaves were too prickly. There was one madrone, but usually madrones were too small and weak. Her favorite climbing tree in the front meadow was the madrone that had a regular oak growing in the middle of it, intertwined: sturdiness and good smooth branches together. This one was a bit smaller and didn't have a companion oak, but she thought it just might be possible to get up there.

At least it was worth a try. She could always retreat and rethink the situation if it didn't work.

She crept back to the base of the madrone, pushing at the trunk to test its strength, measuring its branches with her eyes. It wasn't exactly in the right position, but it was close. Oh well. Spies made do with what they had to work with. If it were easy, everyone would do it, and then it wouldn't be glamorous and dangerous and fun.

She was agile as a monkey, and she got right up the first branch, no problem. The trunk shifted, and the big papery leaves rattled together. A few dead leaves fell to the ground. The Princess froze for a long moment, but nothing else happened. Trees shifting, creaking, and dropping leaves happened all the time.

She resumed climbing, hoisting herself from branch to branch, working quickly but quietly. After a few minutes, she was at the height she needed, but on the opposite side of the tree from the camper. She paused, considering. The branches were far better on this side of the tree, but they did her spy mission no good. She scooted around the branches, moving carefully, very slowly now. Finally, she stopped directly beside the camper, and concentrated.

She heard the voices from inside much more clearly. Alas, she couldn't see a thing, but she couldn't get any closer without falling onto the roof. So she stilled herself and listened.

As Harriet had done before her, the Princess found that the great secrets were not immediately forthcoming when you were a spy. In fact, mostly it was downright boring. For a while, it seemed that Astrid was just hassling at the dogs, who still crowded into the camper, even though they would have been perfectly safe outside. No one else was keeping dogs indoors in the daytime. "Go on," she said, "get off of there." She threatened to put them outside if they didn't behave.

That's dumb. They don't understand you, the Princess thought.

Weed must have been sitting at that little built-in table they had, adorable like in a dollhouse. She heard the table creak as he shifted, and he said something quietly, maybe even just to himself. They didn't seem to be talking to each other. Anyway, the Princess couldn't understand what he said.

She shifted slightly on her unstable perch, remaining careful to not slip and fall or put too much pressure on the thin branch. Her leg was falling asleep. She wouldn't be able to stay here long. Spying was hard work.

Ten minutes or so went by. Astrid and Weed didn't seem to be harboring any secrets. The Princess was increasingly uncomfortable. She shifted again, sending more leaves down to settle on the camper roof.

She was just figuring out how to climb down when she heard someone moving about. So she waited, listening hard. Was it just one of the dogs? Astrid's angry voice rang out: "I said, get *down* from there!"

There was a scrabbling of claws on something hard and a little yip, and then the back door of the camper opened. Elf and Granola bounded out and darted, sniffing at the ground, thrilled to be outside. Elf peed against a tree; Granola looked as if she was going to take a poo. Astrid stood at the doorway, hands on her hips. From her perspective above and slightly behind her, the Princess couldn't see the expression on her face, but she was clearly not happy.

"All right, come on back," she said, after the dogs had done their business. The dogs both ignored her, roaming and sniffing. Elf rolled on the ground. Astrid whistled. The dogs pretended they couldn't hear her.

"Oh, let them stay out a minute," came Weed's voice from inside the camper. With the door open, the Princess could hear a lot better. This was great. Dull, but great.

Astrid turned to look back inside, but still keeping one eye on the dogs. The Princess froze. All it would take would be for Astrid to look up, and she'd be caught. But Astrid didn't. "I'm not letting them stay out there with that thing," she said, tersely.

"What thing?" Weed said, but with no question in his tired voice.

"I'm not having this argument again," she said.

"There's nothing there. It was a mountain lion and it's long gone."

The Princess leaned forward just a hair.

"I am telling you, it's not a mountain lion, and it's still here. I can feel it."

"That was a hallucination! You were freaked out, you were on acid!"

"I don't care if you don't believe me! I just want to leave. It's wrong here, even if you're too insensitive to feel it. If you loved me, we'd already be gone."

"After the party—you agreed. Come on."

"You'll be sorry when I'm dead."

Weed sighed loudly but didn't answer. Astrid turned and looked back out the door. "Elf! Granola! Get *back* in here!" The dogs heard the tone in her voice and moseyed back to the truck. "Get in!" She jerked Elf by his collar, got the dogs inside, then slammed the door behind her.

Now their voices were muffled again, but they were still talking. "(mumble mumble) means so much to him (mumble) next week (mumble mumble)…"

"No you (mumble) me (mumble mumble) dark and cold and just *wrong*!"

"Sweetheart (mumble) come on and (mumble mumble) (something

something murmur murmur).”

Then the Princess heard Astrid start to cry, and Weed get up from the table. There were more murmuring sounds, and then a longish period of silence. Then the camper started to sway, gently. Okay, now that: that was balling.

She started to extract herself from the tree. If she didn't want to fall onto the camper roof while they were hanging out, or arguing, she most definitely didn't want to fall while they were balling.

She painstakingly got herself back down the way she came. She dropped the last two feet to the ground without a sound, letting her breath out slowly. Whew. That was hard work.

But oh my goodness! Astrid had seen the monster too!

The Princess melted back into the woods, planning to circle around and enter the front meadow from about halfway up so that nobody would see her coming from the camper truck, just in case. It was unlikely that anyone would be paying attention, of course, but spies always had to be careful.

She hadn't gone but a few feet when the weird coldness came all around her, and the dark formlessness of the monster appeared before her. As always, she felt strangely calm, as if this was not some horrific murderous beast-creature-thing. She waited for it to speak in her head.

Where are you going, little Princess? it asked.

“I am going back home after spying on Weed and Astrid,” she said quietly, in case she was still close enough for them to hear her.

They can't hear you, the monster said. *Don't worry.*

“But you can hear me even if I think,” she said.

I can.

“Did Astrid see you?”

You heard them. She was on acid. People see things on acid that aren't really there.

“Did she see you?”

The monster moaned, or murmured a little. The Princess couldn't quite hear. She leaned forward just a touch towards the cold dark. *Acid is a funny thing.*

The dark formless mist still hovered in front of her; the Princess wanted to walk up and touch it, but she felt like she always did in the presence of the monster: sort of spacey, dreamy, like she could have thoughts but not really do anything about them. Like she was asleep and awake at the same time. Maybe this was what being on acid was like?

Why didn't she want to run away from it?

Could anyone run away from it? The strange hitchhiker lady couldn't. Or didn't. Or hadn't wanted to.

Then the mist dissipated, and it was like the Princess woke up. She shivered a little, then kept on through the woods, emerging into the meadow as planned. Nobody, of course, saw her.

CHAPTER 10

The morning of the big Land party seemed no different from any other. The folks who generally slept late did so, and the kids got up early and got their own breakfasts. The Mom had been working on getting stuff ready for the last few days, with Junior helping her every chance he could: chopping broccoli for a big soup, gathering whatever was ripe from the garden. He was such a great help.

They had managed one more quick tumble in bed since the first time, and a few stolen kisses and gropes when they were alone in the house, but other than that, it was pretty hard to get safe time together. Everyone was too unpredictable. Anyone could show up in the house at any moment. Plus, Evening Star was watching them like a hawk. They thought about going down to the river together, but that would seem suspicious, especially since the Mom never swam all that much. Or else everyone would want to come with them, and then it would be just torture, to be able to see each other and not touch.

Several times, the tension of keeping the secret, and of dealing with Evening Star with her smirks and knowing glances, got to be too much for the Mom. She would almost go and talk to her husband about it, to confess everything, but then at the last minute, she'd stop. She just was not ready for that conversation yet. But then the longer it went on, the worse that conversation would be when they finally had it. She should have told him right away. Then Evening Star wouldn't have this leverage, and the Mom would stop having to watch herself all the time—herself and Junior. He was not subtle. She was sure he was going to give it away without even meaning to.

She was also reluctant to tell because, well, she didn't want to stop. Not just yet. She didn't know where the situation was going, if anywhere, but even in her misery and tension, she was loving it, adoring it. But the whole thing could end at any moment, and there would be no sense in telling her husband something that would surely upset him if it was just going to be a temporary diversion, a fling. No matter how earnestly they had agreed to be honest with each other if something like this should come up, now it had become real and not hypothetical, she didn't know what to say.

The Mom hated being controlled—by Evening Star, by her husband, by the entire situation. But as more time went on, it got harder to contemplate talking about it and easier to keep putting off dealing with it.

She was chopping up bananas for a giant fruit salad, as Junior stirred the big pot of broccoli soup. The Dad came in, arms full of wood for the fire. "Should we head down to the river?" she asked him. It was late morning, and reasonably warm out.

"Aren't people coming up here first?" he asked, stacking the wood in the wood box.

"I don't know. I didn't make the fliers—what did they say exactly?"

The Dad went over to the desk and got one of the fliers Evening Star had drawn. "There's a map that shows the house and the river. It kind of looks like she was pointing out that parking should be up here, but it's not really clear."

The Mom dried her hands on a rag and came to look. "So maybe there's people down by the river already."

"It's pretty early."

"I guess." She looked around the kitchen. "Well, I suppose I could leave this for a while." She glanced at Junior, who was studiously ignoring the conversation.

"Walk down with me?" The Dad smiled at her.

"Sure." Then she said to Junior, "You want to stay here? I don't know where everyone else is. In case someone shows up?"

"Sure," he said. "Fine."

The Mom and the Dad walked down the path beside the driveway. When they got to the road, there were no cars parked alongside it, which answered the question as to whether anyone was already at the river. Of course, there were no signs or anything, other than a little post with their address on it by the driveway. But still, the map was pretty good. People ought to be able to figure it out.

"Okay, that's fine," the Mom said, preparing to turn back to the house.

"Wanna go for a quick dip?"

Did he have something on his mind? She stole a glance at him, wondering. It really wasn't hot enough to swim yet, though sitting in the sand would be pleasant enough, if you didn't have a huge party to get ready for. The Dad saw her glance and hung a look of exaggerated innocence on his face. Ah, okay then. Her level of sexual frustration was such that, even though her husband wasn't her first choice at the moment, he would certainly do. They had always been perfectly compatible in bed. Or wherever.

So she grinned and took his hand. "Sure." They headed down the path to the water.

Thirty minutes later, they walked back up to the house. Still no one had arrived. The Mom was wet and a little cold, though quite satisfied from the messy balling at the water's edge, where the sand turned to clay. They climbed the front steps and came in the front door.

Billy Goat, Evening Star, and Morning Star had come in and were eating breakfast at the octagonal table. Morning Star was naked, still refusing to put on clothes weeks after the acid had worn off. Junior had left the broccoli soup and was adding more fruit to the salad. The Mom couldn't quite meet his eye. *What is this, now I'm cheating on him? That's ridiculous. I can have sex with my own husband if I want to. Surely he can't ask me not to do that.* Of course, he had never asked her not to do that. But she felt oddly guilty all the same.

"Where is everyone?" she asked to cover her awkwardness.

"They'll be here," Evening Star said serenely, sipping a mug of tea. Her gaze flicked to the Mom. *Yeah, I know,* the Mom thought. *Just sit there and drink your tea, you witch; no one's gonna ask you to lift a finger.*

"I hope so," the Dad said. "That's a lot of fruit salad!"

It must have been noon when the first vehicle arrived—an orange VW bus filled with hippies and kids and dogs, followed closely by a baby blue Gremlin bringing a strange-looking character with a pot belly and no beard. The community was just greeting them and telling them how to get down to the river—and offering them fruit salad and broccoli soup and home-baked bread, and taking their potato salad and cold apple fritters and sliced watermelon and pot brownies, and setting them all out on the makeshift tables in the front meadow—when three more cars pulled up. The Dad recognized two or three of them from the other community down in Vaughn's Corner. Introductions were made, joints were lit and passed. Some dogs started fighting, and then fucking, and having to be pulled apart again. It was a party!

Soon a contingent headed down to the river while another group stayed behind to eat, drink, smoke, hang out, whatever. More cars came, and a few motorcycles. Beer was brought in great big ice chests, and copious amounts of food. Even more copious was the number of hippies. Who knew there were so many around, with all the rednecks in town? The Dad was thrilled. The energy was great.

He started for the river, but kept getting stopped by more people arriving, needing to be shown where to park, where to put their food, where to pee. Some needed to be directed to the back meadow, since the front was already filling up with people pitching tents. He looked around for the rest of his community, hoping someone else could help with the hosting—they knew where things were—but he only saw naked little Morning Star running around with a huge slice of watermelon in one hand and what had to be a pot brownie in the other. Juice dribbled down her chin and onto her protruding chest and belly. The Dad shook his head but smiled. She'd be all right. This group was full of love.

As the afternoon wore on, the Dad began to wonder if he'd ever get back to the river. The weather was heating up, and a swim might feel nice. As opposed to the other thing he had done at the river this morning, which had also felt rather nice, but he didn't see any great likelihood of that happening again any time soon. At least not with all these freaks all over the place.

The crowds of people, all doing their own thing in their own time, diluted the possibility that two people looking for a little privacy would be discovered. And the randy unexpected morning sex at the river had only amplified the Mom's appetite for randy, slightly more planned afternoon sex in the woods. As soon as the crowds began to build and the party took on its own energy, the Mom and Junior looked at each other from across one of the piles of food, and then both wandered off—a few minutes apart—to the edge of the front meadow.

Within minutes, her dress was pulled up above her hips, her bare ass was against an oak tree, and Junior was breathing smooth and easy as he drove steadily into her, over and over again, fluttering those beautiful eyelashes. "Oh god," he sighed. "I do love you."

She felt his come dribble down her thigh as he slipped out. He still held her against the tree, caressing her hips, reaching up to stroke her breasts under her dress. She kissed those eyelashes, then nudged him away tenderly so she could reach down and get an oak leaf to wipe her leg with before the drip went too far. "Junior, sweetheart, you know I care about you…"

He looked downcast. "But you don't love me."

She kissed him full on the lips and took him in her arms again, letting the soiled leaf fall to the ground next to her panties. "Shhh."

The Princess drifted around the party, enjoying all the people there, but wary as usual of actually talking to anyone. She kept the Apricot Boy with her as her mother had asked; he clung to her, but not out of fear. He liked people. He liked watermelon too. Well, they both did. They each ate big pieces of it. It was like candy. Country hippie kids didn't get candy all that often.

She stayed in the middle of the crowd, keeping away from the forest. She had an unsettled feeling about it. Though the monster had never said anything specifically about crowds, she had a bad feeling about him and all these people. She had the sense that he might just like it to be quiet around here. The trouble had really started when more people started showing up. But who knew? All she really knew was that she felt better in the middle of the crowd than out on the edges. She'd be glad when the party was over and all these people were gone.

The Dad finally gave up on trying to get down to the river and just let himself enjoy the gathering. Seemed most of the energy was up here in the meadow anyway. He met some cool folks. The guy in the Gremlin was named Rob, and he had been renting a room in a house in Yokayo, hoping to get connected with the underground hippie community. So far he'd only managed to get to a few David Raitt shows in the Chinese restaurant in town that had concerts on Saturday nights. He had been so excited to see the flier at the health food store. He had had a little trouble finding his way out to the place, until he'd gotten behind the orange VW.

The Dad also met this even weirder guy, Cliff. He had a full head of dreadlocks, and he said his name clearly, making sure the Dad got it, as if he was going to remember in ten minutes. Everyone else seemed to have nicknames, or just one name, or had changed names altogether. It was all so confusing, the Dad just felt more comfortable calling everyone "buddy." As in, "Hey, buddy." "How's it going, buddy?" "Way to go, bud." But Cliff (and of course, the Dad *did* remember his name, after all that) talked his ear off about UFOs and aliens and government conspiracy theories, stuff the Man didn't want you to know. How what you really needed to do was to get away from all corporate influences, get away from the Man, the pigs, get out of the mainstream, go back to the land, drop out. No matter how much the Dad tried to explain that yeah, man, that's exactly what they were doing here, the guy paid no attention and just kept on with his diatribe. The Dad finally got free of him by sending him off to the back meadow, pretending that he thought there were many more people back there who would love to hear his views, and pressing two pot brownies in his hand as he left.

This is so completely cool, the Dad thought, alone in the crowd once more. There were lots of chicks here, single ones as well as ones with dudes in tow, which didn't matter, he was only looking anyway. He just liked to look at the chicks, any chicks, all the chicks, and they liked to be looked at, and it was all mellow…

The monster had tolerated the slight encroachment of the humans before, the ones who had come to live, to care for the Land, to settle here with respect and love. The monster didn't like it particularly, but he sensed that their commitment was light, and that they would move on. The monster was used to their kind moving on.

The monster sensed the presence of the multitude on the Land, and he did not like it. The monster owned the Land, he had always owned the Land, and he always would own the Land. The monster was the Land. The monster punished swiftly and severely the souls who disrespected the Land.

The Princess snapped back to attention, the Apricot Boy's sticky hand in hers. "What?"

"Is your mother here?" A large woman in a huge flowered, multicolored dress was shouting down at her as though she was an idiot.

Well, maybe she was an idiot. For a minute there it had been like she was in the monster's brain, like she understood who he was and what he was thinking. But then she wondered if she had made it all up. It sounded too much like a story. Maybe she was letting her imagination run away with her.

"Yes, she's here," the Princess answered, shaking her head slowly. It felt funny.

"Where is she?"

The Princess looked around the meadow. She hadn't seen her mother in a few hours, but that was nothing new. The Land was a big place, and people could be anywhere on it. Did it really matter exactly where?

"I don't know. She's here somewhere." The Princess kept looking. "There's my dad."

"I know he's here. I just don't know where your mother is!"

"She's here." The Princess took the Apricot Boy and moved away from the slightly disturbing woman.

Cliff lumbered up the path to the back meadow, chewing a brownie and feeling suspicious that he'd been brushed off. But he was also enjoying the cool scene and the pretty land. This was nature the way it was meant to be, with hand-built houses tucked under the trees, and lots of wide-open space. So much better than the life he had in town, and his uptight redneck family. Finally he'd gotten in touch with the freaks! His own kind.

The meadow appeared as he rounded the last curve in the path and stepped through the little dry creek bed. Indeed, there were a few folks out here already, sitting crosslegged in the tall dried grass in a sociable circle. Some guys, some chicks, passing a joint around. Far out.

Cliff approached the circle, and two blonde chicks scooted over to make room for him. He settled in and the joint was passed to him.

One of the guys was an older dude with a grey beard. He introduced himself as Billy Goat, saying proudly, "I live here."

"Cool," Cliff said. "This is a fabulous spot."

"It is." Everyone grinned at everyone else. Good vibes abounded.

The Dad watched the flow of bodies in the meadow. He had eaten one of the brownies—okay, maybe two, three of the brownies, since they were pretty yummy—but they weren't all that potent, not nearly the quality of the weed that he grew up the hill, but that was all right, it meant that you could eat more, and they were really delicious brownies, someone had been so nice to bring them, so incredibly generous, that was such a nice thing to do, really, so uncalled for...

He watched the guy Rob that he had been talking to earlier, the guy who had come in the Gremlin, who hadn't any friends until now, the one who was so excited to finally hook up with other hippies. Rob mingled easily in the crowd, talking to everyone, talking to chicks. In fact, that was really cool: he was talking to Evening Star. He was really making friends here.

The Mom put her panties on, ready to make her way back to the party. Junior wanted to go to the river. "Go ahead," she said, but gently.

"Come with me," he said.

"No, hon, maybe later." She kissed him again, and then again.

"You just say that—you don't mean it." He was deliberately, aggressively not pulling his jeans back up, not ending their scene in the woods, their gorgeous little interlude, their escape from real life.

"I do mean it—I want to swim with you." *And it would be nice to get clean for real*, she thought, looking down at the oak leaves on the ground.

"So come now."

"I can't. I'm the hostess here; I have to make sure everything's going all right, there's enough food, everyone knows where to go to the bathroom," she said. Junior giggled at this, and she smiled weakly back. But then, hurt that he'd jabbed at her and nervous about Evening Star, she jabbed back: "You could help."

It worked. It was so easy to pull at the heart strings of a seventeen-year-old. "I helped a lot already!"

Then she felt bad and melted again. "I know you did. It's all right. You go ahead. I'll be down there real soon, when I can get away."

He pouted a little, then finally pulled up his jeans, did up the buttons, and gave her one last kiss goodbye before finding his way back to the path.

The Dad watched Rob from town as he laughed and talked with Evening Star, leaning in, obviously enjoying her company. Maybe they knew folks in common. She and Billy Goat had lived in town a while, hadn't they? Where was Billy Goat, anyway? The Dad scanned the meadow but didn't see him. The Dad hardly saw anybody he knew. Which was cool, far out, no problem.

Evening Star and Rob headed for the house. Ah, so she was going to show him the place. The Dad was rightfully proud of the house. He started to walk up to the front porch, to help explain the more subtle architectural details to Rob, but then someone interrupted him, and by the time he remembered, they had long vanished.

The Mom re-emerged into the front meadow, glancing around to make sure nobody had noticed her. They hadn't, but she had a cover story ready in case: she had gone into the woods to pee. Normally they didn't go so far from the house to pee, but if your meadow was filled with dozens of strangers, you might go a bit further afield. So to speak.

She mingled into the crowd, introducing herself to people. There seemed to be some commotion over near the picnic tables, so she gravitated towards that. When she got closer, she realized what the strange and unfamiliar sound was: music! Someone had brought out a decent stereo and hooked it up to a car battery, and was playing Pink Floyd's *Ummagumma*.

The Mom stopped, swaying to the music and grinning to herself. She had loved, loved, loved Pink Floyd, back when they lived in the city and had electricity and a stereo of their own. Now she hardly ever heard any music at all, other than what she and Junior managed to make between them. (With his guitar and her singing, that is.) There was the car radio, but no stations reached out here. And the ones you picked up in town were…well, suffice it to say, you didn't hear a lot of Pink Floyd on them. She made a note to find her husband and suggest the car-battery method. How clever!

She felt really, really good. She also felt sort of wicked, but not in a bad way. As the psychedelic music wafted through her head, she contemplated the fact that she had just had sex with two different men in the same day. Wow! She blushed at the thought, but kind of enjoyed it. She had really come a long way from her upbringing.

Pleasantly stoned, Cliff and the rest of the crowd in the back meadow wandered around exploring. The guy Billy Goat followed with the proud air of one who owned the place, but letting the folks explore.

A few other people had joined them, including another dude who said he lived here. It was so cool: a real commune! Cliff wondered if they'd let him come live here too. There was obviously plenty of room. He could get out of his brother's house, build himself a little cabin, maybe right here at the edge of the forest where—

He noticed something. "What's this?"

One of the chicks, a frizzy redhead, came and stood next to him. "Far *out!*"

There was a little patch of mushrooms tucked away under a tree at the back edge of the meadow. They were white and shiny, almost gleaming in the late afternoon sun. And at the head of the patch, there was a small, hand-lettered wooden sign that said *BLISS*.

"Magic mushrooms!" Cliff exclaimed. Behind him, the Billy Goat dude chuckled, but didn't say anything.

"It's like a fairy tale! Shrooms for us all!" The chick leaned over and picked one, brushing the dirt off it as she held it up to the light.

"Are they all right to eat?" one of the blonde chicks said. "How do you know they're not poisonous?"

The redheaded chick laughed. "Of course they're not poisonous! It's like a little garden, look at the sign." She looked at Billy Goat. "You live here—these are Bliss shrooms, right?"

Billy Goat shrugged, grinning. "It's perfect, man. Yeah, they should be utterly Bliss-full."

Cliff shrugged, not getting the joke exactly. That Billy Goat was a weird guy, but then again, the world was full of weird guys. It was all mellow.

So they gathered up a little batch of mushrooms, careful to leave plenty in case anyone else wanted some. "Does anyone know how much we should take?" Cliff asked. "I've only taken them dried."

Nobody knew. Finally they agreed on one mushroom each, cap and stem. They'd go find a quiet place to sit, and if nothing had happened in an hour, they'd each eat another.

"None for me," said one of the blonde chicks, glancing at the other one, who, come to think of it, looked just like her.

The second blonde chick said, "Yeah, man, let's go find someone who wants to ball."

Torn, Cliff looked back and forth between the sexy twins and the shiny mushroom in his hand. But he ultimately followed the group back into the woods.

It started getting dark before anybody realized quite how late it was. *So much for the river*, the Dad thought, realizing for the thirteenth time that he had meant to go down there. He was very stoned. He didn't quite understand why. How many brownies had he had? He didn't think more than a couple. Honestly, he couldn't remember. And oh yeah, so much for the river.

The Princess was feeling a little funny too. She had eaten lots of different kinds of food today, from lots of different plates and pots and piles of stuff. It all looked so good! It was all different, and varied, so unlike her mom's cooking. Maybe she had eaten too much weird stuff.

She wanted to climb up into her little bed-nook and hide, but she had the hardest time getting herself to move. She was thoroughly exhausted and a little dizzy. She knew about pot brownies, of course; she had thought about it, tempted, but ultimately had been a little afraid of them. She couldn't be stoned, could she? Did people put pot into other things? As much as she usually wanted to do drugs with the adults, wanted to play along, she now felt worried and confused. It would be one thing if you knew you were on drugs, and understood why you were feeling the way you were feeling. It was entirely another thing to just be feeling weird and not know why.

She inched her way through the meadow, concentrating as hard as she could on not bumping into things or falling over. Oops, where was the Apricot Boy?

The Mom drifted through the party, grinning, dancing, smoking, drinking nice cold beer, eating great food, having a grand old time. She was pleasantly high by the time someone pointed at a big vat of spaghetti sauce and said, off-handedly, "Oh, watch out for that, it's spiked."

"Spiked?"

"You know—just a little pot. Better than oregano!"

She hadn't eaten any of the spaghetti, but now she wanted some. She dished herself up a plate full, then found a place to sit and eat. True: it was tastier than oregano.

But it made her thirsty again, so she set off in search of more beer, and talking to more people. At one point, she realized there was a small hand in hers: the Apricot Boy had found her. "Sweetheart!" she cried, sweeping him up off the ground. He put his little arms around her neck and hugged her, smiling.

The Dad decided to go check out the back meadow. It seemed more and more of the party was drifting back there. He had sent that guy Cliff there simply to get rid of him, but now it was the place to be. He walked up the path, enjoying the dark night.

The Princess finally made it to the front door of the house, and found that the little latch had been turned from the inside, effectively locking it, though there was no key. She stood there for a while, dumbly, and kept on rattling the door handle, but it wouldn't turn.

She knew what had happened, because she used to play with the latch herself, until her mom yelled at her to cut it out. Who could have accidentally turned it? It was so crazy! All these strange new people on her Land. It could have been anybody.

Fortunately, there was a back door. It didn't have a latch at all. So the Princess, summoning all of her strength, hauled herself back down the stairs, around the side of the house, and up to the Dutch door.

The Dad walked along the dark path to the back meadow. The air chilled, and he was no longer feeling sorry for himself for having never gotten back to the river. The nights sure did get cold fast this time of year. As opposed to earlier in the summer, when it seemed like it stayed hot all night, and you could hardly sleep for it, lying up in the loft, it was like the sauna was on downstairs, although of course they hadn't run the sauna since April, because it was too damned hot, you didn't want to be making it any hotter.

The sauna might be nice tonight, though.

He got to the last curve in the path, went down the dip in the dry creek bed (they would have to get some sort of log to lay over here before winter), and turned the corner. And there was nobody there. Just nobody at all.

Well, how did you like that! There must have been a dozen or more people he'd seen head off back here! It was the place to be!

He stood at the end of the path, hands on his hips, shaking his head. He'd seen Weed come out here, where was he? Where were those cute long-haired blonde twins from town? Where was that weirdo Cliff, even?

He waited a long while. He thought maybe he heard voices in the woods beyond the meadow, like maybe they'd all gone to find a darker place, to smoke pot or drop acid or have some sort of orgy thing or whatever, but after he listened closely, he decided there was actually nothing. And then the dark and the cold and the silence and the emptiness began to creep him out, and so he turned and headed back down the path, back to the big noisy party in the front meadow.

The people in the darker place in the woods ate the mushrooms. Then they all sat in a nice circle, not unlike the circle they'd made in the middle of the back meadow earlier, before Cliff had found the magical fairy-tale mushroom patch called Bliss. They joined hands, and somebody started a chant, the typical pseudo-Eastern-spiritual Om-ish chant. Cliff had been feeling really incredibly cool about the whole thing, but now he was feeling actually kind of weird. Almost sick, maybe. He sat under an oak tree, the guy Billy Goat's hand in his right hand, the redheaded chick's hand in his left hand, but he didn't even feel like making any moves on the chick. Actually he really did feel sick. He was hoping he wouldn't have to go and throw up somewhere. That would be entirely uncool.

How stoned *was* he? He'd had a couple of pot brownies, and then there had been a joint passed around earlier...that shouldn't have created this much trouble. None of it. Even mushrooms just made you a little queasy. But then that passed.

Maybe if he could just lie down. Yeah, that would help. He let go of the hands, and nobody protested. He snuck a look at the redhead and saw that she didn't look a whole lot better than he felt. They were obviously just all too stoned. Or maybe these were really strong shrooms. Maybe fresh was different.

He curled up on the ground, lying sort of on his stomach, snuggling his face into the soft ground. Ah, that felt better already. Perhaps just a little nap…

Weed let go of the sweaty hands that held his and staggered to his feet. Something was wrong. They shouldn't have eaten the mushrooms growing on Bliss's grave. There was something really fucked up about them. There had been such a mellow scene going, everyone was getting off, and then suddenly everyone was just like falling over, face down in the dirt. Now it was a bad scene.

He stumbled a little, trying to reach the back meadow, to find light, safety, other, different, non-fucked-up people. But his head swam, and he sank back to the ground. He leaned against the sturdy trunk of a tree for just a moment before he passed out.

The Princess opened the Dutch door. The two sides rattled on their hinges, as they always did, and then rattled again as they settled together, closing behind her. She stepped into the house without really looking to see who was in there or why they had locked the door. She was still feeling awfully weird, and tired, and whatever, so she couldn't really register her surprise at seeing Evening Star in the middle of the floor with a perfect stranger, a guy, with a big belly, even. Completely unlike the scrawny and peculiar Billy Goat. Evening Star and the strange guy were balling like she'd never seen before—and she'd seen some balling, that was for sure. Not that she had ever wanted to, but it was kind of unavoidable.

The Princess barely hesitated as she took in the situation, in some corner of her confused brain. It was odd, yes, that Evening Star would be balling somebody so fat, but then again, her daughter was fat, so maybe she liked fat people. In any event, they were balling right smack dab in the middle of the big braided rug, in the center of the room. The only room. But there was a little space next to them, near the unlit stove. As long as they kept doing what they were doing and didn't move around any, she could squeeze past there. So the Princess slipped past them right there and got herself to the stairs. Then she climbed slowly, painfully, laboriously, and found her way to her sleeping nook. Once there, she crawled under her covers and tried to hide from it all. If Evening Star and the fat guy ever took notice of her, she didn't have a clue. It didn't matter.

The Mom sat with the Apricot Boy in her lap, swaying gently and enjoying the music. By this time, Pink Floyd had been changed out for the Grateful Dead. The Dead was never the Mom's favorite, but she was still grateful—ha ha—just to hear anything. Besides, the Dead was pretty good music to be stoned to, come to think of it. She didn't feel entirely stoned yet, but it might be coming on.

A guy named Rob with a big belly and no beard walked up and started talking to her. Though she didn't find him at all attractive (and she'd had sex with two men already today!), she enjoyed the idea that he seemed to find her attractive. She laughed and leaned into him when he made jokes, and touched his arm, and all that flirtatious stuff that she thought she'd forgotten how to do, but somehow came right back when it was called for. It was perfectly safe, of course. With the Apricot Boy in her lap, she hardly looked like an available chick, did she? But Rob was flattering and clever, and it was fun to talk to him. At least, until he started coming on too strong, just as the Mom noticed Evening Star watching her. She brushed him off and turned away.

She felt woozy and put her hand to her forehead. The Apricot Boy slipped out of her lap and toddled off; she barely registered the fact. Maybe that was the Dad over there, that he was going to? Probably. And now Rob was gone. Now there was some young blonde girl—well, young woman, nineteen or twenty—or god, she was seeing double, there were two of them exactly alike—holding her hand, touching her hair, giving her a glass of water.

What was the matter with her? If she sat up and focused, she could be almost normal, but it was a huge amount of effort. If she relented at all, leaned forward, closed her eyes for a second or even blinked, then it was like rushing downhill in the fastest car ever, or sliding, falling, whooshing—a ski run—falling off a cliff—it was terrifying and she couldn't make it stop, except with that most enormous of efforts, and then only for a moment, because then she'd close her eyes and it would start again. She reached her hand out to steady herself, and one of the blondes held it—*were* there two of them?—but the Mom felt she was just dragging the girl down with her, rather than being saved by her. The force was too much, it was like she was being sucked into the center of the earth; she was a tiny insignificant speck of a creature and the force was eating her up, swallowing her whole.

"I think I have to go lie down," she moaned. But nobody heard her, and when she tried to get to her feet, it was utterly beyond her. So she sort of sidled down to the ground from the makeshift bench (a sawed-off log), and stretched out on her back on the ground.

Some time earlier, upstairs in her bedroom nook, the Princess heard Evening Star and the guy finish balling. They both seemed to enjoy them-selves, but then, in the Princess's experience of observing or overhearing such things, people generally did seem to find it enjoyable. Presumably that was why they did it. Then the guy got up, ran some water in the sink, and said something about hot water which the Princess couldn't entirely hear. Evening Star laughed at him, or with him; anyway, he didn't laugh very loud. Then he left the house. At least he unlatched the front door. Now other people could come in.

Evening Star stayed downstairs for a little while. She got herself a glass of juice from the cold-box, and then rummaged around in the desk. The Princess heard her opening and closing drawers and then giving a low chuckle. After that, she quickly left, and the house was quiet. Soon enough, the Princess fell asleep.

The Dad rejoined the party in the front meadow, looking around for some of the people who'd disappeared to the back meadow before, to see if they'd come back. But then he saw that someone had hooked up a stereo to a car battery, which was the cleverest thing ever, and it was playing Cream! Oh god, he loved Cream. He never got to hear any decent music on the stupid radio station he could get on the Dart, they played no rock at all. Just stupid pop songs. The only other station was country: forget it.

"In a white room, with black curtains, at the station," he sang along, forgetting all about the back meadow folks. He was still feeling nice and high, a little less extremely so than he was earlier. The pot brownies were working their way through his system nicely. Now he was actually getting hungry. He poked around the tables, looking at all the food laid out. Yum, spaghetti!

The Princess woke from a dead sleep and barely made it to the pee-pan before getting sick. She filled the pan with barely digested spaghetti. Her eyes were watering and she wished her mom was behind her, holding her hair out of the way, like she did whenever the Princess got sick (which wasn't all that often, but it happened).

She finished throwing up, then sat back on her heels, catching her breath and wiping her eyes. The thing about throwing up was, sometimes when you thought you were done, you weren't really. Like the time she'd eaten too many strawberries and had to go throw up in the dry creek bed.

She had thrown up like a billion times then. She hadn't been able to eat strawberries for a long time after that. Thank goodness she got over that: strawberries were her favorite food.

Although they didn't sound all that good right now.

Her stomach continued to settle, though. She was happy she couldn't see what was in the pee-pan, because it was probably really gross. She should go downstairs and empty it. Was anyone down there? It seemed dark and silent. It was her job to empty the pee-pan, and she was supposed to do it in the mornings, but nobody would want her to leave barf in it overnight.

She took a deep breath, made sure she was steady, and got up off the floor. At least the dizziness from earlier had gone away. She didn't know how long she had slept, but she felt wide awake now.

She put the lid back on the pee-pan and picked it up. It was heavy, but not so bad, not as heavy as with a full night's pee in it. And more stable. She walked towards the edge of the loft, moving carefully in case she should suddenly feel dizzy again. But she was fine. She held fast to the railing as she walked down the steep stairs.

It was completely dark downstairs, but there was lots of light in various places in the front meadow. People had Aladdin lamps and candles and campfires and other things lit. Some light filtered through the narrow windows, making eerie shadows on the floor.

The Princess stepped around the pillows that Evening Star and the big-belly guy had left in the middle of the floor and found the back door.

She had been planning to empty the pee-pan in the usual place, at the edge of the woods behind the house, conveniently close but not in any pathway, but there was a small group of people there, sitting on the ground around a small campfire. Oooh, did they know they were sitting in old pee? The Princess stifled a giggle and went farther from the house, back into the back woods, but still close enough so that she could hear lots of people in the meadow.

When she was done dumping the barf behind a tree, she brought the pan back to the house. Probably she should rinse it out with the hose before she took it upstairs again, but she just didn't feel like it. Did she have to do everything? And nobody had been there to help her be sick! She choked back a sudden tear as she reminded herself that sometimes, nobody was there. She knew that.

She left the empty but dirty pee-pan by the back door and went around the house, into the front meadow.

At the edge of the woods that rimmed the back meadow, a lean young mountain lion prowled. He smelled humans, which generally meant danger, but something about this scent was different. He stepped closer, one careful paw at a time, making no sound on the dry grass. There were many humans, but they were not moving, not talking. Still alive, but not alive.

He came closer still, nose working, avoiding the main group of people, instead approaching one human male propped against a tree. Not dead, not quite. The mountain lion took one careful, exploratory bite, from the soft middle of the body. But something was wrong. The blood oozed sluggishly, and the meat tasted like long-dead carrion.

Still, the mountain lion was hungry, and took another bite before moving on. After he crossed the creek to the cattle ranch, he sickened and died.

The Dad was dancing. A big and energetic group had gathered around the car-battery stereo, and Santana's *Abraxas* was now playing. Some very cute and braless chicks were also dancing, reminding the Dad why he loved dancing so much. Nobody was exactly dancing "with" anyone else the way they used to do in high school in the early sixties, a lifetime ago, choosing a particular partner and doing proper steps and all that. Instead, it was hippie dancing, where everyone just moved to the rhythm of the music, feeling the beat, letting the body move whatever way it wanted…and oh, some bodies really felt like moving in interesting ways.

More girls than guys were dancing in the big mix of dancers, too, so that was particularly groovy. Though the Dad did notice that guy Rob moving around awkwardly, trying to get as close to women as possible. The Dad grinned at the thought. Wasn't he doing the same thing?

Rob grinned back, and then moved to dance closer to a busty redhead. Damn, the Dad hadn't even noticed her. Now he wanted to move over there. Not too obvious, though.

After a while, the music changed from Santana, which was really, really danceable, to the Moody Blues, which was less so, although wonderful. The Dad wasn't really sure who was in charge of the music, but he decided to try and find them before the end of the party, ask them how they had set it up. Car batteries weren't that expensive—and you could put them back in the car when they wore down, and they'd get charged up again. What a great idea!

When the music changed from Santana to the Moody Blues, the Mom stirred from her spot on the ground. It wasn't that she had been asleep, exactly, but she hadn't been awake, exactly, either. She remembered the changes of music around her and people coming and going and all that, but she hadn't been an active participant in the scene. Any of it.

The Moody Blues album was her favorite. *A Question of Balance.* Balance—ha!

She sat up a little more and looked around. Someone had covered her with a blanket or a towel or something. She didn't recognize it, but it was warm and soft, and that was nice. She pulled it up over her shoulders as she tried to figure out what was going on.

Wow, that had been some pot in the spaghetti sauce. That had to be it. She still felt rushy-headed as she tried to move or think, but she was getting her equilibrium back. A little.

She sat up all the way, testing the limits of her head. Still seemed all right.

So she got back up onto the stump she'd originally slithered off of. Of course now she was hungry. But she would find something else to eat besides spaghetti, that was for sure.

After she sat here a while.

The Princess wandered through the dark and crowded front meadow, trying to figure out where the Apricot Boy was, where her parents were, where anybody she knew was. Just to get a sense of things, not because she needed anybody. Not any more. The monster hadn't spoken to her for many hours; she hadn't felt his presence, his disapproval. So maybe he wasn't going to cause any trouble, after all. Besides, he would talk to her if he was going to eat somebody else. Right?

But she still wanted to find out where her family was. Or the rest of the community. But all she kept finding were total strangers, dancing, laughing, smoking pot, looking strange in the dark, lit from beneath by all the little campfires and kerosene lanterns.

Dogs ran and tumbled through the meadow too. All the dogs had become one big happy pack of wild animals—mostly happy, there were still snarling and tussling episodes, but mostly, they just tore around knocking things over, snatching food from the tables, humping each other. The Princess watched the dog pack, also looking for dogs she knew, but couldn't tell any of them apart in the dark.

It was hard to tell anything about anything in the dark.

The Mom slowly got to her feet and set out to look for some food. Lots had been eaten, but there was plenty still around. She found a platter of some zucchini fritters and ate two or three, then another. God, they were delicious. The food started making its way around the spiked spaghetti already in her stomach, so she slowed down, wary. But then it seemed it was going to be all right.

She spotted her husband with the dancers. Suddenly she remembered Junior—where was Junior? She hadn't seen him in hours, not since their interlude in the woods. She looked around the meadow, but it was too dark. Some cars had driven off, but a lot of people were staying over, unrolling sleeping bags or pitching tents around the edges of the dance party.

She got up and walked around, enjoying the movement, the fresh air in her lungs, as she looked for Junior, not finding him. Well, he was probably sulking somewhere. Every day, this relationship got more complicated. She really should just come clean and tell her husband about it and take her knocks. Then together, they could have it all out, and he'd help her figure out what to do.

After the party was over, anyway. She couldn't do anything drastic now, with all this chaos and excitement and energy on the property, all these people. There would be plenty of time to deal with it later.

After the mountain lion had come and eaten and gone and died, nothing stirred in the back meadow or in the woods behind. Even the bugs all quieted down for the night. The creek flowed on, spilling ceaselessly into the Eel River.

The Princess watched as people settled in for the night. Little by little, dancers split off from the main crowd and found places to sleep. The music got mellower and a little quieter. The fat guy who had been balling Evening Star walked off with two blonde women who looked exactly alike, heading for a small tent.

She kept circling through the crowd, looking for her parents, for anyone. She saw lots of people trampling her known universe: her best little village spot, her favorite climbing tree, all the spaces that were hers alone.

She knew it should have bothered her, but she felt an unusual blankness, a blandness. There were too many people here. It was just too overwhelming.

Suddenly, she saw her parents climbing the front stairs to the house. They both looked weary. Her Mom had something in her arms: it was the Apricot Boy!

Surprisingly relieved and overjoyed—surprisingly because she had been feeling so blank just a moment ago—she ran towards the house. Thank goodness everything was going to be all right.

CHAPTER 11

The sun had barely begun to peek over the high hills behind the house. The Dad was awakened out of a deep druggy sleep by the sound of someone yelling. At first he thought he heard pounding on a door, which made no sense, because nobody locked any doors here. Maybe it was just feet running up the stairs, or someone knocking something over.

Anyway, now it was a woman yelling. That much was clear.

He rolled over and opened his bleary eyes. He was in his own bed. That was good. His wife was next to him. That was good, too. The woman screaming was downstairs. That was not so good.

He got up and shuffled over to where the pee-pan should be, but it wasn't there. Okay, that was not so good either, but less of a problem than the woman yelling. Whatever that was about.

He looked down: he was naked, and despite the fuzziness in his head, he had a morning erection. Well, he did have to pee something fierce. He found his jeans on the floor by the bed and pulled them up, wincing as the necessary adjustments were made. Where the hell was the pee-pan?

The woman was still yelling something incoherent downstairs, and moving around bumping into things. Now the commotion was making the Mom stir too, and the kids. The Apricot Boy stood up in his crib, and he could hear the Princess moving in her little nook.

He went to the stairs, still buttoning up his jeans, and hurried down. It was Astrid doing the yelling and running around, which was not easy to do in such a small room. The front door was wide open. Many hippies still slept in the front meadow.

Astrid finally focused on the Dad. She turned to him and kept saying whatever it was, which he still could not understand.

He went to her and took both of her small arms above the elbow, firmly. This held her still but didn't do anything about the screaming.

"Astrid!" he yelled directly into her face. "Stop!"

She caught her breath and looked at him, eyes and mouth still wide open.

"I can't understand a word you're saying. What's the matter?"

"It's Weed! He's been gone all night! I don't know where he is!"

The Dad sighed with relief. "Sit down." He eased her into the desk chair.

She popped back up again as soon as he let go of her arms. "No! You don't understand! I can't find him anywhere!"

"Astrid..." The Dad sighed, closed the front door, and took the desk chair himself, if she wasn't going to sit in it. God, he had to pee. "It's a *party*. There's about a billion freaks in our front yard, half of them female. There are tents everywhere, and sleeping bags, and people bedded down in cars and vans. There were lots of drugs last night, lots of beer and wine, lots of fun. I saw people getting really friendly with each other." He paused, then went on. "I'm sorry, but I'm sure nothing awful has happened to him."

Astrid froze, and gave him a dark look. "Weed would *not* have spent the night with another woman, if that's what you're trying to say."

The Dad shrugged. "I don't know him that well, so maybe you're right. But that isn't to say that he couldn't have—I don't know—found himself partying with a bunch of new friends and then just crashed with them when it got late. It's a long walk down to your camper. Maybe he was just stoned and tired, and fell asleep somewhere." He got up. "Now, I'm sorry, but my bladder's gonna burst." He went to the back door and opened it, meaning to step out just into the yard and pee. There were a bunch of people sleeping back there too, though, so he had to go all the way over to the little dry creek bed at the edge of the meadow.

When he got back into the house, the Mom had come downstairs, tying a kimono around herself (which looked pretty good—she rarely wore it). She had gotten Astrid to sit back down and was going through basically the same possible explanations. "He's here somewhere. Don't worry, there's all sorts of people here." And then, seeing the Dad come back in, she asked, "Where's the pee-pan?"

"I don't know," he said. "Ask her."

The Princess came down the stairs, still wearing her nightgown.

"Honey? Where's the pee-pan?" the Mom asked.

The Princess's face went blank as she thought. "I don't know," she finally said, seriously.

"Well, it's your job to empty it. Did you leave it somewhere?"

Again she was silent. "Maybe," she said, and headed for the back door.

"Don't go outside in your nightgown." But the Mom wasn't really paying attention.

The Princess went outside in her nightgown, and returned a minute later with the pee-pan. The Dad distractedly watched her go upstairs with it then returned his attention to Astrid, who said, "I know something's wrong! Something's just wrong here!"

The Dad sighed and rubbed his head. Now that he'd peed, he was thirsty. "What do you want us to do about it?" he asked.

"Come help me look for him!" She sprang up from the chair again and made for the door.

"Whoa, whoa, hold on," the Dad said.

Astrid turned to look at him, her hand on the door handle.

"Sit back down," he said.

She came back to the desk chair but didn't sit down.

"We're not going to go storming all over the Land at the crack of dawn to find Weed." He tried not to grin as his internal jokester added, *Although weed wouldn't be at all hard to find here right now!* "We'll eat some breakfast, let the other people start to wake up, and he'll turn up."

Astrid frowned, then turned to the Mom with pleading eyes. "Come on, you'll help me, won't you?"

The Mom shook her head. "No, he's right. Eat some breakfast, have a cup of tea." She filled the kettle with water, set it on the stove, and peered inside the firebox.

Astrid started pacing again, her eyes wild.

She was making the Dad uneasy. "All right," he said, patting her arm as she went by, trying to slow her down. "If he's not here in an hour, I'll help you find him."

"An hour? We have to go now!"

"Mom! Mom!" the Apricot Boy sang from the loft. He was a mellow and patient boy, but he had apparently had enough of being trapped in his crib while a whole bunch of drama was going on downstairs. The Mom went up to get him.

The Dad kept his hand on Astrid's arm. "He'll turn up. You'll see."

Astrid shrugged his hand off. "I'm not gonna wait an hour. I'll go look for him myself."

"Don't you want some breakfast?" the Mom asked, coming back down the stairs with the Apricot Boy on her hip. But Astrid was already out the back door, heading up the path.

The Princess went back to her sleeping nook after she had found the pee-pan, rinsed it out, and carried it back upstairs. She vaguely remembered dealing with it last night, which was why she knew where to find it. It was all messy and gross and stinky inside. Had she barfed? She thought so, but she didn't entirely remember it. She must have accidentally taken some drugs after all, though she wasn't sure how. She had stayed away from the brownies, after all, even though they had looked really good, and she never got to eat brownies. It was so not fair that the adults would put drugs in brownies.

She liked the idea that she had maybe taken drugs, although at the same time she was a little weirded out about it. It was like the other stuff that had happened to her in her short life that she was weirded out about: somewhat happy that it had happened, it was sort of enjoyable, but she also didn't quite know how to deal with it. She wished she was an adult. Then she would know how things worked, what she was supposed to do. Being a kid was just no good at all.

She huddled under her covers, half-listening to the adults argue downstairs. When Astrid slammed out the back door, leaving the two halves to rattle together the way they always did, she perked up. Where was Astrid going? Her stomach felt strange at the question. So she picked up one of her Narnia books at random and started reading to take herself to another world. At least for a little while.

The Mom considered going after Astrid, but what would be the point? If the fool wanted to go look for her man, let her. He was undoubtedly in bed with some other woman. And why not? Why should he have any more morals than his younger brother? The same brother the Mom hadn't seen the whole rest of the afternoon and evening, she remembered again, annoyed again at the thought.

She settled the Apricot Boy at the table with some sliced apricots, then got out some paper and kindling, and started to build a fire in the cook stove. The Dad gave her a light hug from behind, dispelling the bad, anxious energy Astrid had left behind. "Mmm," she said, leaning back into him slightly. "How you doing?"

"Not bad. A little tired." He rubbed her back for a minute and then moved over to the front window.

"That was some party, wasn't it?"

"It's not over," he said. "It's gonna be all day today too—we may get even more people."

"Wow," she said. "Hard to imagine where everyone will park."

"A few folks split last night. Looks like another gorgeous day, though."

"Mm-hmm." She got the fire lit, then came and looked out the window with him. The sun was just starting to filter down into the front meadow, illuminating the sleeping partyers and their cars, tents, dogs, leftover food, and rapidly accumulating piles of trash. There was not a cloud in the sky. It would be a lovely day.

After reading only one chapter, the Princess put down her book. She had to go outside again to see what was going on. She thought that Astrid knew about the monster—well, she had already figured that out, of course—but the new part of the thought was that Astrid wasn't going to have any idea how to speak to the monster. She would make it mad, she would do something wrong, and it would do something bad as a result. The Princess knew how to talk to the monster, more or less. At least, it seemed to like her, to be her friend. It told her things it didn't tell anyone else.

She didn't want Astrid to mess up. She didn't know what would happen if she did.

So she put her clothes on and went downstairs. Her mom smiled at her. "Want some breakfast?"

"No thanks," she said. "Maybe later. I'm not hungry."

"Okay."

"I'm going out now, all right?"

"Of course."

She went out the back door. Astrid had gone this way. If she knew about the monster, she'd probably look in the back meadow. It was a good place to start, anyway.

The Dad watched out the front window as a few early risers began to find their way out of tents and sleeping bags, stretch, smile at the sun, and look around for something to eat.

He turned back and watched the Mom making oatmeal, now that the cook stove was warm. It was a big pot, the biggest they had, full to the top. Who knew how many people would turn up at the house hungry? There wouldn't be enough for everyone, but they could feed a lot of people. Whatever happened, it would all work out.

The Princess padded up the path to the back meadow. She passed Evening Star and Billy Goat's big green army tent. Inside, she could hear Morning Star whining and her mother whining back. The Princess slowed down briefly to listen.

Now Evening Star was arguing with Billy Goat. "I have his map, see?"

"How can you be sure that's what it is? It just looks like scribbles to me."

"It was hidden in his desk! What else could it be?"

Billy Goat didn't respond, at least not so that the Princess could hear.

Evening Star went on, "Do you have any idea what that's worth? If it's even half of what we think it is?"

Now Billy Goat sighed. "Jesus, woman."

Morning Star whined again and seemed to be about to leave the tent. The Princess quickly kept going up the path as quietly as she could. She didn't want Morning Star following her. It was more important to find out what Astrid was doing than what Evening Star and Billy Goat were hassling about.

She turned the corner, and the back meadow was in front of her. It looked entirely empty, but then she noticed what must be Astrid at the far end, right at the edge of the trees leading up the mountain. Astrid was kneeling, but she was too far away for the Princess to see what she was doing.

I told them not to come here, I told them to go away, the monster's voice slithered into her head. And the morning suddenly became very cold.

The Princess did not want to speak out loud. So she thought back to the monster: *There are a lot of people here.*

Fewer than there were.

What did you do? Did you eat more people?

And what if I did?

You know you're not supposed to eat people. The Princess tried to not sound so bossy, in her head, but the fact of the matter was, eating people was just wrong.

I didn't really exactly eat them. But they were on my Land. I had to do something.

Couldn't you eat the cows next door or wild animals? You're going to get in trouble.

Actually, I won't.

The Princess stopped and thought about that a moment, not directing her thoughts to the monster. After a few minutes, it said, *Aren't you going to go see what the black-haired woman is doing?*

Should I?

If you want. It makes no difference to me. You're the spy.

So she started across the meadow.

The Mom sat on the front porch, eating her oatmeal with raisins and goat's milk and brown sugar, and watching people get up. She was watching for someone in particular, and she was not seeing him. She was also pretending that she was not watching for someone in particular, so she had to remain casual and mellow about it.

She couldn't sit here all morning. Speaking of goat's milk, the goats needed tending to, the dogs needed to be fed, all the usual chores had to get done, party or no party. And she should probably go see if everyone was able to find breakfast and was feeling all right. Oh, and somebody should check out the river, make sure the beach wasn't too cluttered with junk—and weren't they going to try to get that rope swing hung?

She turned to the Dad to say something about this at the same moment as he said, "Damn, the rope swing. I meant to get down to the river all day yesterday, and I never did."

She laughed. "I was just about to say that!"

"Great minds think alike!"

They finished their oatmeal, and she took the dishes in to wash. "Tell you what: I'll take care of what needs doing around here if you go check out the scene at the river. Make sure it's all right, okay?" This way, she could stay close to the house. When Junior finally resurfaced, maybe they could have a private word or two. She had words for him, all right. Vanishing just when she needed the most help.

"Sure." The Dad kissed her. "And I'll rustle up some able-bodied guys to get that thing up there, finally."

"That's going to be fun." But she wasn't sure she wanted to try it. Oh well, it would make the guys happy anyway.

The Princess crossed the meadow towards Astrid. As she got closer, not only did it get colder, but she could clearly see that Astrid was crying or shaking. The Princess knew that the monster had done something awful. The only question was what.

She didn't have to wonder for long. As she walked up behind Astrid, she saw clearly.

Weed sat propped against a tree with several rough bites taken out of his mid-section. The monster was changing its style, she thought. The dead Weed looked nothing like the dead Bliss. Of course, Bliss had been in the creek, which had made her look even worse. Weed had a really bad color to him, although he wasn't all blue and waterlogged. He looked more green, and dark.

The Princess stood silently behind Astrid, just watching her and thinking. An evil monster was destroying the minions of the Princess's realm. When it was the goats or a strange hitchhiker lady, that had been bad enough. But now the evil monster had gone and eaten one of the actual subjects of the realm. Though the Princess hadn't really gotten to know him or anything, Weed had always seemed like a perfectly nice man.

The Princess felt sorry. She should have been able to protect them all better. She was the Princess, after all. She ought to have been in charge here.

But there were too many people to protect. The Princess's realm should have been smaller. This was too much. What could one Princess do?

"Oh my god," Astrid blurted out, suddenly sensing the girl behind her, spinning around to face her.

"I'm sorry," the Princess said all too calmly.

"You've got to get away from here—you can't see this." Astrid scrambled to her feet and tried to cover the girl's eyes, to steer her away.

"It's all right, I know what happened. I know who did it."

"You do?" Astrid froze and stared hard at the girl.

"You do too."

They continued staring at each other for an eternity. Then Astrid broke into a sob and ran back towards the house.

"What the hell was that about?" the Mom asked herself, after Astrid had stormed shouting through the house, then raced off to her camper down by the road. And for once, without her stupid dogs. The Mom, still coming back from the goat shed, hadn't caught what she said. Astrid must have not seen her coming down the path or heard her calling out.

The Mom took the pail of milk into the house and hefted it onto the counter. She again considered going after Astrid. Obviously she'd found Weed and hadn't liked what she saw. So everyone fucked around. Well, Astrid would get over it. The Mom decided to let her cool down a bit, and then maybe she'd try and talk to her. Or maybe even after the party was over and everything had settled back down.

Once she got everything put away, she thought she heard someone coming—sounded like a truck, down by the road—but nothing came up the driveway. Must have been that old rancher, Don whatever his name was. Him with the funny wave. Ha—what he would think of all these hippies if he came up to the meadow?

In that moment of looking through the rancher's eyes, as it were, she saw the scene differently. Now she noticed how wasted people looked, even though it was first thing in the morning. In fact, here was a young woman—barely past her teens, if that—who seemed to be having a bad trip. She shook and cried, and an older woman was holding her arms firmly, trying to comfort her. The Mom knew she should go and help, but it gave her an ugly feeling deep in her stomach to see it. It reminded her too much of her own acid experience.

She glanced away and saw Evening Star hassling her daughter about something. Morning Star, still naked, was whining and pulling on her mother's arm, but Evening Star was just snapping back at her.

Ugh, the Mom thought, and looked around for the Dad.

The Dad walked down the driveway, skirting the majority of the party, determined to make it all the way down to the river today without getting interrupted. It was easy because not a lot of people were awake yet, but he didn't slow down anyway.

When he got to the end of the driveway, he saw dozens of cars parked on both sides of the road anywhere they could squeeze in, some of them half in the ditch. Ah, so this was why the front meadow wasn't as full of cars as it could have been. He wondered what the neighbors might think of this, but there weren't very many neighbors to bother. Probably nobody cared.

He crossed the road and climbed down the path to the river. The beach was in pretty good shape, considering how many people must have been here yesterday. Sure, there were plenty of garments hanging in the clothes tree, and some shoes and other stuff strewn around on the sand, but really not much. Good.

He checked out the big tree they were going to hang the rope swing from, trying to make sense of it. It could be done, with enough people, and maybe a length of chain…then he shivered, and wished he had a cup of hot tea, or even coffee. Something warm. It was too cold right now to swim, but why were there all these clothes still here? People didn't just wander off naked for the rest of the day, did they?

The Dad didn't believe in vibes, so he didn't have a good way to describe how he felt. But "bad vibes" was really the best way to put it. It felt unnaturally abandoned, and sort of bizarre. Come to think of it, the whole party was kind of a bizarre scene. Maybe a two-day all-county freak party had been a bit much. And he was still really hung over.

He hurried up the hill from the beach, wanting to get back to the rest of the people.

CHAPTER 12

After Astrid took off down the path, the Princess stood staring at Weed. Yet another dead body. It was getting to be a familiar kind of situation. But why were the bites different? Weed's face was frozen in shock or disgust or fear, and his arms were splayed as though he had had one final moment of fighting back before it got him.

And why was he propped against a tree? It looked as if he had sat down uncomfortably. Was that before or after he had been bitten? There wasn't much blood around him, not much at all. Not that the Princess was any kind of expert on dead bodies (or at least, she hadn't been, not before this summer), but there was something weird about his position. It was as if someone had killed him, and then decided he would look better if he were sitting up against a tree, passing the time of day. Except with his middle bitten. Which was really gross, however you looked at it.

"You shouldn't kill people," the Princess said to the empty forest. "That's a bad thing."

It is my Land, the familiar voice replied in her head.

"It is my Mom's and Dad's land. They bought it, and they built our house on it, and my room is in our house, and all my books, and you shouldn't kill people!"

It is my Land… It's mine, and I want it back now.

"You let us live here for a year," she protested.

That is true. I did.

"And now you want us all to leave? Or just the party people?"

You were fine. You know that. You were not like the others.

The Princess took a few steps away from the body. It was too gross to stand near. A shiny blue thing in the grass caught her eye. She bent over to pick it up, as she said to the monster, "Do you mean just me, or me and my family?" 'You' could go either way.

But the monster didn't answer. And it wasn't like she could live here without her family anyway.

She looked down at what she was holding. It was a rolled-up Bugler bag full of tobacco, rolling papers, and a cigarette lighter.

Just then she felt a presence behind her and wheeled around, dropping the bag. But it was just Sauron and Galadriel—her big sweet dogs, coming to find her. "No!" She wouldn't let them hassle another dead body. It was too awful, too hideous, too extra-gross. Already it was horrible enough. This would be too much.

She grabbed both dogs by their collars and tried hard to keep them from noticing Weed. They pulled against her—they were big, strong dogs—but they liked to play, which gave her an idea. She let go of the collars and started to run across the meadow, towards the house. "Come on!" she called, urgently.

They scampered across the meadow after her.

One person who didn't need convincing to leave was Astrid. The engine that the Mom had heard was that of the camper-truck as it pulled free from its moorings and hightailed it the hell off the Land. The Dad re-emerged on the road just in time to see the camper roaring past all the crazily parked cars.

The Dad stepped off the road and stood between a couple of cars, though she wouldn't have run him over anyway, probably. He shook his head as he watched her fly by. *Well, obviously she found him,* he thought, imagining that lucky (and then unlucky) dog Weed, caught in bed with some hot new chick—or maybe those blonde twins. Jeez, they were something!

He walked back up the driveway to the front meadow, glad to get away from the silent river and eager to hear the gossip.

The Princess walked slowly back to the house, catching her breath after her run with the dogs. They walked with her, happily.

What was she supposed to do? Did the monster really mean they should all leave? Why had he let them stay this long, if that was what he wanted? He must have meant only all the extra people.

The Princess loved the Land, but she also felt very bad about all the crazy things, the danger, and the dead people. She didn't particularly like the party, with all the strange weird people here. She agreed with the monster, that it would be good if all the party people left.

Things had been fine on the Land before the first new people had come and stayed, the community people. When it was just hitchhikers who came and went, there hadn't been any monster.

Or had there?

The Princess kept walking down the path, lost in thought. When had she first felt the presence in the forest? She couldn't remember if it was before Evening Star and Billy Goat and Morning Star had come to live them, or after.

It had grown so slowly, her awareness of the monster. Like it had always been there, only rising to her conscious attention…when?

The Mom moved through the front meadow, checking in with people, pointing folks to Shit Hill, making sure everyone had enough water and stuff. Most everyone was awake and ready for more mellow, transcendent, far-out fun. She gently fended off three offers to ball and two proposals of marriage. She did not find Junior anywhere, but the chick who was having the bad trip seemed to have calmed down a bit.

She saw her daughter at the top of the meadow, tousled blonde hair glinting in the morning sun, peering around the meadow, looking for someone—probably her. She smiled and started making her way to the Princess.

The Princess spotted the Mom, and started walking towards her. But then she felt a gentle tug on her sleeve. It was the Apricot Boy. "Hi," he said. "Wanna go play?"

"Sure," she said, taking his damp hand off her sleeve and holding it briefly. "In just a minute. I have to go see Mommy."

"I'm coming with you."

She hesitated a moment, then decided. "Sure, okay."

She took his hand again and they stepped into the crowd, and lost the Mom immediately. The dogs were already gone, melded back into the pack.

The first of the Sunday arrivals drove past the Dad as he walked by the side of the driveway. These were not only folks who'd driven back to Yokayo for the night, but also some who were coming out for the first time. The Dad smelled fresh-baked bread wafting out of one modified school bus. Yum! He smiled and waved at the freaks in the front window of the bus, and they smiled and waved back.

The bus pulled up to the top of the driveway and looked for a flat place to park. Of course, all the good places had long since been taken. The Dad walked around, motioning to the driver as he tried to scope out something halfway decent. Maybe he could get some other cars to move. He could move the Dart—where was the Dart, anyway? He didn't see it amid the jumble of cars. Well, it was here somewhere.

"Bring it here." He pointed to a space in between a couple of trees. The bus ought to be able to squeeze in there. They could fine-tune it later.

Then, a minute later, there was the unmistakable sound of another vehicle coming up the driveway. People hadn't shown up this early yesterday! The Dad turned to face the new car. Then he stopped, the wind going out of his sails. The latest arrival was a shiny new green and white American car, with a bank of lights across the top, whitewall tires, and a reinforced bumper. Mendocino County Sheriff was picked out in gold letters on its side.

The sheriff car rolled to a stop at the top of the driveway. It idled a moment, then was turned off. The Dad stared, but in the glare of the morning sun reflecting off the windshield, he couldn't see inside.

Then the driver's door opened and a solid man in a uniform got out. The Dad took one hesitant step forward, then stopped again.

The sheriff (or sheriff's deputy? Who knew about these things anyway? All the Dad's knowledge was from TV, when they'd had one) stood by his car, taking it all in. He had clearly seen the Dad's halting approach. He gave a nod that seemed to imply, *I see you, I'll get back to you, mister, you just hang loose a moment.* The cop put his hands on his hips and looked long and hard at the front meadow.

The Dad also scanned the front meadow, seeing it anew through the eyes of the Man. And it was not good, just really not good at all. He saw joints being passed around openly, pot-laden brownies sitting out on the tables, children running everywhere, and topless women. Well, maybe the cop wouldn't object to that. He was a man, after all, and it was private property. But he saw wine and beer and bags of drugs sitting out for anyone to partake of. And the rest of the whole scene, the general condition of being a hippie. Unlicensed dogs. Unregistered cars. Unwashed children. Unmarried couples. The whole gamut of dropping out of society. A society that was embodied by this one thick fellow in his tidy uniform, standing on the Dad's own property, passing judgment on it.

Indignation rose in the Dad, and he tried to stifle it. Getting uppity would do him no good. So he hung a sweet and innocent look on his face and waited for the cop to address him.

Which he did, in good time. The cop finished his scan of the front meadow, then turned his attention to the Dad, stepping towards him and putting a hand out, cordially. "You the homeowner here, sir?"

The Dad took the meaty hand in his and tried to return the firm but polite handshake. He wished his own palms weren't so sweaty, but hell, cops must be used to that kind of thing. "Yes, I am."

The sheriff, or whatever, finished the handshake and let go, not wiping his hand on his pants, as the Dad imagined he wanted to. He glanced across the meadow again and said, "You got a permit for this gathering?"

The Dad shifted from one foot to another. "Um, well, not exactly... It's just a party."

"Interesting sort of party," the cop mused, voice still casual. "With fliers all over town. You know all these people?"

The Dad's throat tightened and his mouth felt dry. "Sure, um, yeah, they're all mellow, you know..."

"Who's that? Tell me her name." The cop pointed at random at a red-headed chick who was standing over one of the picnic tables, testing to see if the watermelon was still good to eat or if too many yellow jackets had been on it.

"Ah—okay, you got me." The Dad grinned helplessly. "She's a friend of a friend."

"Okay," said the cop, smiling. "What about him?"

"Him? Oh, that's Rob!" The beer-bellied guy was just emerging from the blonde girls' tent. The two tall goddesses followed him, barely dressed. From across the meadow, Evening Star immediately caught sight of him. She left her naked daughter and strode over, hands on her hips.

The cop was obviously impressed with Rob's tent-mates. It was not a very large tent. "And their names?"

"Ah, um, they're with Rob."

The men shared a look. It was the first moment when the Dad thought that perhaps this would work out all right after all. But then the cop said, "Do you mind if I take a look around?"

"Er, do you have to?"

The cop smiled broadly, generously. "Of course not."

"Great!" The Dad was so relieved.

But then the cop went on: "You, as the property owner, can certainly deny me the right to look around your property. So then I would have to drive the twenty-five miles back to town, over that big hill, through that ford in the river, and get myself to the county courthouse. And once I got there, I'd have to get myself a search warrant. Now, it's a Sunday, but I know the judge on call today. He's my brother-in-law, and he's not so lenient about you hippies as I am. He'd be happy to come in and sign a search warrant, even though it's his day off. Then I'd have to drive all the way back out here, serve the warrant, and then I'd have the legal right to search this property. I could do that, but I'll be honest with you, that would be a heck of a lot of bother for the same end result. Don't you think?"

I don't know why cops have to go through such crap just to get their point across, the Dad thought, but smiled amiably and said, "Why don't you go ahead and look around, Sheriff..."—he peered at the man's name tag—"Brooks."

"It's Deputy Brooks. And thank you for your cooperation."

The Dad had one last thought to try to save the day. "You know, I'd be happy to show you around, if you like," he said, as casually as he could manage.

"Oh, there will be no need for that," the cop said, smiling again. "I'll just see myself around. I won't be any bother to you."

Sure, the Dad thought sullenly, as the cop glanced again at the meadow, then turned and headed for the house. He glanced back over to Evening Star. After what appeared to be a few choice words that the Dad was glad he didn't hear, she stalked off, grabbing her daughter's hand as she headed for the back path. She had an ugly look on her face.

The Princess saw the cop car arrive. She stopped, still holding the Apricot Boy's hand. *My goodness! Somebody already knows about the dead body!* Partly she was relieved, and partly she was confused. She knew that Astrid had fled, but she couldn't believe that she had gotten all the way to town already. Maybe she had stopped in Vaughn's Corner and called from the little roadside market. That had to be it. No one could have driven all the way to Yokayo that fast.

Then she watched her dad talking to the cop, and she wished she could hear that conversation, but she didn't dare go close. Her dad looked terribly nervous. But then again, so did the cop.

Then the cop was walking towards the house, so the Princess skirted the edge of the meadow, moving away. She was still looking for the Mom, but she was keeping an eye on the cop too, and she still had the Apricot Boy's hand in hers. It was too much to pay attention to all at once. As soon as she scanned the crowd for the Mom with any seriousness, she lost track of the cop. Had he gone into the house?

She felt a sudden fear at the thought. All her books were in there! Was he going to take her books away from her? And all her little-village supplies and toys? The library books weren't overdue yet, were they? But no, that was silly. The cop didn't want those things, he didn't care about library books. The cop didn't want to go in the house anyway, that wasn't where the dead body was. Hadn't Astrid told them where to find it?

"Oh, *there* you are," she heard, and there was Mom!

"Ah!" the Princess exclaimed, dropping some of her usual reserve. Her mother glanced at her, noticing. "He's been looking for you," she added, handing her the Apricot Boy's hand.

"Come here, sweetie!" the Mom sang, sweeping the child up into her arms. The Apricot Boy giggled. The Princess started to say something to her, but was still confused. What should she say? She needed to figure it out. The monster hadn't told her not to tell, this time.

She took advantage of her mom's momentary distraction to melt back into the crowd again. She knew she should tell Mom about the body, but somehow she just couldn't.

Maybe she could tell her dad. Maybe that would be easier.

The Dad watched the cop go into the house. Well, he shouldn't take too long to search a one-room house, anyway. Good thing all the newly harvested pot had been distributed around the party. And indeed, within a few minutes, the cop re-emerged to stand on the front porch and scan the front meadow yet again.

The Dad walked up to the porch. "Find everything all right?"

The deputy smiled amiably. "Sure, no problem, thanks. Is this everyone, right out here?" He waved a hand vaguely outward, indicating the crowd.

"Well, I guess, more or less…" The Dad glanced towards the path that led to the back meadow. "There might be more people back there, but I didn't see anyone the last time I looked."

The cop started walking down the stairs, holding firmly to the dried-madrone rail, making it creak and sway. He wasn't fat, but it was rare that they had someone so huge and beefy on those stairs.

The cop seemed to notice the same thing, and he paused at the bottom of the stairs, looking back up at the house. "I suppose you got a building permit for this?"

"Uh, yeah, sure!" The Dad smiled. "You want to see it?"

"No thanks. Not just yet." He looked at the path leading to the back meadow. "This way?"

"Yep."

The Princess watched her dad and the cop talking again. They both seemed a tiny bit more relaxed. That was good. And now the cop was walking up the path towards the back meadow. She guessed that was good too, though it gave her a scary, sick feeling in her stomach.

Is the cop going to find the dead body after all? And what will he do to the monster? Or what will the monster do to him? Between the monster and a big scary cop with a gun, she didn't know who might win.

They never understand, a familiar voice murmured in her head. She started and looked all around, but this time there was no dark shape, no unnatural coldness. Had she imagined the voice? "They never understand" was something she might easily think herself. Adults never understood anything, that was true. When she'd tried to tell them things in the past, they'd laughed and waved it off. "You have such an imagination," they'd say.

Of course, this was different. With real live dead bodies to show them, they *would* understand. She needed to just go tell her dad, take him to the back meadow. Then he'd take care of everything.

You know you can't tell them about me, came the voice in her head. This time it was definitely not her imagination.

She veered away from her dad and out of the front meadow, towards the back path. "Why not?" she asked, when she was too far off for anyone to hear.

You saw what happened to Astrid.

"What do you mean?"

She's an adult. It made her crazy.

The Princess thought about this. It seemed to her that seeing Weed dead was what made Astrid crazy, when you got right down to it. But she didn't like to argue with the monster.

Meanwhile, the cop had made the first bend in the path, so she followed him, silently as always on bare feet. She looked around, making sure the dogs didn't notice her. She didn't want them out there again. But they were thoroughly distracted, playing with the visiting dogs.

The cop walked straight along the path to the back meadow without deviating to look at the vegetable garden, or Billy Goat and Evening Star's tent, or anything. He reminded her of a tin soldier marching up the path. She wondered at that, but kept following.

When he got to the back meadow, he walked straight into it, right up to the spot where the goats had been eaten, weeks and weeks ago. He stopped there, peering down at the ground, then kneeling, touching the dirt. Then he stood abruptly up, wiping his hands on his pants, and looked around again.

The Princess watched all this from the dark trees. *Go across, right there,* she encouraged, silently.

But he walked over to Bliss's grave instead. He stood there, peering down at the sign that had her name on it. He didn't bend down this time, or touch anything; he just stood and looked, with his head cocked, like maybe he was thinking or listening to something. *Go to the edge*, she thought again. *Into the woods.* After a minute or more, he walked a few steps further towards the back woods, to the body. From all the way across the meadow, she heard him say, "Oh my god." Then he leaned against a tree and threw up.

The Princess raised her eyebrows. Gosh, this body wasn't nearly as gross as the last one, or even the goats. Then again, she had thrown up last night too, she thought. Or she probably had, anyway. Maybe the cop just had a sensitive tummy.

She thought that he would now go running back to his car and call someone on the radio, or go get to a phone, or something. But after he finished throwing up, he wiped his mouth carefully, then adjusted his collar and stood up straight. Again, he waited a moment, staring straight ahead, very still, as if something had caught his eye. Then he stepped deeper into the woods, vanishing into the darkness.

This was no good. How was she supposed to spy on him if she couldn't see him?

Maybe he sees something else, came the voice. She felt the familiar chill in her tummy. "No," she whispered.

She went around the edge of the back meadow, keeping to the trees and the darkness. It took a long time, but she couldn't risk being out in the open meadow even for a moment. She didn't know how far into the trees he'd gone, or when he'd come back out. Besides, her eyes were adjusted to the gloom now. If she went back out into the open, they'd get dazzled and she wouldn't be able to see. Even temporarily, spies could not be blind.

Eventually, she got around to the other side of the meadow. She heard the cop's tramping boots in the underbrush. He was poking around, a few steps here, a few steps there, muttering under his breath.

But then he stopped. "Holy shit," he said, and then a crashing sound.

She couldn't stand not seeing what was going on! She stole forward one cautious step at a time, hanging behind each tree until she could figure out exactly where he was and what he was seeing.

She peered around an oak tree, and there he was, finally. He was down on his knees. That must have been the crashing sound, as he toppled into the leaves. His head was in his hands, which was a really weird thing to see a big burly cop doing.

In front of him was a whole bunch of people, a dozen or more. They were all lying down. Face down on the ground or curled up like sleeping, but not.

That was strange. People didn't do that, did they?

She crept forward just the tiniest bit. She was only a few feet behind him now; he still hadn't moved. He was kneeling right before a man. Then he reached out and touched him.

But the man on the ground didn't move. The Princess was beginning to think that all these people were probably dead.

They weren't eaten, not in any way that she could see. They were just lying there in all their clothes. And with no blankets or pillows or sleeping bags or tents or anything. It was really creepy. Yes, they must be dead.

She let her breath out slowly. She hadn't realized she was holding it.

The cop whipped his head around: had he heard her? She froze. He seemed to look right through her, his eyes wild and blank. Then he turned back to the body and his shoulders started shaking, just a little.

Oh, my goodness. Was he crying?

Deputy Brooks had been feeling pretty good about finding the hippie land and finally solving the nagging mystery. Once he'd seen the fliers in town, it had all fallen into place. He'd planned his trip specially to come during the party. That way, he could potentially bust the whole county's worth of freaks. What a haul!

Oh, and clear up the matter of the dead person the first hippie woman had talked about. If there actually was such a thing.

Everything had started to go wrong from the moment he drove up the long, crappy, rutted driveway. Sure, there were hippies galore, and an asinine landowner (assuming he wasn't lying) who would be fun to jerk around, and all that. But something didn't feel right.

It just got worse when the landowner sent him to the back meadow. He started feeling...pushed, a little. Nudged. As if he wasn't entirely in control any more.

The deputy was *always* in control. Well, now that he had anything to say about it. That was why he had become a cop in the first place, and then joined the sheriff's department, because that was a more in-control position than one in the city police. He loved his uniform and his big smooth green and white car. He loved his gun, heavy on his hip. He loved how people subtly reacted when they saw him—not just hippies, but everyone. Fear, respect, awe.

But now that was missing. Now he was the one feeling fear. And doubt, and uncertainty, and confusion. Like there was a different person doing his thinking for him, and he was just along for the ride.

Who's doing this? he thought very cautiously, as he walked out to the middle of the meadow. Because if you talk back to the voices in your head, then you're for-sure crazy. But of course there weren't really voices in his head. Just a feeling. Doubt.

Which was bad enough.

Stop here. Check this out, came a thought that was not exactly his own.

"I am not hearing voices." He bent down in the grass and stuck his fingers in the dark dirt.

Goat blood. Then, *How do I know that?*

He got quickly to his feet and wiped his hands on his trousers.

A small sign caught his eye at the back of the meadow, so he walked over to investigate. "BLISS," it read. A few small white mushrooms grew nearby, and more had recently been picked. There were many footprints around, and, although it was hard to tell, it appeared as though some of them led into the woods behind the meadow.

You should go check that out.

He shook his head to get rid of the thought. Of course he would check that out. Any cop would check out footprints leading into the woods.

And then he lost his breakfast, when he saw the first body.

And then he found the rest of the bodies.

And then there were no more nudges. Now that he could actually use one. Now that he had seen the unthinkable, the worst, the absolute fuck-all impossible thing.

The Dad waited for the cop to return from the back meadow. He had deliberately sent the fellow that way because he didn't think there was anything to be found there. The cop could traipse all around in the woods to his heart's content, maybe see a few stray cows from next door, maybe go bother Bill and Star in their tent, see the zucchini in the garden, whatever. Then he could go on his merry way and everything would be cool again.

And, most important, he would avoid the pot garden, which was off the *other* path, up the hill directly behind the house.

The Dad was silently congratulating himself on his craftiness when he saw the cop staggering back down the path. The man's face was ashen and gray, and he was sweating. His cop hat was in his hands, a crumpled-up mess, and the cop didn't even notice.

Uh-oh.

Sheriff Brooks—Deputy Brooks, rather—made it to his car, stumbling a little. He straightened up and steadied himself, holding onto the hood, then yanked the door of his car open and grabbed the handheld radio.

The Dad watched him, stunned. What had he found? What had happened? He sidled over to the car, trying to hear what the guy was saying into his radio. At first it was impossible, but then the man started to yell. "What do you mean, you *can't*? The fuck—well, *call* him! …No, I won't!" Another pause, then, "*Fuck* you!"

The cop smashed the radio handset against the dashboard. A piece flew off, and then the thing was silent.

The Dad went cold in his stomach.

The cop looked wildly about, then focused on the Dad. He gestured at the meadow with an expansive fling of his arm and said, "Get all these people out of here! Now!"

"What?"

"Get them all *out* of here!"

The Dad backed away from the car. What was the matter with this guy? How the hell was the Dad supposed to make everyone leave? He stumbled over to the nearest picnic table, where a few people were sitting eating oatmeal and sipping tea, and watching the drama at the cop car with wary attention. "Um, he says you all gotta go now," the Dad said apologetically, pointing at the cop.

"Aw, what a bummer, man," one of the guys said.

A woman nodded. "Yeah, they're always trying to bust up a scene."

"So, um, would you all mind helping me spread the word?" The Dad looked around for any of the other Land residents, but didn't see anyone. He'd seen Evening Star and her kid earlier, but apparently they'd split after the argument with Rob. Astrid had left, but where was everyone else? Some help would be real useful, right about now.

"Jesus H. Christ," the guy said, but sympathetically. He scraped the last bit of oatmeal out of his bowl and got to his feet. "Sure, man. It was a cool party while it lasted."

"Yeah, well, thanks for coming," the Dad said. He didn't know any of these people's names.

Between them, they got the word around quickly. He found his wife, and after a whispered conversation, she helped too. People muttered and groaned, but started packing up their stuff, putting food in their cars, untangling their dogs from all the others. Soon cars and trucks and vans and buses started wending their way back down the driveway.

The cop had stomped back off toward the back meadow, leaving his car where it was, door hanging ajar. The hippies parked behind him had to struggle to get around. Nobody wanted to scrape a cop car.

After only about half an hour, the front meadow was nearly empty. Of people, that was. There was still plenty of trash. The Dad counted, and only six cars remained. A blue Volkswagen, a dusty beige Plymouth Valiant, a few others. He wondered at this, then remembered the river. The folks who owned these cars must be there. He said to his wife, "You wanna go check on the river? I think he wants me to stay nearby."

"Didn't you just get back from there? Was there anyone down there then?"

"No." The Dad frowned. "It's been a little while, though. I wasn't watching where everyone went."

"I wish we knew what the hell was going on," she whispered. Apricot Boy squirmed and whimpered in her lap.

"I know," the Dad whispered back. "But whatever it is, it's a bummer."

She nodded grimly and started down the driveway. Sauron and Galadriel got up from the shade of the porch and trotted along behind her.

The Mom tried to put the Apricot Boy down about halfway down the driveway. "Ugh, you're getting heavy. You want to walk now?"

"No, Mommy. Carry me. I'm scared."

"You're too big to carry, sweetie. You're a big boy."

"Not." He started to cry, fat tears rolling down his cheeks.

She sighed, shifting him to the opposite hip.

They got to the road, where she saw a few cars still parked here too. So obviously there were folks at the river who hadn't gotten the word.

But when she got down the path and out onto the beach, there was no one. She wouldn't have expected swimming this early—it was still cool out—but whose cars were those? There were lots of clothes in the tree, too.

Sauron jumped into the river and started paddling about, then got out and shook himself vigorously, spraying water within a ten-foot radius.

"Swim?" The Apricot Boy looked at the dog and then up at the Mom expectantly.

"Not right now, honey." She rumpled his hair, and then wiped the water drops off her legs. "Let's go back and see Daddy. You ready to walk now?"

"No!"

Where is the Princess? she wondered as she carried her son up the hill.

The Princess was in the house now. She knew from her spying experience that, except for at night when the lights were on and it was dark outside, a person could watch things from the house and not be seen, even if they were right at the window. The only window that wasn't too high for her to see out of was on the stair landing. She sat there, on the patches of nailed-down scrap carpeting, watching.

It was not all that interesting, though, after the initial excitement of her dad and mom getting all the people to leave. There was a lot of standing around and waiting. After a while, her mom took the Apricot Boy and went down the driveway, and then a little later they came back. Maybe this wasn't such a good spying place after all.

The Dad sat on the front porch and watched the Mom and the Apricot Boy come back up the hill alone. Dully, in the back of his mind, a thought nagged at him, but he couldn't make it bubble to the surface in the face of all that was going on. Something was missing, something he'd forgotten.

Well, a whole bunch of people were missing, apparently. His wife climbed the stairs and shook her head. "Nobody's there. But there's more cars on the road."

"How many?"

"Three or four—I don't know."

She sat on the porch next to him. The Apricot Boy clung to her. They all stared at the cop car. *Something is not right here,* the Dad thought.

Just then, the cop strode back into the meadow and looked around. He seemed confused, as if he was wondering where everyone had gone. As if he hadn't been the one to send everyone away.

Then he focused on the house, on the family on the porch. He walked towards them with a stiff, awkward gait. The Dad's tension deepened, but he tried to put a friendly, harmless expression on his face. Just hangin' out on his porch on a nice summer morning with the wife and kid. Nothing weird here, nope.

The cop walked slowly up the stairs, and when he got to the top of the stairs, he pulled his gun out of his belt, slowly and smoothly. He pointed the gun at the Dad, standing far enough back to encompass the Mom and the Apricot Boy in the threat. "Get up."

The Dad scrambled to his feet, then helped his wife up. She still held the Apricot Boy. Her hands were as clammy as the Dad's.

They stared back at the cop, frightened, silent.

"Go in there." The cop pointed at the front door of the house with his gun.

They went in, and the cop followed. It was a small room, and everyone was very close together. The Dad could smell the man's sweat.

There was a slight movement on the landing. It was the Princess, watching the whole scene with very wide eyes.

The cop slowly turned the gun on her. "Come down here. Stand with them."

The Princess obeyed.

"Sit down," he said to the Mom and the Dad. They sat on the floor in the middle of the room. The Princess sat down beside them. The Mom held the silent Apricot Boy in her lap again.

Still holding the gun in his right hand, the cop fumbled on his belt with his left hand, finally removing a pair of shiny metal handcuffs. He tossed these over to the Dad. "Put these on, cuff yourselves together, you and her." He indicated the Mom, using the gun to point.

The Dad grabbed the cuffs out of the air, almost dropping them, then tried to figure out how to open them. He had no clue.

"Oh for Chrissake." The deputy set the gun down and reached over, cuffing the Dad's right and the Mom's left wrists together, leaving them sitting back to back on the floor. Then he picked the gun up, waving it at them. "Stupid hippies."

I should have grabbed the gun, the Dad thought belatedly. But the whole scene was just so completely unreal, his whole head had gone numb.

Besides, who knew how to fire a gun? Not the Dad, that was for sure.

But still. It might have changed the balance of power. But it was too late now, the Dad realized, as his thought processes slowly reawakened. Nothing was making sense. He'd made everyone leave, just as the cop had demanded. Now what? What was going *on*?

The cop strode around the small room, opening cabinets, looking in the closet where the folding table was kept, peering in the sauna room. "Hey—the kids, in here," he ordered.

"What?" The Mom tightened her grip on the Apricot Boy.

The deputy came back out and waved his gun at her again. "I said, the kids, in the little room back here. Now!" Then he turned the gun on the front door and fired it, expertly shooting out the tiny high window.

The sound was astonishingly loud in the small room. The Mom shrieked and pushed the Apricot Boy off her lap. The Princess reached out for her brother's hand and took him into the sauna.

The cop closed the sauna door, then turned the skeleton key that sat in the lock. He put the key in his pocket. The Dad had forgotten that door even had a lock.

"What the hell is going on?" the Mom asked quietly in her husband's ear, and then glanced at the cop and whispered, "Never mind."

"I don't really know," the Dad answered, anyway.

The cop went back to the front of the house and looked out the narrow broken window in the door. Then he turned back to the Mom and the Dad. "'Go to the back meadow,' you said," pointing his gun at the Dad. "Very funny."

The Dad swallowed hard. "What happened?"

"'What happened?'" The cop mocked him. "What *happened*?" He was practically screaming. "What the fuck happened? That's what I want to know! You stupid fucking hippies! It's not enough that you have to take over the whole goddamn county, but then you have to—" He broke off, gasping for breath, waving the gun around again. "Fuck!" He stomped to the back of the house (all of eight steps), and flung the Dutch door open so hard it almost bounced back closed again, but then hung ajar, rattling. "How can you live in such a fucking shack! You're all animals!" He went outside, leaving the door open.

The Dad pulled at the handcuffs, but they were tight. He would hurt both himself and his wife by pulling further, so he stopped. They did manage to scoot around so that they could sit more side-by-side, still keeping an eye on the back door.

Then he thought he heard a noise in the sauna. He hoped the kids were all right, and that the lunatic cop had forgotten about them.

"Where's the Dart?" the Mom suddenly asked, quietly, a minute or so later.

Ah! That was what he had been trying to remember earlier! "I don't know." Cuffed like this, he couldn't look out the window unless they both got up, working together. He didn't want to risk it until he knew whether the cop was coming back in or not.

He knew where he had parked the Dart—in its usual spot—and scanning his memory of the meadow, he knew it wasn't one of the half-dozen cars that were left. "It's not here."

"Do you think someone took it?"

The Dad gave her a harsh look, then softened. She was just as dazed by this as he was, in fact she looked like she was on the verge of tears. They were both helpless. "I guess so," he said gently.

"Who would have taken that old pile of junk?" she asked.

"Well, it ran."

"Yes, it always started, every time." She was speaking slowly, kind of dreamily. Was she in shock? Was she even all right? The Dad looked at her again, but he didn't know how to tell if someone needed help or not. It suddenly struck him as terribly funny that, of all the times you might want to call the authorities out for help but you couldn't because you had no phone, this would be one of them. Except really, it wasn't funny at all.

The Princess listened for any more gunshots. After a while, when she only heard the evil cop yelling and then slamming the back door and stomping around, she swore her little brother to silence, and then opened the tiny sauna window. In another year, the Princess would be too big to squeeze through it. She was almost too big now, but she was desperate. With one final finger-shake at the Apricot Boy, she slithered outside and let herself silently to the ground below.

She let herself recover for a minute, hiding behind trees, taking refuge in feeling like a little girl, just a little girl who didn't know about bad things. But she couldn't pretend for long, because the scary cop was prowling around near the shed. She needed the scary cop to go away, but not before he let her parents go. The key to the handcuffs must be one of those keys on his belt. How would she get it?

She tiptoed up to the shed, hiding behind it, trying to figure out what the cop was doing. He looked in the shed, then behind it; she scooted around to the side, keeping easily ahead of him. His boots were so big, he wouldn't be able to sneak up on a deaf cow. Certainly not a Princess-spy. Of course, he didn't know there was anyone to sneak up on. He didn't know the Princess had escaped.

Then he left the shed and started nosing almost absently around in the back yard—by the old chicken coops, looking through piles of recycling, even poking at the woodpile. What was he looking for? He was clearly not even focusing on what he was doing.

Then the monster's voice found its way into her head.

He wants to kill you all, you know, it said. *He's trying to talk himself out of it, but I don't know if he will succeed.*

I thought you were my friend, she thought at it. *I thought you helped me with things. Why aren't you helping me now?*

She wasn't sure if she actually believed that the monster was her friend, but she didn't know how else to think about it.

I am nobody's friend, the monster said after a long pause. *I belong to the land.*

Tell me what to do, she pleaded.

You all have to go away. You have to go away now. It isn't safe here.

But my parents are locked up.

So you have to unlock them. And then go away. You don't belong here any more.

It was just crazy, because she had always wanted to go away, to be rescued off the Land, to be a normal girl with normal clothes, living in a town or a city, to no longer be a weird hippie child. But when the monster told her what to do like that, it made her want to resist him.

And then there was the more pressing need of dealing with the bad cop. When she hardly knew how to deal with the monster.

The cop stopped rummaging around and just stood for a long moment, staring into the middle distance. Then he suddenly straightened and started hiking up the hill-path.

The Dad racked his brain for a solution and could only come up with: *Let's not make him angry.* But of course, the deputy already seemed plenty angry. So that got modified to: *Let's not make him angrier.* But since he didn't know what had angered the man to begin with, he was kind of helpless there, too.

Anyway, the man had bumped and crashed around outside for a while, muttering to himself. The Dad heard the word 'meadow' a few times.

Something horrible must have happened in the back meadow, the Dad thought, though he had no idea what it could be. It had been totally empty when he'd checked it out last night. Obviously he'd missed something. *All the cool people were heading back there. It was the place to be.*

All the cool people… Suddenly it came back to him, what he'd wondered when the cop had made him send all the strangers away, what had gotten chased out of his head when the cop had freaked out. Where did everyone go? And where were the rest of the community members?

Now he really began to feel sick. He turned to say something to his wife, but the dull look in her eyes stopped him. No, she didn't need any more shocks.

The cop had been gone again for a while, though the Dad had no idea how long. He struggled against the handcuffs again, just to do something, but of course that did no good.

"Princess?" the Mom suddenly called out.

The Dad turned to look at her again, as they listened to the silence in response.

"Princess? Honey?"

"She's not here," came the Apricot Boy's muffled voice through the door.

"Oh my god." The Mom started to struggle to her feet. The Dad tried to help and not hinder, but it was awkward, handcuffed together as they were. Soon they managed it, and the Mom was on the door, yanking at the handle. "It won't open!"

"He took the key," the Dad said.

She banged on the door with her free hand. "Damn it damn it *damn it!*" She gasped for breath, tears streaming down her face. "Let me in! Where are my children? We have to get them out of here!"

"Shh, honey, calm down," the Dad tried to soothe her. "We're doing everything we can." *Which is nothing. And she knows it. And you know it too.*

They heard the Apricot Boy start to cry on the other side of the door.

Deputy Brooks climbed the mountain trail that led straight back from the house. He climbed quickly but not effortlessly. His breath came in ragged gasps, and sweat drenched his polyester uniform. He didn't notice and he didn't care. He just needed to get as far away as possible. As far away from what had happened to his brother.

Some small, irrelevant part of his mind was aware that he was just bumbling around in a stunned panic. That he was not truly running away from anything; that he would have to return to the scene, convince Dispatch to call in more backup officers, never mind that it was their day off. But he just…couldn't. Not right now. Cliff was dead. Dead as a man could be, face down in the dirt behind the back meadow, poisoned by mushrooms.

The deputy clutched his gun as he climbed. Not that there had been any love lost between him and his sorry-ass brother. But that didn't mean he wanted him dead. He'd given him a piece of his mind for hanging around with hippies, yesterday. The last time they'd talked. Forever. He'd threatened to kick him out, make him get a job, a place of his own. Straighten his ass out. Cut his goddamn hair. *He can't be dead*, Deputy Brooks thought.

He turned a corner and movement caught his eye. He paused, looking. Was someone there?

The deputy left the trail, pushed through some trees, and suddenly he was staring at the biggest, lushest pot garden he'd ever seen. The plants grew almost as tall as he was, so it took him a moment to notice the woman. She was bent over, pulling plants out by the roots. A plump, naked child was with her, holding a bag. A crudely drawn map was on the ground next to the child.

His brain was not working like it should. He knew it wasn't. His finger was on the trigger, gun pointed directly at the woman. Something in his brain warned him that this was wrong, this was not why he was up here. But it was hard to think. He itched to pull the trigger, but could not understand why. He gave a strangled sound, resisting…himself?

The woman jerked her head up, frozen with a fragrant, resinous plant in her hand. Her gaze fixed on the gun.

There was too much that was wrong here, too much that didn't make sense. He started to lower the gun.

And why was it so cold?

The deputy heard a noise behind him, and his stomach froze in fear.

CHAPTER 13

The Princess followed the deputy at a stealthy distance, hurrying up the familiar path that led past the hidden pot garden to the top of the mountain, from which she could oversee her entire realm, along with the neighboring realms. Before she reached the pot garden, she heard noises: he'd stopped, and something was happening. Rustling, thumping. She froze, stock-still on the path. Should she duck into the bushes?

"Hey!" she heard. The cop's loud voice, raised in fear or anger. Had he spotted her?

There was another thump and a crash, and then silence.

She stood motionless for a minute. The silence continued. She had just started to creep forward when suddenly—*bang, bang!*—two gunshots in rapid succession, and a shout, ending in a strangled cry. The Princess clapped a hand over her mouth, stifling a squeal of terror.

Silence reasserted itself, though the echoes of the gunshots hurt her ears.

She stood still for so long, straining to listen. Her legs started to tremble, and her heart pounded. But she heard nothing further from the pot garden. At last, she began to steal forward once more. Through the oak and madrone trees, she made out the barest outline of the bright green firs surrounding and obscuring the garden. She paused, still hearing nothing. So she crept closer and closer, leaving the main path, approaching the garden.

Whatever she found, she knew it would not be good. Even before the gunshots, she'd known that. The monster hadn't said anything in her head for a while, not since the deputy had been rummaging around the yard. It worried her. There was some comfort in hearing from him, as if what he said made sense. As if she had any control over him.

She padded closer, avoiding fallen leaves on the dirt path. It grew colder in among the thick trees…no, colder even than that. A familiar coldness.

Hello? she thought at the monster. It did not respond.

She smelled the heady fragrance of the pot, and something else with it. It was too strong, too much. Her stomach gave a little turn, and she remembered barfing last night, all that gross spaghetti in the pee-pan.

I don't think I like the smell of pot anymore, she thought.

It felt like the wrong sort of magical realm in here, under the dark trees. Not a fabled kingdom, not a Princess's safe domain. This was the underworld, the spooky side, the land of the demons and monsters and ogres.

Run away! her mind insisted. Not the monster's voice. Just her own thoughts.

She forced herself to creep forward.

At last, the garden came into view. Some of the big, gorgeous green marijuana plants stood tall, but many of them lay on the ground, yanked rudely from the soil, strewn about. The Princess swallowed another shriek as she saw the dead bodies. Morning Star and Evening Star. Evening Star had a big pot plant in her hand; her eyes stared blankly at the sky. There was alarm on her face, the blank eyes, the wide-open startled mouth. Her shirt was wet with blood, right in the middle of the chest.

Morning Star lay next to her, her own naked chest covered in blood. She held a paper grocery bag; a sheet of paper lay on the ground beside her.

The cop shot Morning Star and Evening Star! The Princess trembled, swallowing a fearful lump in her throat. It smelled horrible in here. Like the dead goats.

Where was the cop?

She nearly stumbled over him. He lay about three feet from them at the entrance to the garden, half-hidden by a pile of uprooted plants. His throat bled from double holes; his dead face was a frozen mask of fear and anguish.

Much of his body was laced with weird white ropy stuff. His right arm was rigid by his side, clutching the gun. The Princess was strangely fascinated by the dark, cold-looking thing. She had never seen a gun before today, except in pictures. Somehow, it seemed like the most evil thing here.

The Princess took a couple of steps forward and sighed, letting her breath out slowly, heart still pounding. The cop was dead. That was good. But what was all this white stuff?

Stepping around the cop, she walked over to Morning Star. A few leaves had fallen out of the bag the little girl clutched, but it was mostly empty. The Princess leaned in to look at the wound in her chest, then pulled back, shuddering. She had never liked the girl, but she wouldn't wish this on anyone.

Shivering, she went back to the cop's body. She leaned over him, reaching out to touch the white ropes. They were very sticky. She pulled her finger back in alarm, and the stuff tried to hold her, stretching out like bubble gum before finally letting her go. Her finger felt funny afterwards, and she rubbed it on the palm of her hand, but the feeling wouldn't come off.

His keys were on his belt. She needed to get the keys so she could unlock her mom and dad. The white stuff was all over him, though. She took a step back into the woods. *A stick. I have to find a stick.* Her thoughts seemed to come slowly, sluggishly, as if from a great distance.

She looked around the ground. She found a stick.

Back at the body, she poked the stick at the white ropes. It clung, of course, but she was able to shove enough of it aside, freeing the belt. She tossed the stick aside. Then, trying to control her squeamishness, she reached down to unhook the heavy ring of keys. It jingled as she picked it up.

Under the sound of the jingling, the Princess thought she heard something else. She wheeled around, but nothing was there.

She turned back to look at the garden one last time. *Think.* Was there anything else she needed here?

Then she heard the sound again. She whipped back around and saw, through the trees, a large, black shape hurrying up the path.

"Sauron!" She laughed, relief pouring through her. How the dog had scared her! Silly dog.

The creature bounded into sight, and it wasn't Sauron.

The Mom and the Dad had gotten themselves first into and then out of a panic. They were still handcuffed together, standing at the door to the sauna. After they had both banged on the door to no avail, the Mom had had the idea of trying to find something else to stick in the lock, something that might mimic the skeleton key.

She rummaged around in the kitchen drawer with her uncuffed hand and found a paring knife. "That's too thick," the Dad said, but she shrugged and tried it anyway. It didn't work.

Back in the drawer, she rejected a fork, a bamboo chopstick, and other various spoons and spatulas and gizmos.

"What's that?" the Dad asked, pointing with his free hand.

"Huh." She pulled out a little sharp-ended implement, a little ring at the opposite end. "This might work."

"What's it for?"

She snickered. "Turkey. After it's stuffed, you do it up with these. I didn't know we still had them."

"Wow. Okay, let's give it a try."

They moved back to the door, and she stuck the pointy end in the lock. After a lot of fiddling and some choice swearing, it released.

The Apricot Boy sidled out, still wiping away tears. He reached up to take the Mom's hand.

"Where's your sister?" the Dad asked gently.

"She went out." The Apricot Boy pointed at the open window.

"Oh god," the Mom breathed, veering toward panic all over again. "Where?"

"Out." The Apricot Boy shrugged.

"We have to find her!"

"We will," her husband said, his voice aggressively calm.

She gave him a look, over the boy's head. *Don't freak him out too,* the Dad's eyes seemed to suggest.

Fuck you, she thought, biting her lip. But she nodded. "I don't suppose that turkey lacer opens handcuffs."

"I'm happy to try."

She sighed. "Sure."

He began fiddling with the lacer, one-handed, clearly getting nowhere. The Mom fought down her panic as best she could. Tried not to think about being handcuffed together, with an insane armed cop prowling the Land, and their daughter loose out there…somewhere…

The Princess stood frozen, the deputy's keys in her hand, staring at the thing that came around the corner. It was the size of Sauron, but it was not Sauron. It was actually rather hard to see, half in shadows, as though it was dark out. She tried to focus on it, but couldn't quite make her brain believe it, or grab onto it. It kept slipping away, visually.

It reminded her of nothing so much as a gigantic black spider.

Spiders were the worst things in the whole wide world. The Princess *hated* spiders.

I am your worst fear. Did she hear that, or just think it?

All the seeing and thinking and reacting and maybe-hearing took place in a heartbeat, the amount of time it took for the thing to move up the path and stop before her. It didn't move like a spider or a dog. It kind of…became somewhere, when it had been somewhere else before.

Even though that didn't make any sense.

The Princess was so frightened, so completely scared out of her wits, that it was as if she had crossed all the way through scared and had come back into not-scared. Like fear was a circle, and she'd made a full turn.

"You're the monster," she said, voice utterly calm.

The blurry-edged creature drew up and surrounded her, without exactly moving. She felt that it was gazing at her, though she could see no eyes. Didn't spiders have lots of eyes? It was really hard to look at.

I am, came the familiar voice in her head. Didn't this body speak?

Was it actually real?

"What happens next? What do I do?" The Princess still did not move. The dead cop lay at her feet. She gripped the heavy ring of keys in her sweaty hand.

The monster-spider-thing stood motionless before her, around her. *You should go.*

"Go where?"

Just go. It's what you've always wanted, isn't it?

"Sort of?" Had she? Yes and no. "Are you going to stop killing people if we do?"

Maybe.

"My parents—" the Princess started.

You cannot tell them about me, you know. Or about the dead people. You just have to take them and go.

"Why can't I tell them?"

If anyone finds out about the dead people, then more bad cops will come. Your parents will be arrested and sent to jail forever. You and your brother will be orphans.

The Princess stared hard at the thing, still not feeling the fear she knew was there, in her stomach. The monster seemed even less real than it had a minute ago. It was almost as if—

Nah. She shook her head. Of course it was real.

As if in answer, it grew more substantial, more in focus.

Or it's not real, she thought, experimenting. It faded slightly.

"You're not real!" she shouted at it.

Of course I'm real, the voice came in her head. *If I'm not real, who is doing the killing?*

"The cop killed Morning Star and Evening Star."

And who killed the cop?

"I am the Princess of this realm and I say you're not real!" She put her hands on her hips, trying to seem strong. The ring of keys slipped out of her sweaty hand and jangled to the ground at her feet, startling her. Fear spiked through her heart.

The spider-monster suddenly sharpened. Now she could see its many eyes, terrible and glassy, and its many legs, hairy, shiny. It reared up, waving its first two feet in her face. It smelled gross, like the back seat of the car after a long trip to town on a hot day, or something left in the cold-box too long.

That mundane thought steadied the Princess and allowed another, even more rational thought to wander through her brain. *It's only here when you're afraid of it.* So she stood taller, not flinching in the face of the monster. "I'm not afraid of you because you're not real."

The spider faded noticeably. *I am real and I will kill you all!* The voice just about shrieked in her head, but the Princess now understood the game. She smiled.

"Poof," she said, flicking her fingers at it. It faded further. Emboldened, she took a step forward. The fuzzy monster faded even more and seemed to cringe back.

The Princess picked up the keys, and started down the path. The spider vanished before she had taken two steps. As she walked through the space where it had been, the air was very cold.

The Princess hurried down the hill and into the house. Her mom and dad and the Apricot Boy were sitting on the floor, looking dazed and lost.

"There you are." Her mother turned to look at her, eyes wide and anxious.

"Here I am." The Princess smiled at them. She had faced down the monster and now she was going to save her family. She closed the Dutch door behind her. "We have to go away now," she announced.

Her dad started at this. "We can't."

"We have to," she said. "We have to go now."

"We can't go away, honey," he said in that fake-patient voice that parents use when they say things that mean no, and they don't want you to have a tantrum about it. "The cop wants us to stay here." He lifted his handcuffed arm up, along with the Mom's, of course.

The Princess held up the keys. "Here. We have to go away now."

Her dad reached out with his free hand and grabbed the keys. "Where did you get these?"

Her mom leaned forward too, her eyes shining. "Where is the policeman, honey?"

She couldn't tell them the cop was dead. The monster, who didn't exist, told her she couldn't tell.

The Dad fumbled with the keys, finding the one that unlocked the handcuffs. It was awkward with his left hand, but he finally identified it, then jammed it at the lock.

The Princess reached out to take the keys from him. "Here, I can do it," she said, quietly, unlocking the handcuffs.

Her parents pulled their hands away from each other gratefully. Her dad massaged his wrist.

"Oh my god," her mom said quietly. "That feels so good." She reached out to take the Princess in her arms.

"Okay." The Princess squirmed away from her mom's clutches. "Now we have to go away."

"Honey, stop saying that, please, just for a minute." The Dad glanced at the Mom quickly, then away. "You didn't answer your mother: where is the cop?"

The Princess shrugged, mouth tightly shut. The monster had said she couldn't tell about any of the bodies. But then that gave her an idea. "He's out there somewhere, I don't know, with his gun, so we have to get away."

"Where did you get these keys?"

"I found them."

Her parents looked at each other for a moment. The Princess couldn't read their expressions. That bothered her. Then the Dad said softly, "We can't just leave the others."

The Princess stared at him, wide-eyed. "Yes we can! We have to go!"

"Now, stop that," her mom said, but gently. She frowned and massaged her wrist where the metal cuffs had left an angry red mark. "Your father is right. We'll go find the others, quickly, and then we'll all leave together."

The Princess was near tears. She hadn't seen every single Land member dead, but where else could they be? But she couldn't tell her parents that. Whether the monster was real or not didn't matter: her parents wouldn't believe her. They would insist on seeing for themselves. "We *have* to go away." She could see they weren't going to be convinced.

The Dad looked at his daughter, his mouth grim. The Princess waited. The monster wasn't going to stop now. It had let them live here for a year. Maybe it had taken a while to wake up to their presence. But now it had, and it most certainly didn't like all the extra people, or especially the evil people. So now they had to go. Everyone. It was perfectly simple and perfectly clear to the Princess. She wouldn't get away from the monster so easily the next time. It would wear her down, would wear them all down.

Even though it wasn't real.

(But who killed the cop?)

The Dad shrugged, frowning. "We're not going to go away without the others, honey. I know you're scared, but we have a responsibility." He turned away from her, his mouth set. She knew the argument was over.

Well, she had made the monster vanish. By not believing in it. Maybe they had a little time. She just had to hold onto its unreality.

Her parents whispered together for a moment. Mom clearly disagreed with Dad, but then turned to the Princess. "We're going to go out and look around. I want you to take your brother upstairs, and don't go outside or open the door to anyone. Okay?"

"No! Don't go out there!" But her mom's face had that same closed, stubborn look. Blinking back tears and trying to swallow over the lump in her throat, she took her brother's hand and led him to the loft.

She set him in his crib and whispered for him to be quiet, then crawled back to the edge of the loft and perched on her belly.

Her parents were talking quietly as they put their shoes on. "They'll be safe in the house," Dad was saying.

"No they won't!" her mom whispered. "The doors don't even lock. I think she's right."

"Since when does a ten-year-old girl call the shots?" The Dad's voice was high, almost whiny. "We'll just glance around, then we'll go."

Silence for a minute, then the Mom sighed. "Let's just go check out their tent."

"Okay, fine," the Dad said. "But where's the cop? How did she get those keys?"

There was another minute of silence. The Princess inched forward, straining to hear better. Then the Mom said, "I guess we gotta find out what the fuck is going on. This is too weird."

The Dad sighed. "All right, then. Let's go."

After shutting Sauron and Galadriel in the shed, the Dad and the Mom walked up the back path. As they got to Billy Goat's tent, the Mom glanced at the Dad. He nodded, and they approached, wary.

They paused outside it for a moment, listening. But they heard nothing. Finally, the Dad lifted the tent flap, and they both peered in. Just jumbled-up blankets. Too much stuff. Too few toys.

The Dad let the flap fall, and they walked out to the back meadow.

It was no longer pristine. "Looks like someone had a party here," the Dad said, in an attempt at levity.

"Right." The Mom didn't smile. She started across the meadow, looking at the trash—beer bottles, paper plates, someone's halter top. The Dad followed, letting her meander about, letting her lead.

At Bliss's gravesite, the Mom paused. "Have people been walking on this?" she asked, aghast.

"Looks like." The Dad knelt down near the little sign. "Someone picked mushrooms, I think."

"God, I hope no one ate them."

"Yeah."

The Mom shrugged, holding her arms as if she was cold. "It feels weird here. I've never liked this meadow."

They both stood silently a moment, listening. They did not see Weed's body in the shadows at the edge of the woods.

"Well, there's no one here," the Dad said. "I guess we keep looking."

"Right." They turned and walked back across the meadow, rejoining the path.

When they got to the cutoff path, they stopped and looked at each other again. "Well, where the fuck *is* everyone?" the Dad asked. The silence around them was deeply unsettling.

"Where's the cop?" the Mom asked.

The Dad shrugged and shivered.

"And where's our car?" the Mom asked, very quietly.

"I wish I knew." He thought a moment. "Well, we can hot-wire one of the other ones, if it comes to that."

"Right." She glanced at the path. "Well, shall we?"

"Do you really think anyone's up here?" He wondered if he had mentioned the pot garden to anyone last night. He'd been awfully high, maybe he had actually lost his mind and done so. There was a path, anyway, most of the way to it.

"We have to check."

They quickly joined up with the mountain path. They walked in silence for a time, listening for signs of anyone—friend or cop. "Some party," the Dad said, quietly, testing the words out.

"Yeah. There were a lot of weird drugs going around last night," she said. "I think I might have been dosed."

Then she stopped abruptly on the path. Had she heard something?

The Dad almost ran into her, then stopped, his hand on the small of her back. "What is it?"

"Shh," she said. They both strained to hear, but there was no sound. "I thought I heard something over there." She pointed to the thick woods to their right.

He stared into the trees. "I don't see anything. I don't hear anything either."

"Hello," she ventured. Then whispered to the Dad, "I just wish I knew where that cop was."

"Maybe we shouldn't call out."

She nodded. They waited a moment longer, and then she whispered, "Well, there's nothing there now."

They started up the trail again. The woods grew darker and thicker around them, and the trail became steeper, and she realized she hardly knew where she was. She never came up here, not since they'd first found the pot garden site. But god, it was cold.

Suddenly a darkness overcame her. She cried out as pain flashed through her body, and then she knew nothing.

Fear spiked through the Dad's chest as he faced the—what was it? He'd had the anticipated threat so firmly in mind, it took him a moment to realize that this wasn't the cop.

Before him on the trail, bent over his wife, was a darkness. There was no other way to describe it; he could see no detail. It turned his eyes away as he struggled to look at it. But he couldn't let it take her. "Stop!" He leapt forward to save his wife.

He heard a low noise. He still couldn't see anything, almost couldn't see where he was going. He focused on her. He had to get her away from here, away from the thing.

Pain stabbed through his right leg, and he barely saw a piece of the thing retreat. "Shit!" He grabbed at his leg, which felt warm. He was dizzy, but his eyes never left the Mom. He had to get her. That was all that mattered. He staggered forward and reached for his wife.

The darkness overtook him.

He woke up, lying on his back on the path, staring up at the dark trees. Everything hurt. His right leg was a swarm of pain, and his left arm was throbbing. He tried to move his arm, and it obeyed, but sent more shocks of pain up to his shoulder.

He pushed himself up with his right arm, then looked around. He avoided looking at his leg. Something told him he didn't want to see it.

The Mom lay on the path in front of him, motionless. "Oh god..." He crawled to her, pulling himself along with his good arm.

She was curled up in a fetal position. He touched her shoulder tenderly. It was warm, and yielding. Was she alive?

He tried to shift her onto her back so he could see her face. She was hard to move at first, and he didn't want to hurt her, but he managed.

Her color was very pale, but then she took a tiny breath.

He almost fainted with relief. He sat back hard on his tailbone, in the dirt. Then he forced himself to look at his right leg.

It was bleeding badly from the meaty part of the thigh muscle, just above the knee. His jeans were torn and soaked through with blood. Through the hole, he could see the wound. He quickly turned his face away.

His gaze rested on his left arm, which was also bleeding, though not as badly. Looking at it seemed to make it throb.

"Oh god..." Another wave of sick dizziness overtook him, and again he lost consciousness.

In the house, the Princess waited. She pleaded silently in her head with the monster: *I tried, I did everything I could! When they come back, we'll go! Please don't hurt them!*

But the monster didn't speak to her. Because it didn't exist.

So she waited.

When the Dad woke up for the second time, his arm had stopped hurting quite so much. His leg, well, he couldn't think about that. He had to get himself and his wife out of there, had to stop passing out. How long had he been unconscious?

The Mom was still breathing quietly. The darkness, whatever it was, was gone for now. Maybe he'd only been out a few seconds. He had no idea. He just knew it—the thing, the threat—could come back.

He pulled himself excruciatingly to his knees, fought off a spell of dizziness, and then got to his feet. Still avoiding looking at his leg, he leaned down over his wife. "Honey. Wake up, honey." He shook her gently. Her head lolled, and she did not wake up.

He would have to lift her, carry her down the hill. He couldn't wait for her to wake up. She wasn't a large woman, but, unresponsive as she was, it was a challenge. He got around behind her, worked his hands under her shoulders, and tried lifting her from under the armpits, but it was awkward at best, and he was so very weak. When he almost dropped her to the ground, he sat back down beside her and tried to catch his breath.

He had to get her to the house.

He struggled to his feet and tried again. After a good deal of experimentation, he finally settled on a sort of half-drag, half-carry, holding her under the armpits, cradling her head against his chest. Walking backwards down the path, he could pull her along with her feet dragging.

After he had gone a few yards, he had to stop to rest. He leaned against a tree, again out of breath. Sweat poured down his face, dripping down his neck and onto his shirt, getting some on his wife. He didn't let go of her to wipe it off.

He realized he had been hoping against hope that all this maneuvering would wake her up. But it didn't.

"Okay, buddy, carry on," he said to himself. He pushed off the tree and moved a few more yards down the path.

Each time he stopped to rest, he strained to hear anything of their attacker. He wished he'd gotten a better look at it. Some kind of animal. It was obviously rabid, or it wouldn't be attacking people like this. Wild animals were supposed to be wary of humans. There was not supposed to be anything dangerous in these woods.

He pressed on as much as his strength would bear. Blood dripped down his leg, and he almost passed out again several more times. He forced himself to stay conscious.

Finally, after what seemed like a thousand years, he saw the house. He stumbled backwards along the path though his muscles screamed in protest and his breath came in ragged gasps. He just about fell the final few yards but made it to the door. He heard the dogs in the shed, whining to get out, scratching at the door. Too bad. He'd deal with them later.

He laid his wife down on the stoop as gently as he could, and then leaned against the door, panting, too spent to even reach up for the handle.

The door opened, and the Dad almost fell over. He grabbed at the door frame, and a shock of pain knifed through his arm. The Princess stood there, eyes wide. "You're hurt!"

"Help me get her in the house," the Dad said.

The Princess started trying to help carry her in. She did manage to shift her a few inches, and then the Dad recovered enough to help. They settled her on the braided rug with her head on one of the big floor pillows, then the Dad collapsed back onto another pillow. He closed his eyes for a moment, then leaned forward to look at the Mom.

She was breathing. She was muddy and covered in blood, but at least she was still breathing. He'd made it to safety.

But it was so dark in the house. "Sweetie, can you light a lamp for me?" he asked his daughter.

"Okay." She found the matches, checked to make sure the kerosene well was full, turned the wick expertly, and lit their brightest lantern. She picked the lamp up with both hands and carried it carefully over to her dad.

"Thanks," he said, rolling painfully to his side, pushing himself up with his unwounded arm. He set the lamp on the floor beside the Mom, trying to assess the damage. But other than the fact that she was unconscious, he couldn't see anything wrong with her. All the blood seemed to have come from him.

"You're hurt," the Princess said again. She looked at his leg with a very serious expression on her face.

"Yes, and we need to bandage that, but your mother is hurt too."

"She just looks like she's sleeping. But you're hurt."

"Where's your brother?" the Dad suddenly remembered.

"Upstairs. I left him in his crib." The Princess got up and went to the sink. She got a clean dishrag out of the cabinet and ran water on it. She brought over a bottle of Dr. Bronner's Pure-Castile Peppermint Soap, which they used as everything—dish soap, bath soap, shampoo, dog wash. "We have to fix this," she said, pointing to his leg.

"All right." He surrendered, lying back on the pillow.

The Dad struggled to keep from screaming as she dabbed at the wound, pulling aside torn bits of his jeans in the process. The excruciating pain kept him from wondering, for the longest time, why she hadn't seemed surprised or curious at what had happened to them in the woods.

Finally, she got another cloth and wrapped his leg tightly. It was still bleeding, but more slowly now. It didn't immediately soak through the cloth. "There," she said, still serious but clearly proud of her work.

He closed his eyes and whispered, "Thank you, sweetheart."

Then he must have lost a little time, because he woke up again. He couldn't tell how much later it was, but now the Apricot Boy was downstairs as well, and the Princess was feeding him slices of cheese.

She looked over at the Dad as he stirred. "We have to go now."

He sighed and closed his eyes again. His head was swimming, and he was having a hard time making sense of things.

"If you eat something, you might feel better," the Princess said.

He shook his head. "I can't eat."

She brought him one of the cheese slices. He stared at it in her hand, then finally took it and tried to nibble at a corner.

A wave of nausea quickly flowed over him, but then it passed. Maybe she was right. No, of course she was right. He took another nibble and swallowed slowly.

They needed to get help, that was what they needed to do. Damn their stupid decision to not have a phone all the way out here in the middle of nowhere! His parents, and hers especially, had objected strenuously to this, but he and the Mom had stood firm. There was no point in doing a half-assed job of dropping out of society, it was all or nothing.

A phone would come in real handy right now, though.

"We have to go now." It seemed like the millionth time she'd said this, and the Dad didn't know what to say to her.

"We're safe for now here in the house, honey." He reached up to tousle her hair. "And our car is gone, and I can't drive anyway." He nodded at his bandaged leg. "And your mom needs to wake up too. We'll go soon, I promise."

"No! It has to be now! We've already waited too long!" She pulled away from him and ran for the front door.

The Princess panicked. She ran for the front door and threw it open. She had to get out of there and her dad would not help so she would just go by herself! She would run right down the driveway and out onto the road and off the Land forever!

"Stop!" her dad yelled before she'd even gotten out the door. She didn't stop.

"Jesus H…" she heard behind her, and then a groan.

She ran down the steps and into the front meadow, looking around wildly. What could she do? She couldn't run all the way to town. She couldn't even drive.

Then she wheeled to a stop, noticing the abandoned cop car.

CHAPTER 14

The radio! Cop cars had radios! The Princess could call for help! Driving wasn't the only thing cars were good for.

She yanked on the door handle, but it was locked. She hesitated a moment, glancing back at the house. But they really had to *go*, and now. She darted into the meadow and found a big rock that someone had made a campfire ring with.

Her first blow at the window was unsuccessful. But then she took a deep breath, steeled herself, and hit it as hard as she could. The glass shattered everywhere and she dropped the rock, startled but pleased.

She reached inside and opened the door, trying not to cut herself on the broken glass that rimmed the window.

She carefully brushed away as much glass as she could from the seat. Then she sat down behind the wheel, trying to figure out all the complicated devices. That's when she saw a tangle of wires and the broken thing on the ground, and then she remembered that the cop had smashed the radio. The cop had been strange and scary from the moment he arrived—scarier than cops generally were.

She shivered as she thought she heard a low chuckle. She whipped her head around, looking out the windshield at the empty meadow, then back at the woods behind her. But no one was there. Was it the monster in her head again?

She took a deep breath and thought to the monster, *We're going to leave. I'm trying to get us to leave, you know I am.*

There was no answer.

Well, the radio was broken, but what else was there in the car? She scanned the dashboard, pushing buttons randomly, pulling at everything that looked like it came away and could be useful, that could perhaps communicate with the outside world. Did the car have to be on? She had no idea.

She still had the keys in her jeans pocket, the ones that she had used to unlock her parents from the handcuffs. She'd watched her parents turn on cars enough times; it didn't seem too hard. She couldn't tell which key was the right one. So she tried each key in the ignition, but finally had to admit to herself that none of them was a car key.

She sighed and leaned back against the seat. Her panic had slowly ebbed, but she couldn't call anyone, and she couldn't very well run away by herself. She needed to help her parents. They were both hurt. And she couldn't leave her brother. So she climbed out of the car and walked slowly back to the house.

The Dad lay on the floor, eyes closed, fighting off another spell of dizziness. He knew he should go after the Princess, but he could hardly move. The Apricot Boy played with his little cars over by the front window, oddly quiet, even for him. The Mom had not moved. She was still breathing, anyway.

I have to pull myself together. With a colossal effort, using his good arm, he heaved himself up to a sitting position. He anticipated the dizziness and didn't succumb to it. When it passed, he crawled to his wife, kneeling on the floor beside her with most of his weight on his good leg.

He picked up her hand and caressed it. He touched her face lightly and whispered her name. She moaned a little, or sighed, but didn't wake up. It was too creepy, her being unconscious like this. He pushed away thoughts of what it might mean: he could not afford any more panic now.

Maybe a glass of water would help. Assuming he could get her to drink it. Again, he remembered movies he'd seen, TV shows. He could lift up her head gently, touch the glass to her lips, letting in the merest drop. She would taste it, her eyelids would flutter open. Maybe she'd give a delicate little cough. She would look up at him, see him bending tenderly over her…

He crawled to the edge of the room, then pulled himself to his feet using the cabinet handles and the edge of the counter. He knew the Apricot Boy was watching him silently. Too bad the boy wasn't a little bigger. The Dad opened the cupboard where they kept what passed for their set of dishes and serving bowls—mismatched pottery plates, mugs, and some garage-sale Tupperware—and there, propped up right in front of the stack of dishes on the bottom shelf, was a note. Addressed to his wife.

He pulled the note down and stared at it. It was just a folded-over piece of paper. He didn't recognize the handwriting.

He looked back over at her. She was still unconscious.

The glass of water forgotten, he slowly opened the note.

I am sorry babe, the note read. *I have to go away, I no you understand. I am sorry to have to take your car but you no my bike dont work no more. I will leave it in town at the auto body store and sumbody from the party can give you a ride to town and you can get it. Im sorry.*

I love you so much and I no you dont love me as much thoug you seem to like me pretty well. But I saw your face today in the woods when you left me after we did it and I new I had to go away.

Please dont try to find me, I am long gone. Tell my brother and Astrid goodbye too.

Love, Jr.

The Dad folded the note and looked back at his wife. She still lay on the floor, head propped on the pillow.

Suddenly he felt dizzy all over again. His leg throbbed, and he couldn't catch his breath. He reached a hand out and steadied himself on the counter. The room grew blurry, then reset. He gulped in a breath of air. It tasted different. Flatter. The Apricot Boy still played with his cars, murmuring quietly to himself across the room.

The front door opened, and there was the Princess. She looked at her father, and her mother, and her brother. "Can we leave now?"

"Yes," he said.

The Princess looked closely at her father. He stood by the sink, holding on to the edge with one hand. In his other hand was a piece of paper.

But he was on his feet and had agreed to go, and that was the important thing. So now they had to figure out how to move Mom.

"How do we wake her up?" she asked her father, at the same time as she sent a silent appeal to the monster. *Please, wake her up.* But the monster still did not respond.

"I can't," her dad said, but then he seemed to remember something. "Wait, I was going to try this." He reached for a cup from the cupboard, but he had the piece of paper in his hand, and he couldn't pick up a cup and steady himself on the edge of the counter and still hold the paper. She watched him puzzle through this and eventually set the paper on the counter. He was moving very slowly and deliberately, much more so than he had earlier, even though he seemed to be feeling better in his leg. She didn't know what was the matter with him. And she didn't want to ask.

Despite everything, she wanted to trust him. She wanted him to be in charge. She had always wanted to trust the adults she loved, but sometimes they didn't understand the situation. Sometimes they just made things worse. She had already learned that no matter how much you wanted to trust somebody, you only had yourself to rely on.

If her dad didn't start seriously hurrying and stop being so paralyzed with fear, he could easily make things worse. The Princess understood about monsters. If you were afraid of them, then that made them happy and they wanted to hurt you, because they were evil and that's what evil monsters did. Fear gave them more power. Even someone who hadn't faced down a monster knew that. It was in all the books.

But maybe that was something you forgot when you got older. Maybe her dad didn't know that any more. Even though he read the books to her, maybe he wasn't paying enough attention when he read.

All the more reason to try to convince him even harder.

The Dad poured some water into the cup and carried it over to the Mom, moving slowly and carefully. "Help me give her some." He reached out for his daughter.

She knelt on the other side of her mom. "How are you going to get her to drink it? She's asleep."

"I don't know—I'm going to try with just a drop." He reached under her head and lifted it a little. She moaned and turned her face away from him slightly. The Dad and the Princess froze.

"Is she waking up?" The Princess leaned in close.

"I don't know—she's done that before." They waited, but she didn't make any more sound. "Here, let's try some. You hold her head steady."

The Princess complied as best she could, and the Dad lifted the glass to the Mom's lips. They were slightly parted, but when he touched them with the water, it dribbled down the side of her mouth. A drop or two fell onto her neck.

"Stop, you're getting her wet!" the Princess said. The Dad pulled the cup back and set it down, still slowly.

The Princess's panic started to rise again. She fought it back. It was very weird to be telling her dad what to do, and she didn't like that. She returned to what she knew. She knew that they needed to go, and soon, but she didn't know how to wake up the Mom. Their car was gone, and nobody could drive anyway. So they had to walk off the Land and go for help, but it would be very hard without the Mom awake.

If only there was an easier way to carry— The Princess leapt to her feet. "I know! My wagon! We can fill it with pillows and make her a traveling bed!"

Her father looked back at her, puzzled and vague. "It's not that big."

But the Princess was already out the back door.

She ran out to the shed where she had stored her little red wagon. She had been so excited to get it for Christmas last year, even though it was obviously not new. New toys were scarce on the Land. The wagon's paint was still pretty fresh, the wheels all went around smoothly, and the inside was hardly scratched up at all.

But she had gotten kind of bored with it after a while. The Land wasn't the greatest place for something as big and clunky as a wagon. Her little-village toys were so vastly smaller; it was all out of scale. It would get jammed up if she went over rough ground, so she had had to stay on the driveway or the road. She obviously couldn't take it up into a tree, or down to the river, or really anywhere fun. So after a while she had stashed it in the shed. She had stopped thinking about it by the time spring rolled around.

Now she opened the shed door. Sauron and Galadriel came rushing out, just about knocking her over in their excitement to be set free. She wondered if she should try to catch them, but they had gotten away already anyway. She just hoped they would be safe. She stepped into the shed and found the wagon easily enough, even though it was dark inside. She pulled on the dusty wagon handle as the door slid shut, leaving her in complete darkness.

The wagon was lodged between stacks of other stuff, which she could no longer see; it didn't come loose. She pulled again. It budged a bit, but still wouldn't come.

Okay, it was really creepy in the dark. She went and opened the door, jammed a rock under it to prop it open, and went back inside.

That helped, but now that she had begun to feel creeped out, she couldn't push the feeling away. And it was still pretty dark in the shed, even with the bit of light coming in the doorway.

Stop thinking about it, just do it, she told herself. She grabbed the metal handle of the wagon and pulled. Again, it moved a little, but it was really jammed. "You stupid thing! Come on!" she yelled at it, and pulled again, as hard as she could.

You catch more flies with honey than with vinegar, the voice in her head said, surprising the pee out of her, almost literally.

"What?" She tried to stifle her sudden terror.

Save your anger for those who actually mean you harm.

"You do not mean to harm me," she said boldly. "You are my friend."

I am nobody's friend. The voice was more sinister than she'd ever heard before. *I told you to leave.*

"I am! That's why I'm getting the wagon!"

So you do believe in me after all.

She gave the wagon a huge tug, and it came a little bit more loose before catching on something again. Unfortunately, it also started knocking loose some boxes that were next to it, shoving the wagon sideways. The impact of the shifting boxes made her hand slip off the handle, and she fell down hard onto her butt, on the dirt floor of the shed.

Then the door closed.

She bit back a scream and took a huge deep breath. It was very dark now. She took another breath and very calmly said, "Stop that. You're trying to scare me."

I think I am scaring you.

"Why do you want to do that? I've been trying very hard to get us off the Land. We're going now, honest, for real."

That's not what it looks like to me.

"I'm getting this wagon so we can leave."

You had the right idea earlier. You ran out the front door. Why did you stop?

"My dad, my mom…my brother. They have to come with me. I couldn't go alone."

You could leave your family here.

"No way!" She yelled louder than she meant to, out of guilt from having considered doing just that.

They're only going to get in trouble with the police anyway, when they find out what happened here. What happened to all the people, and the cop.

"No way!" The Princess shivered. "My brother won't get in trouble. He's only a baby."

Your parents are going to be thrown in jail for the rest of their lives.

"No, they're not! We're all going to leave! And you're going to let us leave, because I'm telling you to."

There was a moment of silence in the Princess's head. She breathed heavily but tried to be as still as she could.

But then she heard, very quietly—it almost might have been her imagination—*You do believe in me, don't you?*

She sat very still, trying to calm her breath. She had hurt its feelings, up on the mountain, when she had made it go poof. "Of course I do. I always have. You know that." She moved her hand around in the dark, feeling for the wagon handle. Finding it, she slowly got to her feet, and then tried, "Can I get the wagon out now? We really are going to leave." Her hand was sweaty on the handle, but she didn't dare let go.

I suppose you think you're going to put your whole grown-up mother in that tiny wagon?

The Princess's heart still pounded and her breath still came in ragged gasps, so it was kind of hard to concentrate, but she tried to think about it. Yes, that was true. Her mother was a little bit bigger than the wagon. Actually a lot bigger. But maybe if they curled her up, if she kept sleeping, and didn't move much... All she knew was that her dad couldn't carry her. And if he couldn't, certainly nobody else could.

"I don't know," she said. "We have to try."

Too bad your car is gone. Too bad your dad is so hurt.

Too bad you're so evil, she thought. "I'm going now," she said.

There was a breathless stretch of silence. And then, just maybe, the sound of a sigh.

The door swung open, and the wagon nudged at her. She pulled the handle and the wagon came free, rolling across the shed floor easily.

She pulled it out of the shed and back to the house.

"Where were you?" her father asked, desperate, worried. At least he looked more awake, healthier.

She sat with him on the floor by the still-unconscious Mom. "I was getting the wagon. I told you."

"You were gone forever! I almost came and got you!" His rising panic freaked her out. She had just been managing to calm herself.

She tried again, taking a deep breath and speaking slowly and quietly. "I had to get it out from behind the boxes. It took a lot of time." It was as though he was the child and she was the parent. She felt very adult, very calm. Weirdly calm, given how frightened she had been in the shed.

Now she once again felt that she understood the monster, how it worked, how it thought. She understood the rules. The rules said they had to go now. She was working on making them go. She was doing everything she could.

Her dad was having trouble with the rules. It was too bad she couldn't explain about the monster to him; she knew that would just slow him down. The Apricot Boy was too young to understand the rules in the first place, and the Mom was too unconscious to be doing anything about any rules at all. So it was up to the Princess.

She said, "Okay, so, I got the wagon. We'll put blankets in it and make a bed for her." She started to rush upstairs to grab some blankets.

The Apricot Boy had clearly grown tired of his car game. "I'm hungry," he whined, pushing one of the cars into the wall repeatedly.

The Princess stopped at the landing and looked at the Dad.

"We should feed him," he said. Now he seemed weak and slow again; his panic gone, and with it his energy.

"No way. We have to hurry." Fear built up in the Princess's stomach anew. She pushed it down and continued up the stairs.

"I'm hungry too," the Dad said sadly.

The Princess stood in the loft. What else could she bring? She wanted to bring her things! She didn't have any bags! Were they really leaving for good? This was her home! Would they ever come back?

But she couldn't think about this stuff either. She grabbed the big army blankets off her parents' bed, and turned to hurry back down the stairs. "We have to go."

"Would you stop *saying* that?" the Dad said, but weakly.

The Princess ignored him, carrying the blankets to the back door.

"I'm *hungry*," the Apricot Boy whined, harder than the last time.

"There's apples and cheese here," the Dad said. "Maybe we could just slice him up something…"

"No." She opened the back door.

The Apricot Boy started to cry. "I want Mommy to make lunch! Why won't Mommy make lunch?"

"Shhh." The Dad glanced at the Mom in alarm. Though of course that was ridiculous, thought the Princess. Didn't they want her to wake up? Of course they did! That was what they wanted more than anything in the world! Then they wouldn't have to carry her in the wagon. Then she could help the Dad walk on his hurt leg.

But she didn't wake up. So the Princess placed one of the blankets in the wagon, making a nice nest in there that was obviously way too small for the Mom. But what other choice did she have? She arranged it as best she could, and then went back into the house.

Just then the Mom moaned and stirred a little. Everyone stared at her. Even the Apricot Boy leaned forward, watching her intently, his tears forgotten. But the Mom didn't move again.

Please wake up, she thought at her. *Please, Mom, please.*

The Mom lay there, inert.

The Princess sighed. "Okay, let's go."

CHAPTER 15

The Princess watched as the Dad laboriously brought the Mom out to the wagon and started to lower her into it. "Give me a hand here?"

The Princess tried to help, but it was awkward, and she wasn't quite sure what to do. "Keep her hands and feet in," her dad said, so she did that as best she could.

Now he was working quickly, at least. He had caught her urgency. They spent a few frantic moments tucking and folding and organizing the Mom into the wagon, until she looked as if she might be reasonably comfortable. "She shouldn't fall out, at least," the Dad said, looking worriedly at the bumpy driveway.

"I'll walk right next to her and you pull it," the Princess said. "Let's go."

"Right."

The Apricot Boy stood at the back door, watching them.

"Ready?" the Princess asked him.

"Why do we have to go?" he whined. "I'm hungry."

"We can get food later. We have to go now."

"Nooo!" He began to cry.

Desperate, she said, "Ice cream. We'll go to town and get ice cream."

Her father gave her a sharp glance, but the Apricot Boy said, "Okay."

She went to take her brother's hand. Galadriel and Sauron wandered around expectantly, nosing at the Mom, waiting to see what would happen next.

Suddenly the Princess said, "Wait a minute," and dashed back into the house, letting the door clatter behind her.

She darted upstairs and hurried to her little nook and rooted around the tiny eaves. Aha, there they were. She pulled out her well-worn Narnia paperbacks and ran back downstairs.

Her dad saw what she had. "Honey, you can't bring those, we can get you other books."

"No, I have to keep *these*."

Ignoring his look, she stuck the seven books in around the nooks and crannies between her mom's tucked-up limbs and the edge of the wagon, nestled into the blankets. She was very satisfied with this arrangement. It was like the books were bricks laid around the Mom, protecting her.

The Dad shrugged and picked up the wagon's handle.

The Dad pulled the wagon down the long winding driveway. It was slow going, even as they tried to hurry. His leg throbbed miserably, and he favored it as much as he could. The Princess walked alongside with one hand on her mom's shoulder and her other hand holding the Apricot Boy's. The wagon rocked and bumped and jostled wildly. Each time it hit a rut or a rock, the Dad glanced back at his wife. She seemed to be sleeping peacefully, as if she were in bed. The dogs scampered off ahead, every now and then turning back to see what was taking the people so long, then rushing ahead again, eventually disappearing down to the road. Probably they'd gone on to the river. That was the only place people went on foot.

When the little caravan got to the turn in the driveway by the big intertwined oak and madrone tree, the Dad felt a chill in the air. At the same moment, he sensed that the Princess had stopped, so he stopped as well, letting the wagon settle to a gentle halt. What was she doing now? He barely understood what was going on. Everything he thought he knew had come crashing down, falling apart, all of a sudden, and he didn't have anything to replace it.

"What is it, honey?" he asked.

She stood frozen, face utterly pale, staring at the tree. "No," she whispered. "We're going. You said."

"Yes, we're going," he said. "I thought you wanted to hurry. What's the matter?"

She turned her head slowly to look at him. "You can't see it?"

He saw a normal oak tree, with a madrone's dense red branches reaching all around the oak's limbs as if in a sensual embrace. "It's two trees," he said, uncertainly.

"No," she said quietly. "The monster. It's in the tree. It says you should be able to see it now."

Monster? the Dad thought, panic slowly rising again. The Princess had seemed so calm and in control, she had bandaged his leg and gotten the wagon and the blankets, and he had trusted her. He stared at the trees, but saw no monster. Just the big flat madrone leaves rustling in the breeze, high up. "Um, no, honey, I don't see it." If she fell apart now, just when he had begun to rely on her...

She wasn't listening to him. She addressed the tree: "You said we could go. We're going, and you have to let us." Then a pause. "But you have to do what you said. You said you'd let us go. It's the rules."

The Dad watched in growing horror as his daughter had an argument with a tree.

In some part of her mind, the Princess had known that they wouldn't get off the Land easily, no matter how hard they tried to. That was not part of the rules. The hero had to be challenged again and again, in order to win the right to achieve their goal. In the Narnia books, Peter had to fight the evil queen in order to become the king. Harriet the Spy had to endure having her notebook stolen, and then actually had to apologize to people for the things she wrote in it, even if they were perfectly true. Who knew what Frodo and Sam and all the others would have to go through to destroy the evil ring; she and the Dad hadn't gotten to the end of those books yet. But it would be a big deal, she knew that much. So it made sense that she would have to do battle with the monster one last time.

But still, she was tired, and they had a long way to go, and the Apricot Boy was already starting to drag on her hand, to whine again about food. He wouldn't last long on this journey.

Now she could see the monster more clearly than ever. It sat on the branch, leering down at her and her hapless little family, a hungry look in its yellow eyes. It easily covered the whole of the madrone branch upon which it was perched. It was very, very black, with way too many arms and legs—she still couldn't count them all, she was so busy staring at it, horrified and fascinated. It didn't have horns or a tail, but it did have pointy teeth that poked out of its mouth and long sharp claws on all its limbs. It still looked like some awful spider, more than anything else, although not exactly. She shuddered anyway, taking it in. She hated spiders more than anything else in the world.

And it was trying to break the rules—or, looked at another way, it was following monster-rules. It was pretending that she had failed. But she hadn't.

She stood her ground. "But you have to do what you said. You said you'd let us go. It's the rules."

Who's going to make me?

It was like arguing with her little brother, she thought, exasperated. The thought made her chuckle just a little, deep inside. The sudden release of tension, however tiny, helped her to regain her footing, as it were. She stared at the monster, finally seeing it entirely, every crevice in its scaly black skin, every limb (yes, there were eight of them), the narrow black centers of its beady yellow eyes. *Spider monster, spider monster, go away, nasty spider monster!* She put her hands on her hips, took a deep breath, and said, "I am the Princess of this fair land, and I command you, remove yourself from my tree and let us pass."

Next to her, her dad started to say something. She put a hand out to make him stop. He would only mess things up, he didn't even believe in the monster. He ignored her and moved towards the tree. "Dad, stop!" she screamed, but he pushed on.

The monster seemed to grow, slopping over the edges of the branch. She shivered as a gust of icy air came off it. Her dad shivered too, she noted with minuscule satisfaction. *It is* not *your land!* the monster thundered, in her head.

She stood firm. "Yes, it is, and we are doing you the favor of leaving, so you must let us pass."

The monster stretched and grew to cover two adjacent branches and part of a third. It dropped its head down low and stared back at the Princess. *Whose idea was it to come here, anyway?*

Her mouth dropped open as she stared back at it. "No. No, you can't do that."

Was it your Mom's?

"No!"

Was it your Dad's?

"You can't! You can't do that!"

The Mom woke up. Her body came back to her and she sat up, rubbing her eyes and swallowing a sour taste. She found herself curled up in a tangle of blankets and paperback books, children's books, were they the Princess's books? And was she in a wagon, in the middle of the driveway? Why?

She thought she heard people yelling, but she couldn't quite focus.

She pushed the books aside and tried to get out of the wagon.

A minute or two earlier, the Dad shivered. At least his delusional daughter had been right about one thing: they had to get out of here. Though why she was making self-important speeches to trees, he didn't know.

He also didn't know how much longer his leg would hold out. If they could just get to the road, they'd be able to flag down a passing car, sooner or later. He took a step forward.

His daughter blinked and looked back at him. "Dad, stop!" she yelled. Then she looked at the tree again, and returned to her argument with the tree.

"Come on, now," the Dad said, firmly. If she was going to go nuts on him, he was just going to have to reassert control. He gave the wagon a gentle tug to get it rolling again, and moved a few feet forward. The Mom's head lolled about, and then she gave a small moan and started struggling to her feet.

"No," the Princess said, and grabbed the wagon hard, jerking it to a stop. "No, you can't do that."

The Dad pulled harder, getting it moving again. Again the Princess grabbed at it, making it stop. Was he going to have to wrestle with her too? His arm hurt like a sonofabitch, and he could hardly put weight on his leg.

"Sweetheart," he said, through clenched teeth, in the tone of voice that says *I mean business.* "Let go of the wagon. We have to go."

"No!" She seemed wild, desperate, not really focusing on him, still shrieking at the tree. "You can't! You can't do that!"

The monster focused on the Dad. *It's him*, it said, voice laced with wicked pleasure. *I might have known.*

"No!" She grabbed the wagon to make it stop.

He dragged you all out here, when nobody wanted to be here. I suppose he should stay, don't you think?

"No! You can't have him!" She dropped the wagon and clung to her dad, after a quick glance to make sure the Apricot Boy was still safe behind her. He was watching the whole thing, eyes wide, thumb in his mouth—a habit he had broken ages ago. She wheeled back to face the monster, clutching her father's arm.

The monster filled nearly the whole tree now, making itself almost a third tree, intertwined with the other two.

"*I am the Princess and I forbid this!*" she commanded, with all of her strength. "You are the evil monster and you must follow the rules! Begone from this tree right now and let us pass!"

The monster laughed and swelled.

"Enough of this, sweetie." The Dad pulled his arm loose of hers and tugged the wagon forward firmly. He stepped within a few feet of the tree.

The Princess shrieked and grabbed hold of the back of the wagon again, but her strength was no match for his, even wounded as he was.

The Dad marched directly into the blackness that was the monster.

The monster screamed with laughter, its voice catching in its throat as the Dad walked right into it. The Dad fell into the blackness as the huge horrible spider-demon sank its mandibles into his flesh.

The Mom cried out and scrabbled out of the wagon. She ran a few yards into the meadow before collapsing.

The Princess stood frozen, holding the Apricot Boy's damp hand in hers. *Rules…rules are funny things*, she heard in her head.

She pulled her brother into her arms, turning his face into her chest so that he couldn't see, covering his ears. And she watched as the monster did the awful thing, right in front of her eyes.

Her dad howled with pain and surprise. His hurt leg buckled under him, but the monster had its arms and legs all around him, holding him up off the ground. The thing sank its teeth into the Dad's stomach, then came up. Blood dripped from long fangs. The Dad screamed again, and then his head lolled back. The monster went back for another bite. Its mouth was enormous, and its body was still growing, growing. In the tree, she saw more of the white ropy stuff—the biggest spider web ever.

Then the monster lifted its head and looked right at the Princess. She heard no voice, but she knew she would be next.

The Apricot Boy whimpered against her chest and tried to pull away. She yanked him up off the ground, still keeping him from seeing. He was almost more than she could carry, but she had no choice. Ignoring his protests, she ran down the driveway as fast as she could.

The Mom ran a few yards before her legs gave out on her. She collapsed into a little tuft of soft meadow grass, scraping her hands on the way down. She didn't understand what the hell was going on, but she was sick with dread. She'd been unconscious for a while, she had no idea how long, but now she just knew she had to get away.

Something had attacked her on the trail. A wave of nausea overtook her, and with a sudden convulsion she vomited up a warm soup of tea and oatmeal and green bile.

A moment later, she wiped her mouth and looked around. She saw the thing in the tree. It had her husband in its grasp, and was eating him from the middle outwards. Just like Bliss had been eaten.

Blood splashed off the leaves and pooled on the ground beneath the tree. There was a terrible smell in the air.

She bit back another scream and tried to get to her feet again. Her legs would barely move, but she had to get away. She knew it had already tasted her blood, and it would not stop until it had had its fill, until it had eaten everyone. She vomited again, and felt her bowels and bladder threatening to let go.

She struggled against her body and half-ran, half crawled deeper into the meadow, and then down into the dry creekbed before collapsing again.

The Princess ran down the driveway, but it was a long way. She could still hear the horrible sounds of the monster eating her dad behind her. No matter how far she went, the sounds never got any quieter; the crunching of the monster chewing, and the sloppy, wet, licking sounds of it slurping up her dad's blood and other bodily juices. She fought the urge to throw up. She had nothing in her stomach anyway.

The Apricot Boy still struggled in her arms, but she couldn't let him go, she couldn't let the monster get him. But it was so long to go, and she was so tired. And it was cold, and it felt like it was getting dark everywhere, though it was still just the middle of the day. There were no clouds overhead, though it was as if there were clouds everywhere.

The driveway had never seemed so long in all her life. She tripped on a big rock and stumbled, but recovered because she had to. The Apricot Boy whined and pulled at her hair. She batted his hand away, readjusting her grip on him.

Finally she turned the last corner. She could see the road from here, but the driveway had become narrow. The trees had suddenly grown long and rambling, reaching towards each other, choking off the escape. Thick branches filled the air in front of her. She pushed into them, scraping her face, protecting her brother as best she could.

Trees are my friends, she thought desperately. *Trees won't hurt me.* She knew trees, understood them. She slipped and struggled between the branches, finding passageways where there seemed to be none.

And all the while she heard the sounds of her father dying.

And then she was free. She stumbled out onto the road and put the Apricot Boy down. She gasped for breath; he had been starting to really squirm and cry. "No, no, stop!" he whimpered.

It was lighter here, out of the trees. She sucked air into her lungs—it had grown warmer. And it was quiet here. She could no longer hear the monster.

She took one last deep breath and grabbed her brother's hand again. She hurried down the road as fast as she could make him go. Which wasn't very fast, as he was continuing to resist, and was too small, and never speedy to begin with. "Where's Mommy? Where's Daddy?"

"We have to go get help," she said. "We have to help them. The monster hurt them and we have to go get help."

"I want Mommy!"

"We're going to get her!" she yelled, out of patience. "Stop whining!"

Sauron and Galadriel reappeared from the river side of the road and followed along behind them, happy to be on the move. In the distance, an engine could be heard, working its way along the winding country road.

CHAPTER 16

The case worker looked through the tiny window at the children in the hospital room. "They look normal enough," she mused. "A little dirty."

"I've bathed them three times," the nurse said defensively, crossing her arms. "And changed their clothes."

"Sorry—I didn't mean…" She trailed off, staring through the window again, taking the measure of the children.

The little blonde girl was sober, serious, talking to her brother nicely on the bed. He seemed undisturbed, smiling as his sister wove some kind of a tale about the toys spread out between them.

"You say the neighbor found them?" the case worker asked, checking her clipboard again. She knew the whole story, she'd gone over it with the police and then again with the doctor, but something kept her chatting with the nurse out here. Something kept her from opening the door and walking into the room.

"Oh, yes, just driving his truck down the road, almost ran into them. He came around a corner and there they were, hand in hand. He says they didn't even wave."

"Sad." She looked into the room, studying the girl. She would have to go in there. She would have to talk to them. "How much do they know?"

"Ohhh, they know it all. Dr. Ridgeway told them right off—he doesn't believe in coddling them, at any age." The nurse stood taller, warming up to a favorite topic. "He's modern, that Dr. Ridgeway, you know. He's from the university, and they have all the new ideas there. He told the little girl straight out: 'Your father's dead, and your mother is here in the hospital. She may or may not survive, but we're doing everything we can to save her.' And then he offered to take both of the children in to see her."

The case worker leaned against the door, her clipboard at her hip. "Did they go see her?"

"Yes, can you believe it? They both went in, sober as little church mice. They looked at her, and then the girl said, 'Okay, thank you.' Then Dr. Ridgeway brought them here, and that's when they called you. Oh, I don't know what you're going to do with them."

"Well, we'll find a foster home for them as soon as possible." The case worker looked at her clipboard again without really seeing it. "You said there's no other local family members?"

"There must be grandparents, but we haven't turned them up yet. Maybe your department can find them."

"Well, I do need to talk to them first, see how traumatized they are by the whole thing." *So walk in there and do it already*, she told herself. She wasn't sure why she was feeling so reluctant. Not like herself at all.

"It was pretty awful, I heard," the nurse said conspiratorially. "All the bodies, and Deputy Brooks still missing. There's a search party out there now."

"Have they found anything?"

"I guess we'll hear." The nurse straightened a few items on the shelves, unnecessarily. "Those poor children!"

"I know." The case worker shook her head. It was completely unconscionable, what people let children see these days. Parents had no sense of responsibility, no maturity. They just followed their whims, taking drugs, sleeping around, doing whatever they wanted to do, expecting their children to raise themselves. Or, worse than that: expecting the state to step in and raise them when their own faulty parenting failed. And the state did. Here she was, ready yet again to clean up somebody else's mess.

And such a mess it was. A property full of dead bodies, some overdosed on drugs, others torn apart by some wild rabid animal that should have been hunted down and shot long ago; abandoned, trash-strewn cars; a scene of utter poverty and deprivation. Likely there had been sexual molestation as well. She wouldn't be surprised, that sort of thing was par for the course with these kinds of people. She would need to interview the girl separately from her brother to give her some space.

She shuddered, trying to clear her imagination. She needed to focus on what was in front of her. And that was two frightened, traumatized children in the next room. Children who, God willing, she could help. She *would* help. She knew what to do.

She took a deep breath, straightened her clipboard, and opened the door.

On the Land, the evil energy settled away, the disruption nearly gone. Searchers found and carried away all the poisoned and shot and mutilated bodies. Except for Bliss. No one managed to find her grave.

More disruption might come, in the future. For now, the Land was once again at its uneasy peace.

In a sterile hospital room in town, the Princess sighed as she felt the evil dissipate. Her domain was at peace, and she was the Princess, in charge once more.

Then the door opened, and a strange woman came in, smiling and holding a clipboard.

THE END

ABOUT THE AUTHOR

SHANNON PAGE was born on Halloween night and spent her early years on a back-to-the-land commune in northern California. A childhood without television gave her a great love of the written word. At seven, she wrote her first book, an illustrated adventure starring her cat Cleo. Sadly, that story is out of print, but her work has appeared in *Clarkesworld, Interzone, Fantasy, Black Static,* Tor.com, the Proceedings of the 2002 International Oral History Association Congress, and many anthologies, including the Australian Shadows Award-winning *Grants Pass,* and *The Mammoth Book of Dieselpunk.*

Books include *Eel River;* the collection *Eastlick and Other Stories;* and *Our Lady of the Islands,* co-written with the late Jay Lake. *Our Lady* received starred reviews from *Publishers Weekly* and *Library Journal,* was named one of *Publishers Weekly*'s Best Books of 2014, and is short-listed for the Endeavour Award. Forthcoming books include *The Queen and The Tower,* first book in The Nightcraft Quartet, and a sequel to *Our Lady.* Edited books include the anthology *Witches, Stitches & Bitches,* from Evil Girlfriend Media, as well as several well-received novels from Per Aspera Press. Shannon is a longtime yoga practitioner, has no tattoos, and is an avid gardener at home with her husband, Mark Ferrari, in Portland, Oregon. Visit her at www.shannonpage.net.